"Sanctuary Bay is better for having you come here, my lord."

Her quiet praise, praise he knew he did not deserve, eased a few of the bands around his heart. Those strictures had tightened each time he was faced with a decision and could not make it. He wanted to believe that she saw something in him that he had failed to see himself. Maybe he was fooling himself again, as he had when he had believed Lady Eloisa loved him, but he yearned to lose himself in the delusion while he stood beside Miss Fenwick.

"I don't know how to respond to that," he said with all honesty, "but I do know, as we are working together on this project to rebuild the church, it seems it might be simpler for you to call me Edmund."

He had shocked her, he could tell, because her eyes widened as she said, "Simpler, but not proper."

"Are you always the vicar's proper sister?"

Books by Jo Ann Brown

Love Inspired Historical

*The Dutiful Daughter
*A Hero for Christmas
*A Bride for the Baron

*Sanctuary Bay

JO ANN BROWN

has published more than one hundred titles under a variety of pen names since selling her first book in 1987. A former military officer, she enjoys telling stories, taking pictures and traveling. She has taught creative writing for more than twenty years and is always excited when one of her students sells a project. She has been married for more than thirty years and has three children and two spoiled cats. Currently she lives in Nevada. Her books have been translated into almost a dozen languages and sold on every continent except Antarctica. She enjoys hearing from her readers. Drop her a note at www.joannbrownbooks.com.

A Bride for the Baron

JO ANN BROWN

⬨ HARLEQUIN® LOVE INSPIRED® HISTORICAL

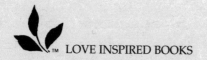

LOVE INSPIRED BOOKS

ISBN-13: 978-0-373-28256-2

A BRIDE FOR THE BARON

www.Harlequin.com

Printed in U.S.A.

Trust in the Lord with all thine heart; and lean not unto thine own understanding. In all thy ways acknowledge him, and he shall direct thy paths.

—*Proverbs* 3:5–6

For Tina James.

Thanks for sharing my enthusiasm for this series and your wonderful guidance, kindness and patience.

Chapter One

Meriweather Hall, Sanctuary Bay, North Yorkshire
February 1817

"'Tis the church in Sanctuary Bay! It's on fire!"

The words still resonated through Vera Fenwick's mind as they had in the moments right after her bosombow's wedding. The original plans to hold the ceremony in Sanctuary Bay had been changed after more than half of the church's ancient roof had collapsed beneath the winter's heavy snows. Even though her brother, who served as vicar of the Sanctuary Bay church, had not been able to officiate at the ceremony in Norwich, which was the groom's home parish, Vera had been filled with joy for Catherine and her new husband, Jonathan Bradby. Then the messenger from Sanctuary Bay had raced through Norwich Cathedral's gate.

After long days of traveling by carriage, Vera would soon see how much damage had been done to the church and the vicarage that had been her home for the past decade. Her composure had chipped away a little more with each passing mile that brought the carriage closer to Sanctuary Bay.

A gentle hand covered her clenched ones. She looked across the carriage to where Lady Meriweather, Catherine's mother, leaned toward her. Forcing a smile, which she could not hold long, she knew she should thank the widowed baroness for her compassion. She feared if she opened her mouth that she would be sick.

"We are almost there," Lord Meriweather, who had inherited the title from Catherine's late father, said from where he sat beside Vera. They were riding facing backward so the baroness and Miss Lillian Kightly, who had come with them from the wedding in Norwich, could travel in more comfort.

She nodded. The messenger had been sent as soon as the fire was discovered, and he could tell them little other than that the church was engulfed in flames.

"Then we shall know the truth of what has happened," the baron went on when she did not speak. "Let's hope that our imaginations have painted a dreary picture of the truth, and the situation won't be as dire as we fear."

Vera glanced at him. He had come to claim Meriweather Hall in the autumn. Even sitting, he was a head taller than she was. His tawny hair blew into his brown eyes as an icy wind off the sea swirled through the carriage. His features were interesting rather than classically handsome.

She appreciated his attempt to put her at ease; yet nothing but seeing the damage with her own two eyes would do that now.

"Look!" Miss Kightly said in an attempt to be cheerful. "There's the gate to Meriweather Hall." The blonde was the most beautiful woman Vera had ever seen. During their journey north, she had noticed how men could not keep from staring at Miss Kightly while none of them had taken a second look at Vera.

Not that she had cared when every thought in her head was of getting back to Sanctuary Bay.

They came to a stop by Meriweather Hall's gate, and Lord Meriweather opened the carriage door.

"Why are we stopping here?" asked Miss Kightly.

Instead of answering her, he said, "Lady Meriweather, I trust you will forgive me for asking you to walk into Meriweather Hall."

The older woman nodded and motioned for Miss Kightly to precede her out of the carriage. Miss Kightly complied but frowned when Lady Meriweather said she believed they both should wait at the manor house while Lord Meriweather assessed the damage.

Vera drew in a deep breath to say she would not be kept a moment longer than necessary to see what was left in the aftermath of the fire, but a footman burst through the gate. He glanced at her, then away.

She had wished her brother would have left a message here to prepare her for what she would soon see. Hope leaped inside her. Maybe the damage was not bad. That hope faded with her next heartbeat. If it had been believed the fire could be doused, there would have been no need to send a messenger with the bad news.

God, give me strength to face what lies ahead. Help me hold up Gregory.

Vera raised her head as Lord Meriweather started to climb back in. He paused as Lady Meriweather murmured something too low for Vera to hear. The baron nodded and gave her a tight smile before he reentered the carriage.

"Miss Fenwick, you will enjoy a better view of the sea if you sit facing forward." His voice held not a hint of emotion.

Relieved that he was not asking her to wait at Meriweather Hall, she edged past him to take the other seat. He sat and faced her as he slapped the side of the carriage. It lurched into motion, headed toward the village farther north along Sanctuary Bay.

Again Vera clasped her hands. She wanted to thank Lord Meriweather for accompanying her, but the words stuck in her throat. Her limbs felt heavy, then light, then a ripple of sensation like a million frantic insects. She tried to relax. She could not. She and Gregory had spent the past ten years serving the church set on the cliff above the village. She had grown up there, for she had been a girl when they had first arrived.

A foolish girl who nearly had ruined her brother's career. Even though Gregory never spoke of it, neither of them would ever forget her stupid belief that the son of Lord Hedgcoe truly loved her. Her youthful foolishness, for she had been barely fifteen, had led to disaster and Gregory being removed in shame from the parish Lord Hedgcoe controlled. If the late Lord Meriweather had not offered Gregory the living at Sanctuary Bay, she was unsure what they would have done.

She looked toward the sea. How she had come to love this bay with its turbulent waves and its capricious winds! A sunny morn could end in a wild storm. She caught a view of the village where it clung to the cliffs, the gray-and-red roofs bright against the winter fields.

The road turned before she could glimpse the church. Or what was left of it.

Lord Meriweather cleared his throat. "Lady Meriweather asked me to remind you that you and the vicar are welcome to stay at Meriweather Hall as long as necessary." He stared out the window rather than meet her eyes. "Assuming it is necessary, of course."

"Thank you. I appreciate you coming with me to th-th-he ch-ch-church." Her voice broke on the last two words. In so many ways, Sanctuary Bay was her church as much as it was her brother's. Since she had almost cost Gregory his career in the church, she had slipped into a life of helping in the background. More and more often, she had taken on the task of writing his Sunday sermons while Gregory kept himself busy with other parish duties. When he read her sermons from the pulpit, she could not keep from sneaking glances at other people in the pews, always wondering if her words had touched their hearts.

Lord Meriweather's gaze focused on her. "Miss Fenwick, I am sure there are many pretty words that might offer you solace at this time, but I am sorry that I am not a man accustomed to speaking such words. Before I served the king, I spent my days working with rough men who are as skilled with crude cant as they are with tools." He drew in a deep breath and sighed it out loudly enough that she could hear it over the breeze from the sea.

Vera tried to think of something to say but was afraid that if she opened her mouth sobs would come out. Again her emotions went up and down like a storm wave, crashing her hopes into many shattered pieces.

She continued to gaze at the sea until she heard Lord

Meriweather pull in a sharp gasp. She sat straighter and realized, while she had been making an effort to think of nothing, they had reached the top of the village where the church and vicarage were. Shouts rang through the carriage, but she did not catch any of the words.

The tone was unmistakable, though. Anger. Fear. Regret. Pain. All those emotions and more were woven through the voices.

Odors of smoke and wet wood hung in the air, tainting every breath she took.

She remembered that smell from when a fire had burned through a side street in the village. The reek of soaked wood had lingered over the village for almost a month. Each new storm brought it forth again until the cottages were rebuilt.

Her stomach dropped as the last drops of hope evaporated. She turned to the other window, but Lord Meriweather's hands clamped on her shoulders. Surprised, she looked at him. His mouth was drawn, and she saw lines on his brow and gouging into his cheeks that she had never noticed before.

"It is bad, isn't it?" she whispered.

He nodded.

"Very bad?"

Again he nodded.

"All gone?" She had to force the words past her lips.

"Yes." His jaw worked, then he said, "If you wish to return to Meriweather Hall now and come back here when you have had a chance to rest from our long journey, say so."

It was tempting. To push aside the problem and pretend it did not exist, but that was not her way. "I appreciate your kindness, my lord. However, delaying will not make my first sight any easier."

"I thought you would say that. You are fortunate to have a quiet courage, Miss Fenwick, that is admirable."

Even though she guessed he intended to warn her to be prepared for what awaited her, his words sent a surge of warmth through her to ease the cold surrounding her fearful heart.

Lord Meriweather stepped out of the carriage and offered his hand to assist her. As she reached for his hand, the courage he had complimented deserted her. She still had not been able to look out the window toward what was left of the two buildings. The church and *her home*. Once she emerged from the carriage, she would come face-to-face with the disaster.

"It can only get better from this point," he said quietly, as if she had spoken her thoughts aloud.

She clutched his hand as she climbed out of the carriage. When he winced, she realized she had a death grip on his fingers. She released his hand, but he took hers and placed it on his sleeve. Without saying a word, he led her around the carriage. The wind battered them. Ashes rose into the air in miniature cyclones before falling, turning the ground into a gray wasteland.

Vera's knees threatened to collapse beneath her when she saw nothing remained of the church. The stone walls had fallen to the ground, scorched by the power of the fire. Upon first glance, the vicarage appeared as if it had survived with less damage. Smoke stains, like dark gray fingers clawing out of the windows and the doorway, warned that the fire had reigned inside the cottage, gutting the interior. The roof was gone, and she wondered if it had burned or fallen into the flint cottage.

"Say the word," Lord Meriweather murmured, "and we can go back to Meriweather Hall at any time."

She looked past him. "Where is Gregory?"

"Over by the church." He continued to keep his hand over hers on the sleeve of his dark brown greatcoat as they walked to where her brother stared into the church's cellar.

The few men who had been gathering up debris and piling it near the edge of the cliff stopped working as they watched her and Lord Meriweather come toward the church.

"Maybe you should wait here," he said. "I don't know how stable the foundation is."

She shook her head, and they walked to where her brother had not moved. His shadow dipped over the edge of the cellar, and he seemed unaware of anything or anyone else.

"Gregory?" she called.

He was silent.

"Gregory?"

When her brother gave her no answer, she glanced at Lord Meriweather. Again his mouth was taut, and furrows had dug back into his face.

He drew his arm out from under her hand and strode to her brother. "Vicar!" His voice was as sharp as the crack of a whip.

Gregory flinched, then turned to look at them. Tears filled his eyes when he saw Vera. She ran, wending her way past the gravestones in the churchyard, and flung her arms around him.

"Do you know what happened?" she asked.

"All I can figure," her brother said, "is that another section of roof fell in and struck the wood stove. Embers must have fallen out. That set the church on fire."

Vera shook her head. "Gregory, that can't be what happened. We didn't use it anymore."

"It is the only explanation I have." His shoulders sagged, and Vera embraced him again.

Edmund Herriott, Lord Meriweather, stepped away to let Miss Fenwick and her brother comfort each other. He spoke to the men cleaning the site and was glad to see many were his tenants. He thanked them. Was he expected to do more? He had no idea. Now that his cousins Sophia and Catherine were both married and gone, he would need to turn to Lady Meriweather to help him make proper decisions.

Or any decisions at all.

He refrained from grimacing as he walked around the ruined church. How was Meriweather Hall going to function if its baron could not even decide which cravat to wear each morning? Now there was the matter of rebuilding the church and the vicarage. He did not want to burden Lady Meriweather, but he was unsure where else to turn.

His gaze settled on Miss Fenwick. He had suspected, since shortly after his first meeting with the vicar's sister, that she handled many of the parish responsibilities. Mr. Fenwick was a learned man who made every effort to serve his congregation, but the vicar's duties often kept him riding from one end of the parish to the other. Would Miss Fenwick help Edmund, too?

Miss Fenwick went with the vicar to examine the

damage, and Edmund looked away. He did not want her to discover him staring at her. She was his cousin Catherine's best friend, but Edmund had to own that he scarcely knew the vicar's sister. Any time they had spent together prior to the journey back to Sanctuary Bay had included her brother or his cousins, and there had been no time to learn more about her during the days in the carriage because Miss Kightly's prattle had monopolized the conversation from morn until they stopped at another coaching inn each night.

The sickening reek of wet ashes erupted with each step as Edmund walked around what was left of the church. The roof had burned. The joists supporting the floor had failed, and everything that had not been consumed by the flames had fallen into the cellar.

But there was another odor. Fainter, yet there nonetheless. He sniffed and frowned. Brandy. There must have been a lot of brandy to leave the scent after a fire. That could mean one thing and one thing only.

The rattle of carriage wheels resounded, startling him. He turned as a small carriage rolled to a stop beside his carriage, its wheels crunching on the filthy snow. Edmund recognized it, even before he saw the baronial crest on the door. It was from Meriweather Hall. Who had driven here after them?

When the door opened and Miss Kightly stepped out of the carriage with the help of a footman, Edmund was not surprised that she had been unwilling to remain at Meriweather Hall as he had requested. An astounding beauty with golden hair and perfect features, she was, as always, a pattern-card of style. The crimson pelisse she now wore was the lone bright spot among the ruins.

She held on to her ermine-lined bonnet to make sure it was not twisted off by the wind as she hurried to them.

Tears blossomed in her eyes when she placed her fingers lightly on Miss Fenwick's arm. "I had no idea there would be this much devastation. I know my great-uncle will be willing to help you rebuild." She gave Edmund a swift smile because she must know that Edmund, like most of the people in North Yorkshire, considered her great-uncle, Sir Nigel Tresting, a very eccentric man. "He likes coming here for services."

"That is very kind of both of you," Miss Fenwick said.

"I am sorry this has happened to you." The blonde flung her arms around Miss Fenwick, giving her and her brother a big hug.

Edmund looked away, feeling as he had too often, like an outsider in this close-knit seaside community. Before the war, his only worries had been how to keep his import and construction businesses profitable. That had changed when he had inherited the title of Lord Meriweather. Now, he had three vital duties. He needed to keep the estate running and make sure its residents saw to their responsibilities. He must attend sessions of Parliament. Last and most important, he had to find a woman to wed and give the baronage an heir, as well as a spare or two.

He had been somewhat successful with the first two, even though he still had much to learn. On the last, he had failed. Oh, he had thought he was on his way to success on the third when he had begun courting Lady Eloisa Parkington after the young woman had shown her interest in him. He had bought her items she admired, and he had escorted her to gatherings where the door might otherwise have been closed to her after her family's reputation was sullied by her older siblings' wild behavior. He even, to quiet her pleading, had introduced her to a man he had served with during the war, a man who had recently become a marquess. Edmund had regretted the decision when Lady Eloisa had quickly persuaded the marquess to propose to her.

Introducing them had been the last decision Edmund had made, and it had been as wrong as too many others had been when he had watched men die on the battlefield following his orders. The night he had heard of Lady Eloisa's betrothal was the night he admitted that he would be a fool to attempt to decide anything else on his own.

He was not going to think about that now. He went back to the hole that once had been the church's cellar. Kneeling on its edge, he scanned the dusky shadows. Again he sniffed. Again he caught a hint of brandy.

One of his tenants, a man who farmed land west of the manor house, came over. "Excuse me, m'lord, but could you use this?" He held out a lantern.

"Thank you, Sims," he said as he took it and held it over the side.

A flash of white marked where the stone font had fallen. When he saw several reflections, he guessed the light might be hitting brass candlesticks or pieces of broken glass. Anything made of wood had been burned beyond recognition.

Almost everything.

Edmund held out the lantern at full arm's length and squinted through the sunlight off the sea. He lowered the lantern into the cellar, hoping to get a better look at what was beneath the joists. He gasped when he saw a black area where the foundation's stone wall had been broken. From what he could see, the opening looked big enough for a man to walk through. Someone had cut out a section of the wall and, with what he had smelled near the cellar, it was not hard to guess who or why.

The bane of Sanctuary Bay was a gang of smugglers who practiced their illegal trade brazenly. His predecessor had tried to halt them, but had failed. Both of his cousins had been threatened by the smugglers who, he had recently learned, were led by someone they spoke of as *his qualityship*. That must mean that the leader was of wealth or of the peerage or both. It explained how they had eluded capture for so long and also why they grew bolder with each passing month.

Getting to his feet, he brushed dirt off his buckskin breeches. He handed the lantern back to its owner, then shrugged off his greatcoat. "Sims, can you hold this up while I go down?"

"Go down?" The thin man gulped, his Adam's apple bouncing like a ball as Edmund took off his coat and tossed it on top of his greatcoat. "Go down *there?*"

"Hold up the lantern so I can see when I get to the bottom." He tugged the hem of his wrinkled waistcoat and looked into the cellar.

Sims hesitated, then nodded, "Aye, m'lord, but let me see if I can find a ladder. Someone in the village must have one."

"No!" He held up his hand to halt Sims. His voice resonated, and everyone stared at him. He must look like a madman standing in the icy wind in his shirt-sleeves. But if Sims alerted the villagers to what they were doing, the smugglers who lived among them would hear. He could not risk them coming to halt him now. "I don't need a ladder. These beams offer me a good path to the bottom."

Miss Fenwick rushed around the church's perimeter. Strands of her black hair flapped on her shoulders, and she pushed them impatiently back under her bonnet. Her bright blue eyes were wide. "My lord, what are you doing?"

"I know why the church burned, and I think I know who burned it." Maybe he should have phrased it differently, Edmund thought, as he saw the faces around him become as pale as milk.

Miss Fenwick stared at him, her eyes widening as understanding dawned. She whispered, "What did you see?"

"I don't want to say until I am sure of my suspicions."

"Smugglers?" Her voice remained hushed.

He nodded grimly. "Take a deep breath. What do you smell?"

She did and shivered. "Some sort of distilled spirits."

"Brandy, I would guess. A lot of it if the odor lingers after the fire." He let his breath sift past his clenched teeth. "Brandy burns fast and hot."

"You think someone used it to start a fire in the church?"

"Possibly. I need to check the cellar to see if there is a clue there." He put his foot on the closest beam. It cracked and tumbled into the cellar with a crash.

Mr. Fenwick stormed toward them and pushed between Edmund and his sister. "My lord, it may not be my place to tell you what you should do, but we lost your predecessor barely a year ago. To have you risk your neck now would be foolhardy."

"Aye," chimed the men who had gathered by the cellar.

Miss Kightly, who had followed the vicar, grasped Edmund's arm with both hands. "My dear Lord Meriweather, there are others who can go down into the cellar in accordance with your directions."

"You cannot believe," Miss Fenwick said with a serenity that contrasted with the panic in the other voices, "that Lord Meriweather would ask someone else to do what he himself would not. He is not that sort of man."

"But, Vera," began her brother.

"Have you forgotten that Lord Meriweather fought heroically for our nation?" she fired back.

"Of course not," Miss Kightly said, "but—"

"Then trust that he would not do something risky without having a good reason." Miss Fenwick faced him. "But he also must see the good sense of taking one or two others with him in case the debris shifts."

Edmund was pleased by Miss Fenwick's defense of his plan. Suddenly the wind seemed less cold and the sunlight brighter because he had an ally. Her eyes glinted like the sapphire sky above them. A man could lose himself in eyes like hers. Maybe he already had, because he had no idea how long he had gazed into her eyes or how long he would have continued if one of the men had not sneezed.

Clearing his throat, he thanked her for her good idea. He asked for volunteers. Every man, except the vicar, raised his hand. In dismay, he wondered which one he should choose.

"If I may make a couple of suggestions, my lord," Miss Fenwick said.

Grateful and hoping his face was not blazing with embarrassment, he said, "Most certainly."

"Mr. Sims is slender and able to squeeze into small places." She smiled when she added, "Mr. Henderson may be the strongest man in Sanctuary Bay. If one of the timbers slips, he will be able to hold it while all of you escape."

Edmund did not doubt the man was the strongest in the parish. He was built with thick shoulders and looked as if he could lift one of the fishermen's cobles—their small deep wooden boats—out of the sand and hold it over his head.

"Thank you, Miss Fenwick." He nodded toward her as if it were the most ordinary matter in the world that the vicar's sister should make such a decision. "Men, come with me."

The vicar began praying for their safety as Edmund put his foot on another beam. Edmund added a few prayers of his own as he shifted his weight onto it, and his boot slid slightly. The beam held. With one foot still on the ground, he gave orders for the men to follow one at a time, testing each step they took and never allowing more than one man on a beam at the same time. Without knowing how the joists had been weakened by the fire, they must take extra care.

Edmund eased down into the cellar, feeling more alive than he had in months. The only decision he had to make was where to put his foot next, and he was relieved to see there was no choice. The crisscrossed joists offered a single path. He reached the bottom and frowned at the broken font to his right. For how many centuries had it been part of baptisms? Now it was rubble.

The odor of brandy was very strong, and he saw several crates of empty bottles in a dark pool. He knelt by the pool, dipped his fingers in and tasted the liquid. Water.

He pushed himself to his feet and leaned toward a joist. The odor of brandy was strong on it. Whoever had started the fire had soaked the floor with enough smuggled alcohol that the reek remained. But had it been the smugglers?

The lantern was passed down to him, and he edged toward the place where the opening was cut into the stone wall. The work had been done fairly recently because the chisel marks where the stones had been torn out of the wall still had rough edges.

He peered into the opening. He slapped his hand against the wall when he saw earth and stone blocked what once had been a tunnel. Someone had pulled down the ceiling only a short time before because the stones still had dirt clinging to them.

Taking a step toward the opening, he stopped when his foot struck something soft. He bent down. It was a water-soaked coil of French lace, another favorite item among the smugglers. He had no further doubts. The smugglers had been using the cellar and had burned the church. It was not the first time they had used fire to intimidate, because there had been a suspicious fire in Meriweather Hall's kitchen before Christmas. But who had given the order to set the church aflame? The order had to have come from their leader, a man who would have no compunctions about burning the parish's church.

He heard a warning creak. He looked up to see Henderson and Sims dashing up the beams. Dirt and ash fell on him. He did not hesitate. He was close on their heels by the time he reached ground level. Jumping off the beam, he whirled as several joists caved in to the cellar. A gray cloud rose up. He waved aside the ash and coughed.

Edmund motioned for everyone to get back from the edge, then thanked Sims and Henderson and the other men. They nodded and went back to piling debris closer to the cliff. But he did not miss their troubled expressions.

He picked up his coat and pulled it on, listening to make sure the men were not within earshot. As he drew on his greatcoat, he asked, "Mr. Fenwick, when was the last time you were in the church's cellar?"

"At least eight or nine years ago." His nose wrinkled. "Shortly after I accepted the living here, I had everything stored down there brought up so it didn't molder away. The door into the church has been locked shut, and the key was lost years ago."

"So the smugglers had the perfect place to hide their cargo."

"Smugglers! In my church?" The vicar shook his head. "Impossible."

"The evidence is in the cellar." Edmund outlined what he had seen.

The vicar's face grew long with dismay. "This is an outrage. When I heard the story that a previous vicar counted himself among the smugglers' ranks, I had hoped it was untrue. Now…" He choked, unable to continue.

Patting her brother's arm, Miss Fenwick said, "We must make sure it does not happen again."

"That may be easier said than done," Edmund said. "They need a place to hide their illicit cargo. Who knows how long they have been using the church? At least since we made it impossible for them to use the dower cottage at Meriweather Hall. All worked well for them until a section of the church's roof fell in. They must have feared someone would check the cellar to make sure the joists could support a new roof."

"So they set the church on fire," Miss Fenwick said, looking from him to the cellar, "to hide that they had been using the cellar."

"That is exactly what I was thinking." He appreciated her acceptance of the facts.

Her brother remained less willing to see what was right in front of them. "But why would they burn this church? We have been discussing building a new church—"

"They could not take a chance that the decision would be made to fix up the old one instead." Miss Fenwick's face hardened. "But where will they go next? It could be anywhere."

Miss Kightly gave a soft cry of fright and wobbled as if she were about to faint. Mr. Fenwick jumped to keep her from falling. He helped her back to her carriage where she could sit and recover her composure.

"I should go back with her," Miss Fenwick said. "It appears that Gregory and I will be accepting your invitation to stay at Meriweather Hall."

"For as long as you need to." Both he and Lady Meriweather would be happy to have company in the huge house that would seem empty now that both his cousins were married to his two best friends, Jonathan Bradby and Charles Winthrop, the earl of Northbridge.

"Thank you. We will need to depend on your hospitality until we can live in the vicarage again. That must wait until after we have a church, of course." She turned to go, then paused. "Before I go, I must ask you one question."

"Certainly."

"You are familiar with constructing buildings. Will you help us rebuild our church?"

She had no idea what she was asking. Overseeing the building of a church would require dozens of decisions each day when he could not make a single one.

"Please, say yes," she went on. "We need your help."

What could he say? That he had plans to go to London for the Season? That was not true. That he had to entertain Lady Meriweather? Miss Fenwick would know that was a lie. But he could not speak the truth. He had seen enough pity in his friends' eyes. He did not want to see more, especially in her eyes. But she was right. He was the man for the task.

God, if this is what You want me to do, I will need Your help more than ever.

"All right," he said. "I will try to do my best."

Instantly, he wished he could retract his words. This was the first decision he had made in more than a year, and he feared it would prove to be as bad as the last one.

Chapter Two

Other than the steady plop of thick, cold raindrops outside, not a sound could be heard when Edmund stepped into the entrance hall of Meriweather Hall. He followed the vicar and Miss Fenwick and Miss Kightly. Other than Foggin, the footman who had opened the door, nobody could be seen. Lady Meriweather must have retired to her room, exhausted by the long journey north from Norwich.

The footman, in Meriweather Hall's black livery, took their coats, then stepped aside as another footman burst into the entrance hall. He skidded to a stop on the stone floor, almost bumping into one of the benches set against the raised panels on the lower half of the walls.

"Jessup," Edmund said with a frown. He was still learning how a baron should act, but he knew that a footman never behaved that outrageously. "I trust you have an explanation."

The footman gulped. "I was asked to deliver this message to Miss Kightly the moment she arrived at Meriweather Hall."

"Perhaps you should not take such requests quite so literally."

Nodding, the footman said, "I won't. From this point forward."

"I am pleased to hear that." He motioned for Jessup to hand the message to Miss Kightly, and the footman held out a folded sheet to the pretty blonde.

As she opened it, he shifted his gaze toward Miss Fenwick. She stood beside her brother, her hand on his arm in a comforting pose. Not that he was surprised. Miss Fenwick was very supportive of her brother and his ministry. He had known that before, but her request by the remnants of the burned-out church was proof of her devotion to him.

Edmund looked away. Miss Fenwick's determination to help her brother with his parish must have been what had persuaded her to ask Edmund's assistance in rebuilding the church. How long would it take for her to realize she had made the request of the wrong man? His gut churned at the idea of having the respect he had seen in her eyes turn to pity.

Pitiful.

He had heard others whisper the word when they thought he could not hear. Even though his closest friends had never spoken so, he knew what was in their heads. It was a pity that Edmund Herriott, who once could be depended on to make a quick decision, now could make none at all. Not good. Not bad.

Pitiful.

A groan sounded in the entry, and, for a moment, he wondered if it had escaped from him.

Miss Fenwick rushed to Miss Kightly's side, asking

her what was wrong, and he shoved away his thoughts that punished him over and over.

Miss Kightly's smile was forced. "Forgive me. I am simply surprised at the message from my great-uncle."

"Do you want to share what Sir Nigel has to say?" Miss Fenwick asked.

"Yes, I guess I should. He says that…" Her voice trailed off.

Miss Fenwick looked toward Edmund, and he shrugged. He could think of several possible subjects Sir Nigel might have written about, especially in light of what had happened at the church and what had been discovered.

He was not surprised when Miss Kightly said, "My great-uncle has sent word that I should be ready to return to his house."

"When?" he asked.

She looked at the note, a lovely golden strand of hair slipping across her pale cheek. "It says only that he will come for me today." Again a strained smile edged along her lips. "'Tis good then that there has not been enough time to unpack my bags." She folded the page and looked around.

The footman jumped forward to take it from her at the same time Edmund reached toward her. Jessup backed away with an apology.

Edmund nodded toward him, then said, "If you wish to sit in the small parlor, I will have a hearty tea brought for us."

"Sit?" Miss Fenwick said with an unexpected laugh. "We have been doing far too much of that."

He savored the sound of her laugh. It lilted like a lark over a spring field, bringing the warmth of sunshine into the entry hall. When she looked at him, he chuckled, caught up in her amusement.

"I stand corrected," he replied.

That set off another round of laughter from both ladies, though the vicar remained as somber as his dark clothes. Edmund had to pause to realize what he had said that was funny.

"No," Miss Fenwick said, "*we* all stand corrected."

Were her words a gentle reminder that his guests were exhausted? Maybe so. Maybe not. As with everything else, he could not decide.

But, even if the words were meant only as a jest, he needed to think of his guests' needs. And his own. His clothes were wet, and they stank of ashes and brandy. He glanced toward the stairs, wondering which rooms were ready for guests. At Christmas, when his other cousin had wed, the Meriweather women had overseen all such preparations.

As if he had spoken aloud, Jessup said, "Lady Meriweather left instructions for where the vicar and his sister and Miss Kightly would stay."

Thank God for Lady Meriweather's foresight. He was able to wear a genuine smile as he said, "Jessup will show you to your rooms whenever you wish."

Miss Fenwick turned to her brother who had not said a word since they had left the church. "Gregory, why don't you rest? I doubt you have slept an hour since the fire."

"I can try." The vicar's voice was a shadow of its usual booming warmth. "I probably won't sleep. Every time I close my eyes, I see that inferno rising up from the depths to consume the church. Every time I let my mind wander, it takes me immediately to the moment when I first saw the flames and knew all I have worked for was being destroyed."

Edmund had to look away before the vicar saw that hated sympathy and pity on *his* face. He did not want to subject any other person to that expression.

"Try to rest today," Miss Fenwick said quietly. "You are going to need to be rested for the work yet to be done in rebuilding the parish church."

"So they can burn it down again?"

Miss Fenwick gasped at the venom in her brother's voice. "Gregory—"

"Someone should have put a halt to these smugglers by now." His fury focused on Edmund. "Why haven't you? Is it because *your* life's work isn't in danger?"

The vicar's words lashed through Edmund. Through Miss Fenwick, too, if he judged by how her face became a sickly gray. Miss Kightly stared at the vicar as if she had never seen him before. No one spoke as the last echoes of Mr. Fenwick's words faded from the entry hall.

Again it was Miss Fenwick who spoke first. "You are exhausted, Gregory. You barely know what you are saying." She put her arm around him, and he wove like a sailor on a ship in a storm. He leaned on her as his head lolled, and she began to buckle.

Edmund leaped forward to pull the vicar's other arm over his shoulder and help keep both Mr. Fenwick and his sister on their feet. He got the man steady only when the footman Foggin grasped the vicar's arm that was draped over Miss Fenwick and drew it over his own shoulder. Miss Fenwick stepped back, her blue eyes wide with despair. She grasped Miss Kightly's hand like a lifeline.

"Jessup and I can get him upstairs to rest, my lord," Foggin said.

"I want to see that he is settled in," Miss Fenwick said in a crisp voice that suggested nothing anyone said would change her mind.

"And, if someone could escort me to where my bags were taken," Miss Kightly said, "I would greatly appreciate it."

A glance he could not read flashed between the two women, and Miss Fenwick asked, "If you don't mind, my lord, can Jessup assist Miss Kightly while we see to Gregory?"

It sounded like a reasonable solution, though he knew he could never have come to it on his own. Everyone looked at him, so he nodded. He loathed admitting, even to himself, how grateful he was for Miss Fenwick's suggestion. He had no idea how long they all would have stood in the entry hall while he tried to determine what to do next.

With a smile and a nod to Jessup, Miss Kightly went up the long staircase, with the footman following like a well-trained puppy. No man of any class could be immune to the blonde's ethereal beauty. She was like a fairy tale princess come to life.

He shook the thought out of his head. Now was not the time to admire Miss Kightly. The vicar needed his help. Telling Foggin that they would start at the count of three, he took a deep breath. The vicar was completely senseless and, therefore, dead weight.

As they climbed, Edmund wondered if he could have managed to help lug the vicar up the stairs before he had gone to the Continent. The life there had hardened his muscles in ways he had never imagined.

In comparison with hefting cannon and gunpowder casks, the vicar was a light load. It had not been an officer's place to handle such tasks, but, in battle, everyone pitched in to help where they could.

Just as Miss Fenwick asked you to help with the church.

He grimaced at how easily she slipped into his thoughts when he was not on guard to prevent it.

"I can send for another footman, my lord," Foggin said.

"If you need to be relieved…"

"Nay, my lord." The footman stumbled over his words as he added, "I meant to take over for you."

"No need." That the footman had misread his grimace was probably the best thing that had happened all day. It would not do for the household staff to start whispering about how their lord could not get his mind off Miss Fenwick.

That would be insulting to the vicar's sister. She had endured enough without him saying something that would be repeated and distorted throughout Sanctuary Bay. It was not she who monopolized his thoughts, but the project she had asked him to work on with her.

The vicar swayed in spite of their grasp on his arms; then he steadied. Edmund looked back to see Miss Fenwick with her hand against her brother's back.

"Move away," Edmund said. "If he falls, he could take you with him."

"I am just helping, even though I know you won't let him fall." She gave him a bolstering smile.

That smile did something unexpected to him, making him feel—for a moment—that he could do anything. Even coming to a simple decision would be possible if she smiled at him again with that expression that suggested she believed he was capable of again becoming the man he once had been. It was oddly comforting to have someone believe the invisible wounds he carried would heal.

"Thank you," he said.

Her crystal-blue eyes widened, and he realized he had put too much fervor into those two words. What a beef-head he was! She was thinking of her brother's welfare, not his. Hadn't he just noted what a devoted sister she was to the vicar? She appreciated Edmund's help. Nothing more. Nothing less. He must not forget that again.

Vera closed the door to the room where Gregory now slept. She guessed Mrs. Porter had slipped some valerian into Gregory's tea, because he had calmed and grown sleepy after drinking less than half of the cup. Maybe with a good night's sleep, he would be more himself in the morning.

Thank You, Lord, for letting him find rest. We will need Your help even more than usual in the days to come.

She walked along the corridor to the room that Lord Meriweather had offered for her use. Going inside, she faltered. Many times she had sat in this room because it had belonged to Catherine Meriweather before her wedding. Here, while seated on the settee in front of the large arched window, she and Cat had talked of every possible subject and read books they both had enjoyed. Occasionally, she had brought a small bag of mending from the vicarage while Cat worked on her needlework. They had sometimes simply looked out at winter snow, summer blooms and the ever-changing sea. She had been here so often that every piece of furniture was as familiar as any in the vicarage, and she knew every contour of the coffered ceiling.

But she had never imagined she would sleep in that grand bed with its bright pink curtains and lush covers. She never had coveted it, being satisfied with the simpler bed in her tiny room at the vicarage. The house she and Gregory had used on Lord Hedgcoe's estate had been larger, but she had been grateful every day that they had a home in Sanctuary Bay.

Now she would be sleeping in this magnificent room until the vicarage was habitable again. She had no idea when that would be. Both Lord Meriweather and her brother had insisted it was too dangerous for her even to peek inside the burned house, so she could not guess how much work it would need. The first priority was rebuilding the church.

No, they needed to find a place to hold services. If the fire had happened a couple of months from now, winter would be past and services could be held out-of-doors. There was no place in the village big enough to hold the parishioners. Maybe Gregory could do several different services for a short time. It was logical, but she knew how important it was to the parish to worship together. That was why, at the time of the previous lord's death, the talk had begun about building a larger church. Recently, the population in the village had grown.

Her fingers clenched on the coverlet. She hoped the arrival of more people to the village set on the side of the steep cliff had nothing to do with the smugglers. Easy money could entice criminals who would change

Sanctuary Bay forever. With all the preparations for Cat and Jonathan's wedding, she had spent very little time in the village during the past six or seven weeks. Maybe she should make some calls on longtime parishioners and discover more about the newcomers.

"Is there a problem, Miss Fenwick?" asked Lord Meriweather.

She released the covers and whirled. She had not expected him to come and check on her. She had assumed he would return downstairs where he could talk with Miss Kightly or seek his own rooms in order to change out of his smoke-stained clothing. His hair was still damp, and it curled at the back of his collar.

"Of course not," she hurried to say before he could notice that she was staring. "Not beyond the obvious ones, I should say."

He nodded, and she expected he would urge her to rest and be on his way. Instead, he lingered by the door. "I have assured your brother as I have you that everything humanly possible will be done to rebuild the church."

"I am sure." She smiled, astounding herself because she had been thinking only moments ago of surrendering to tears. "With your expertise, my lord, all should go well."

He looked past her as if unwilling to meet her eyes. "About that, Miss Fenwick. I hope you understand that I have never been involved in building a church."

"Nor have Gregory or I."

"True." A smile flitted across his lips as he leaned one shoulder against the doorjamb. "I will need guidance." He looked toward the ceiling before lowering his gaze to meet hers. "Not just from above, but on a more practical earthly plane."

"We will do everything we can to help."

"Good."

She sensed there was something more he wanted to say. Perhaps she was mistaken. She did not know him well enough to discern his true feelings, but her intuition whispered she was right.

"And," she said with a smile of her own, "I am grateful that you have offered such a lovely and comfortable place for Gregory and me to stay. We both will understand if a time comes when you need our rooms for other guests."

"Nonsense. I'm not tossing you out when you have no place to go. What sort of fellow would I be then?"

Tears rushed into her eyes, and she lowered them before he could discern how much his words meant to her. If Lord Hedgcoe had shown that kindness, she and Gregory would not have feared being homeless and facing starvation.

"Have I said something wrong, Miss Fenwick?" Lord Meriweather asked, sincere concern in his question. "If I have said something unseemly, forgive me. I have spent too many years with men who spoke plainly."

She met his gaze with her own. "You have not said anything unseemly. You are being far kinder than I dared to hope."

"Kinder?"

Oh, dear! Had she offended him when all she wanted to do was thank him? Every word that came out of her mouth today seemed to be the wrong one.

When she said that and asked for his forgiveness,

he chuckled. "I could say the same thing to you, Miss Fenwick, and beg your indulgence. I daresay fatigue and shock have more control of our tongues than our brains do."

"I agree." For the first time since she had heard of the fire at the church, her shoulders sagged from their rigid stance. A shudder of pain rushed down her back as her strained muscles protested.

A good night's sleep. That was what she needed as much as her brother did.

Vera did not realize that she had swayed until Lord Meriweather's hand closed around her arm and he asked if she needed to sit. Warmth slipped from his palm, strengthening her, but her head remained light.

"Maybe I should sit," she murmured.

"May I help you?"

"Yes." She did not want to tumble on to her nose in front of him, so she allowed him to guide her to the settee in front of the largest window.

He sat her as if she were made of the most brittle porcelain. Brittle. That described exactly how she felt. Every inch of her seemed to feel too much and be about to crack at the next bit of bad news.

Kneeling beside her, he held her hands between his calloused ones. She wondered why his fingers were trembling; then she realized the quivering came from her own fingers.

"Tell me what you need, Miss Fenwick," he said, his face turned up toward her.

She gazed down at him. A low mat of tawny whiskers emphasized the planes of his jaw and cheek. How had she failed to notice that tiny scar beneath his right eyebrow? It was no bigger than the nail on her smallest finger, and she was curious if he had received it, as his friend Lord Northbridge had, during the war. Or had it been there before he joined the fight against Napoleon?

"Miss Fenwick?"

"Yes?" she asked as she seemed to fall into the brown depths of his eyes. They had seen so much. Things she could not imagine. Things she did not want to imagine.

Again the tired tears scorched the back of her eyes. She needed to be more like him in the wake of the fire at the church. Be strong and keep her focus on the task that lay ahead.

"Tell me what you need me to do," he said again.

For you to tell me that everything will be all right, that this is only a nightmare. She could not say that. Instead, she struggled to smile and found it was not as difficult as she had expected when he regarded her with kindness.

She began, "I need you to—"

"Lord Meriweather!" came a shout from the hallway.

A ginger-hackled footman careened to a stop by the open door.

Vera recognized him but was not sure of his name. Heat slapped her face when his gaze focused on Lord Meriweather's hands cupping hers. She hastily jerked her hands away, clasping them on her lap.

"Oh, my lord, I didn't mean to intrude. That is…" The footman's face became as ruddy as his hair.

Standing, Lord Meriweather said, "Carl, Miss Fenwick would like tea and something to eat brought here as soon as possible."

The footman nodded but carefully did not look again at either her or the baron.

"What is your message?" Lord Meriweather asked.

"Sir Nigel's carriage has come through the gate." Carl's voice was so low that Vera had to strain to hear it.

"Has Miss Kightly been informed?"

"I am on my way there now, my lord." He rushed away.

Lord Meriweather turned to face Vera again. "If you will excuse me, Miss Fenwick. Perhaps we can finish our discussion later."

"Whenever is convenient for you." She was surprised that he acted as if the footman's reaction to discovering them alone in Cat's bedroom was nothing out of the ordinary. She decided to follow his lead and pretend that there soon would not be whispers belowstairs about the baron and the vicar's sister holding hands. "Or we can finish it while we walk downstairs."

"Don't you want to stay here and rest?"

"Yes." She sighed as she pushed herself to her feet. "But I want to thank Miss Kightly for being such a good companion on our way north from Norwich. She let me babble on about my hopes and fears for the parish church, and not once did she say what I'm sure was in her mind—that she was tired of hearing me say the same things over and over."

"If you would like, I can convey that to her."

"No. I should thank her myself."

"As you wish." He offered his arm.

She hesitated. Nothing would add to the gossip about him holding her hands more than being seen only minutes later with her hand on his arm.

He smiled coolly. "Miss Fenwick, surely you know from your long association with my cousins and this household that nothing we do or say can halt the wagging tongues of those who misconstrue my attempt to comfort you in the wake of the fire."

"I understand that, but…" Again the warmth surged up her face.

"You are worrying needlessly. Exactly as you know the people here and the village well, they know you and will give no credence to any whispers of you acting like a featherbrain."

Vera put her hand on his sleeve so she could avoid meeting his eyes. If he had any idea of how she had been extremely foolish before she and Gregory had found a haven in Sanctuary Bay, he would not be offering that assurance.

She was glad that Sir Nigel bustled into the entry hall as she and Lord Meriweather descended the stairs. Sir Nigel had snow-white hair and the wide stomach of a well-fed man. His greatcoat was spotted with rain. He ignored the footman waiting to take it as he looked up the stairs and scowled.

"Where is Lillian?" Sir Nigel demanded without the courtesy of a greeting.

Beside her, Lord Meriweather stiffened as they stepped into the entry hall, but his smile appeared genuine as he said, "She has been alerted of your arrival."

"Didn't she get the message I sent here for her? It told her what time I would be here." The baronet puffed up like an affronted rooster.

"I got it," Miss Kightly said as she came down the stairs, her steps light on each tread. Behind her, Carl carried her bags and kept his gaze focused on the floor. "Here I am, Uncle Nigel."

Vera stepped aside as Miss Kightly walked past her to give her great-uncle a kiss on the cheek. The blonde stepped back, glanced toward Vera with what seemed to be a meaningful expression and then turned to Lord Meriweather. What message had Miss Kightly been trying to convey? Whatever it was, Vera could not decipher it.

"Oh, my dear girl," Sir Nigel gushed. "When I heard you were riding back here from the wedding, I wanted to get you to my house right away. It may not be safe here in the wake of recent events."

"Don't be silly," Miss Kightly said with a light tone that Vera had never heard her use before. She gazed up at Lord Meriweather with unadulterated admiration. "I am perfectly safe while in the company of one of England's great heroes."

The tips of Lord Meriweather's ears turned red, but Vera could not guess if he was embarrassed or pleased at Miss Kightly's praise.

There was no question how Sir Nigel felt, because his forehead ruffled as his scowl deepened. "Meriweather, this has been a sorry situation." He shook his head. "A very sorry situation. What do you intend to do about it?"

"Do?" repeated Lord Meriweather, clearly astounded by Sir Nigel's question.

"Yes! You are the lord of Meriweather Hall, aren't you? You are responsible for the parish church in Sanctuary Bay, aren't you? You must have some sort of plan of what to do since it burned down."

Vera almost said, *Since it was burned down by the*

smugglers. She pressed her lips closed, knowing it was not her place to speak up during a conversation between her social betters. If she humiliated Lord Meriweather in front of his neighbor, he could turn his frustration on her and Gregory as Lord Hedgcoe had. Not that she believed the baron was as vindictive as Lord Hedgcoe had been, but she could not take that risk. Not when Gregory's living depended on Lord Meriweather's good will.

"Lord Meriweather intends to rebuild the church," Miss Kightly said with a broad smile. "Isn't that marvelous? And generous." She almost cooed the last words as she put her hand possessively on Lord Meriweather's arm.

Vera lowered her eyes, but not quickly enough to miss Lord Meriweather's shock at Miss Kightly's bold motion. Maybe that was how members of the *ton* acted with one another. Neither she nor the new baron had much experience in that direction. Was he as uncomfortable with Miss Kightly's actions as he was with her great-uncle's verbal assault? As uncomfortable as Vera was?

"It is," Sir Nigel said in the same uncompromising tone, "the very least he could do for the parish when he was not here to help."

"Uncle, be fair," Miss Kightly implored. "We were attending his cousin's wedding." She raised her eyes back to Lord Meriweather's taut face. "He hurried here as soon as he could."

"The church should have been torn down when the roof caved in." The baronet seemed to notice Vera for the first time. "Now neglect has led to this fire that has destroyed not only the parish church but the vicarage."

Vera met his gaze steadily, but as with Miss Kightly, she could not read what Sir Nigel's narrowed eyes intended to convey. When he looked away first to stare at his great-niece, she was curious about the unspoken conversation she was not privy to. Something was going on, something that had to do with Miss Kightly's oddly brazen behavior and her great-uncle's ridiculous accusations.

"Come along, Lillian," Sir Nigel said, motioning for the footman to take her bags out to his carriage. "There is no need to linger here any longer."

Miss Kightly gave Lord Meriweather a long hug that startled him and made Vera ill at ease for reasons she could not quite explain. Her stomach tightened painfully, and she could not pull her eyes from the embrace, even though she knew she should. Instead, she waited for Lord Meriweather to put his arms around the blonde. He did not before Miss Kightly released him. For some reason, seeing that allowed Vera's stomach to unclench ever so slightly.

It compressed again when Miss Kightly turned to throw her arms around Vera. As she hugged Vera, Miss Kightly whispered, "I'm sorry."

She did not know how to respond because she had no idea why Miss Kightly had said those two simple words. Were they to express again her dismay about the fire at the church, or were they an apology for something else?

"Come along," Sir Nigel said again when Miss Kightly had accepted his help in putting on her coat. "It's a cold, wet drive back home." As he put his arm around his great-niece's shoulders, he said, "Now that you are here, Meriweather, I trust you will *decide* what to do to make things right."

The baron recoiled as if Sir Nigel had struck him, and, in a way, he had. The baronet had targeted Lord Meriweather's most vulnerable spot.

Before she could halt herself, she said, "Sir Nigel, Lord Meriweather has already made some excellent decisions toward rebuilding the church. Both my brother and I are very pleased that he has offered his expertise to assist. I am sure you are glad to hear that, as well."

"Yes, yes," the baronet said before hurrying Miss Kightly out the door.

Vera tilted up her chin, pleased with her efforts to halt the baronet's uncharacteristically cruel jabs at Lord Meriweather. As she turned away from the door, she realized that, except for her and the footman by the door, the entry hall was empty. Lord Meriweather must have left while her attention was on the others' departure. His cousin had told her how it pained and mortified the baron that he could not make a decision.

She considered trying to find him, but climbed the stairs to the room she would be using until they returned to the vicarage. She had offered up prayers earlier to ask God to help her be there for her brother through the trials ahead. She also needed to pray that she would be able to do the same for Lord Meriweather.

Chapter Three

The next morning, Edmund found only Lady Meriweather seated at the table in the breakfast parlor. She put down the newspaper she had been reading.

"Good morning, Edmund," she said with the warmth that suggested he was her son rather than her late husband's distant cousin.

"And to you, my lady. Do not let me interrupt your reading."

She laughed. "This newspaper was sent from London. It is nearly a week old, so waiting longer to read it is no problem."

Helping himself to eggs and sausages, he placed his plate at the seat across from the baroness. She poured him a steaming cup of coffee from the silver pot that had been left on a ceramic tile by her right hand. He reached for a muffin from the basket that was set beside him by one of the well-trained footmen.

He buttered it as he said, "I have not had a chance to thank you for making arrangements for Mr. Fenwick and his sister to stay at Meriweather Hall."

"It was my pleasure. Dear Vera has been a steadfast

friend to my daughters, and it is not as if we don't have the room." Her laugh sparkled through the space. "She tells me that you have agreed to help with rebuilding the church."

"It is my place."

"To provide the funds, yes, but Vera suggested you were going to provide more than that."

He poured cream into his cup and stirred it. Setting the pitcher on the table, he wondered when the two women had talked. No doubt, it had been after he had scurried away like a hurt child from Sir Nigel's barbed comments. He snuck a glance at the lady across the table from him. Had Miss Fenwick told her about that conversation? If so, he saw no sign of pity on her face.

"You know of my work before I came to Meriweather Hall," he said when he realized the lady expected him to answer. "I know something of building projects."

"Quite a bit, according to my new son-in-law." She chuckled. "Jonathan mentioned something about seeking your advice for the larger house he plans to build for him and Cat."

"He said nothing about that to me."

"Because he knew you would help when the time came. You, Jonathan and Charles learned to depend on each other's skills in the army, and that will never change." She picked up her coffee cup. "You have been given a great gift, Edmund. Such friends do not come along often."

"I realize that."

"Have you heard more about the tunnel that led into the church?" She must be as curious as he was to learn how and when the smugglers had gotten into the church.

"Sims brought me a report this morning. The tunnel appears to have been collapsed completely. We cannot guess where it might go."

"Nothing aboveground suggests its direction or destination?"

He was impressed with the baroness's question, though he should not have been. All the Meriweather women had sharp minds and cared deeply about the estate and the people of Sanctuary Bay.

With a shake of his head, he said, "The smugglers are too careful to allow that. Otherwise they would have been found out years ago."

"I see." After Lady Meriweather took a sip of her coffee, she changed the subject to her plans for the gardens once the weather was warm enough to plant flowers among the hedges and perennials. He listened with half an ear as he thought of what she had said. He and Northbridge and Bradby had been melded together in the crucible of war. That bond had been strengthened as they had faced the smugglers' treachery since he had first arrived in Sanctuary Bay. He could depend on their assistance again, if necessary.

He hoped it would not be, because Bradby was on his honeymoon and Northbridge and his family were settling into his ancestral estate in the south of England. But it was good to remember that, if he needed them, they would come.

Maybe fulfilling Miss Fenwick's request to help rebuild the church would not be impossible, after all.

When Foggin came to announce a guest later that morning, Edmund assumed either the vicar or Miss

Fenwick wished to discuss the plans for rebuilding the church. Instead, a dark-haired man with an air of arrogance strode into the room as if he were lord of the estate and Edmund his least minion. Edmund suspected women would find Lord Ashland handsome, but his sharp features and hollow cheeks reminded Edmund of how disdainful the viscount had been when Edmund went to his estate in hopes of obtaining help in halting the smugglers.

"Ashland!" Edmund pushed himself to his feet. "I had not expected you to call."

"This is no social visit." He drew off his gloves and tossed them in the direction of Foggin.

The footman scrambled to catch them both along with the greatcoat the viscount shrugged off. The poor footman looked so dismayed that Edmund wanted to assure him that Ashland treated everyone with the same contempt.

"I heard," Ashland went on, as if he had not taken note of the footman, "about the fire at the Sanctuary Bay church, and I thought I should come and discover how bad it was."

"It was very bad." He hid his surprise. The viscount had never shown the least bit of interest about anything in the village. A hint of suspicion bubbled through him. If the viscount were the man the smugglers called *his qualityship,* he would be curious if anything pointing to the smugglers had been discovered in the ruins. "The building is completely destroyed."

"I am sorry to hear that confirmed. Rumors reach one's ears all the time, but I prefer to discover the truth for myself. If you have no objections, I would like to ride into the village and see what remains."

"There is not much to see."

"Even so, I would like to see it with my own two eyes."

"Certainly." He paused, then said, "As you have removed your outer coat, I assume there is more you wish to discuss with me before we leave for the village." He gestured toward a chair near the hearth. "We may as well be comfortable by the fire before we venture out into the cold."

"Quite so." Ashland selected a chair as if he were doing Edmund a great favor.

How did one come to possess such hauteur? Ashland's bearing suggested that his place was at the center in the universe and that everyone should acknowledge it. Did that mien come from being raised as a peer from birth? Could it be learned later in life? Not that he wanted to act as self-important as Ashland, but he could use the confidence such comportment inspired.

Another item to put on his list for his next conversation with Northbridge. He could ask his friend and former military commander such questions without the ridicule he would face if he addressed those questions to Ashland. That lesson he had learned all too well when he had asked Lady Eloisa about life among the *ton*. She had answered him, but later made a jest about it at his expense. The Beau Monde could be scathing to outsiders too eager to join the elite of the elite. They labeled those people encroaching mushrooms, but he had not expected, as a new baron, to be described in such terms.

Not until he had overheard Lady Eloisa use that exact term along with his name.

Edmund sat after offering to ring for a cup of something warm for the viscount. When Ashland said that was unnecessary, Edmund asked, "What did you want to discuss?"

"Rumors."

"You will need to be more specific. Sanctuary Bay is always rife with rumors." He allowed himself a cool smile. "Some are true. The trick, as I learned during my time in the army, was to determine which are true and which are simple conjecture fueled by repetition."

Ashland's eyes narrowed, and Edmund knew that the viscount had not anticipated such a retort from him. If Ashland thought him nothing but a harebrained newcomer to the Polite World, reminding the viscount that Edmund had seen battle on the Continent was not a bad thing.

"That is true," Ashland said, continuing to appraise Edmund. Was he surprised by what he saw? No hint of his thoughts were revealed on his carefully schooled face.

"Are there particular rumors that you wish to discuss?"

"Rumors about the smugglers who work out of Sanctuary Bay."

Edmund kept his fingers from digging into the upholstery and his shoulders from stiffening. The viscount's words disclosed more than his face did, and Edmund suspected his cool composure was a pose. Two could play that game, so he sank back in his chair, crossing one foot over the opposite knee.

"Again," he said, "I need you to be more specific. Smugglers and their exploits are a major source of rumors throughout Britain."

"True. I shall be specific." He pyramided his fingers in front of his face. "Rumor says that the vicar and his sister are now living here at Meriweather Hall. Is that true?"

"Yes." He was shocked by the abrupt turn in the conversation. Why would Ashland be interested in where the Fenwicks were staying in the wake of the fire? "I thought we were talking about rumors of the smugglers."

"We are. Other rumors have reached my ears. Rumors of smugglers using the church as a place to store their shipments."

It took every ounce of his control to ask in a placid voice, "Are you accusing the Fenwicks of assisting the smugglers?"

"The facts speak for themselves."

"Do they?" He lowered his foot to the floor as he met Ashland's stare with his own. "Then you clearly are hearing more than rumor, Ashland. The facts are not that straightforward to me. I have seen what was left behind in the church's cellar, and I have seen the Fenwicks' faces when they heard that information." He faltered as he recalled the pain and grief on Miss Fenwick's face during the long ride back from Norwich. Tears had glistened in her eyes when she had beheld what was left of the only home she had known for the past ten years. The memory of her face as she had fought to remain strong for her brother and his parishioners was etched on his mind. "I believe they have been victims, twice over. First, when the smugglers used Mr. Fenwick's church for their crimes, and second, when the church and the vicarage were burned."

"You come to their defense easily."

"The truth is easy." Keeping his answers short prevented his anger from bursting forth.

The viscount smiled coldly. "Truth, like beauty, is bought by judgment of the eye, if I may misquote Shakespeare. You rush to the defense of the Fenwicks."

"Because they are, as I have said, victims in this heinous crime."

"Maybe they are, but I am not as certain of that as you are."

Edmund borrowed the viscount's chilly expression. "Why?"

Again he sensed that his question had astounded Ashland, because the viscount did not shoot back an answer. When Edmund had gone to Ashland's estate last year to ask for his help in halting the smugglers, he had been shocked at the viscount's disdain and disinterest in taking action with him. He had stuttered over his words and left feeling like a pup with its tail curled beneath its legs…as he had when Lady Eloisa had tossed him aside.

"You are a newcomer to Sanctuary Bay, Meriweather," the viscount answered as he regained his poise. "I have lived nearby my whole life."

"Then you should know that the Fenwicks would never be mixed up with the smugglers."

"No?" He laughed icily. "I would leave you in your ignorance, Meriweather, but the situation requires action. May I suggest your first action would be to speak to the vicar and his sister about assistance they have offered the smugglers?"

Edmund looked away from the triumphant glitter in Ashland's eyes. The viscount must have directed the conversation to this point so he could shock Edmund with such a revelation. No, it was not a revelation. Only innuendo.

"I shall." Standing, he said, "And there is no time like the present. The Fenwicks have gone to see what they can recover from the church, as well as any personal possessions. Why don't we go and ask them together if your insinuations have any basis in truth?"

"I thought the church was completely destroyed." Ashland remained seated, but his smile had vanished into a deep scowl.

"The building was, but items can survive even such an inferno."

He leaned forward, his eyes slitting again. "What did you see when you climbed into the cellar?"

"I see gabble-grinders have been doing a strapping job of spreading the tale of my actions at the church." He folded his arms, after ringing for a footman to bring the viscount's outer wraps, as well as his own.

"Why are you avoiding giving me an answer to my question?" He set himself on his feet. "Are you trying to hide something, Meriweather?"

"Are you accusing me of being in collusion with the smugglers?"

"You? Working with the smugglers?" Ashland surprised him by laughing.

The viscount was not laughing at his question. Ashland was laughing at *him*. And why not? A baron who could make no decisions was hardly a man fit to give the smugglers orders of when and where to obtain their illegal wares. Did the whole world know of his humiliating affliction? It would seem so.

Vera heard the rattle of harness and carriage wheels and looked up from where she was placing a broken plate back on the ground. Brushing away the cloud of ashes that swirled on the sea wind, she was not surprised to see the Meriweather carriage slowing to a stop between the ruins of the church and the charred vicarage.

Happiness burst through her as unstoppable as the waves rolling out of the sea. And just as powerful. She was glad that Lord Meriweather had come from Meriweather Hall. He was calm and sturdy and…handsome. She ignored the end of that thought. He made her feel that her problems were his. He made her feel safe. He made her feel…lovely.

Was she addled? The last time she had let her mind lead her in that direction, she had almost destroyed her brother's career. But lying to herself was foolish. When she was with the baron, she felt as if she were someone special, someone who could be described as more than the vicar's sister, someone who had worth of her own.

The carriage door opened. She wiped her hands on her apron and straightened. Her spine protested, and she realized she had spent hours bent over as she picked through the ashes around the vicarage. With the roof falling in, she had not dared to go inside. Some of the men who had fought the flames had tossed some items out of the vicarage's small kitchen, but only a handful of items had survived.

Her brother stared at the window where his office had been. He had not moved from that spot for the past hour. Her single attempt to comfort him had been for naught. When he'd asked her to leave him to his thoughts and prayers, she had agreed.

Shouts sounded around what remained of the church. The men working there had noticed Lord Meriweather's carriage. They paused in their tasks, and she wondered if they were as eager as she was to listen to any plans the baron might have for rebuilding.

Her welcoming smile wavered when Lord Meriweather stepped out of the carriage, every inch of him bristling with the fury displayed on his face. That anger was hidden when another man emerged from the carriage.

Lord Ashland! What was the viscount doing here? He seldom came to the village, though he had attended services at the church several times in the past year.

Vera walked toward the men, curious what had caused even-tempered Lord Meriweather to wear such a grim expression. "Good day, my lords," she called.

They paused when they reached her and greeted her politely. It was clear they had other issues on their minds.

"I'm glad you are here," she said when silence fell between them. "The men have been working hard, as you'll be able to see."

"They aren't the only ones." Lord Meriweather's face transformed as he smiled.

"What do you mean?"

"It appears you have been poking around the ashes, too, Miss Fenwick. You have a line of gray streaking your cheek." He raised his hand, then drew it back with a glance at Lord Ashland who watched without comment.

"Oh, that must have happened one of the times I pushed aside my hair." She looked at her filthy hands.

"Allow me." Lord Meriweather pulled out a lawn handkerchief and handed it to her. When she looked at him in confusion, because she was not sure which of her cheeks was dirty, he pointed to the left side of his face.

"Thank you," she said as she dabbed at the soot on her face. When she looked at the handkerchief, she was shocked how dirty her cheek must have been. She wondered why nobody else had mentioned it. Maybe they had not wanted to embarrass her, telling her that she looked like a chimney sweep.

She noticed Lord Ashland walking toward her brother. Maybe the viscount could offer Gregory solace on this difficult day.

"Have you found anything that was saved?" asked Lord Meriweather, drawing her eyes back to his.

She saw concern within those dark pools, but the storm that had raged there when he had exited the carriage could not be hidden. She almost asked what was amiss. She halted herself before she could overstep her place as the vicar's sister.

"The cooking pans are blackened, but they can be cleaned and made useable again." She looked at where her brother talked to Lord Ashland. "Not one of Gregory's books was spared. I haven't seen him this upset since…" She halted herself before she could spill the truth of what had happened before Gregory was given the living in Sanctuary Bay by a very generous Lord Meriweather. "There aren't many things he prized as much as he did his collection of books."

Lord Meriweather sighed. "He is welcome to use any books in Meriweather Hall."

"Thank you, and he will avail himself of them, but he had some favorite volumes he will sorely miss."

"I am sorry to hear that. I have contacts in London who may be able to find copies to replace them."

Vera smiled. "I will let him know." London prices would be too dear for a vicar, but she appreciated Lord Meriweather's offer. She hoped Gregory would, as well, though knowing copies existed that he could not afford would add to his frustration.

She started to put the soiled handkerchief in her apron pocket, but Lord Meriweather said, "I can take that."

"Are you sure? It's dirty."

He gave her a sad smile. "I daresay by the time I leave here, I will be far dirtier." He held out his hand.

"That is true."

His troubled expression drew his mouth down farther at the corners. "May I ask you a question?"

"Certainly. What about?" She placed the handkerchief on his outstretched palm.

A gust of wind threatened to steal it. She clamped her hand down on the fine linen at the exact same time he closed his fingers around hers. A shock rippled up her arm, a shock that was startling and pleasing at the same time. He drew in a quick breath, and she looked up at him. She saw her conflicting reaction mirrored on his face.

"Miss Fenwick..." His voice was as breathless as if he had run down the village's steep street and back up. Twice.

"My lord..." She was unsure what to say after that, but she must say something. She could not stand with her hand in his. After what the footman had seen at Meriweather Hall, gossip would spread far and fast... exactly as it had last time.

That memory spurred her to slip her hand from his.

"Thank you, my lord, for lending me your handkerchief."

He did not reply as he gazed at her, as if he had never taken note of her before, and he was intrigued by what he saw.

Vera turned away as someone shouted, glad for the excuse to sever the invisible link between them. She closed her eyes and prayed, *Dear Father, I must not forget what happened before. Lead me on the path I should walk, the path that makes sure I never risk Gregory's work for You.*

When she opened her eyes, Lord Meriweather was loping toward a man by the cellar. The man was waving excitedly to him.

Curiosity sent Vera after him at a slower pace among the gravestones that seemed lonely without the church standing guard over them. Both Lord Ashland and her brother passed her; by the time she reached the hole, the men were grouped around something on the ground. Lord Ashland was looking over the side but stepped back hastily before someone bumped into him and sent him down to the bottom of the cellar.

"Just brought it up, my lord," someone said from the center of the group. "Can you believe it?"

Squeezing among the men, Vera gasped when somebody took her arm and popped her out of the crowd like a grain of sand between her fingers. She smiled at Gregory when he drew her to stand beside him. He gestured toward the ground in front of them.

"Oh, my!" She stared at the baptismal font that rested in three pieces by the cellar hole. The pedestal had broken twice, but the bowl was intact. Smoke and water stains brought the carved figures on the stone into higher relief. "I thought it was shattered."

"So did I." Lord Meriweather bent to examine the ancient font. One side was badly chipped. "Astounding! When I saw it in the cellar, I was sure it was destroyed."

The men grinned.

A tall man she recognized as Luther Hinchliff, the village cooper, said, "We thought so, too, then realized the broken pieces were from the ceiling. The pedestal will have to be put back together, but otherwise it's useable."

"We can put it in the new church," Gregory said, and Vera patted his arm. "God has shown His love by allowing this vital part of our church to come through the flames. Let us thank Him." He took her left hand and reached out to the man on his left.

When a hand grasped her right one, the warmth coursing through her at the simple touch could have come only from Lord Meriweather.

She bowed her head as Gregory led them in prayer and added her silent thanks that her brother seemed revitalized by the discovery. A good night's sleep had helped, too, but she had been worried about his state of mind when he had stood by the vicarage so long.

Everyone chorused heartfelt amens when Gregory finished. He reached past her to shake the hands of the men who had brought the font up from the cellar without damaging it further.

Beside her, Lord Meriweather said, "It's a beginning."

"Yes," she said, unable to stop smiling. "We may not have a roof over our heads when we worship, but we can catch heaven's rain to baptize our newest members."

"A lovely thought, Miss Fenwick." He squeezed her hand, and she pulled in a sharp breath. She had not realized he still held it, for it seemed natural to have her fingers enfolded within his. "With this beginning to inspire us, who knows what other blessings lie ahead of us?"

"Blessings? Finally some good news." The voice came from behind her. She drew her hand out of Lord Meriweather's and turned as the others did to see a pudgy man. His greatcoat was worn at the elbows, and the collar was frayed. His dark hair needed to be cut. Any hint of a shine had vanished from his boots.

Lord Ashland stepped forward. "Ah, Brooks, I should have known you would be here posthaste." He motioned toward the rest of them. "You know the vicar and Miss Fenwick, of course. Have you met the new baron?"

The chubby man nodded his head toward Vera and her brother, then dipped his head more deeply toward Lord Meriweather. "Haven't had the pleasure until now, though I did see you at Sir Nigel's fall assembly. Too crowded to get to you so we might speak, my lord, that night. So many art lovers eager to admire Sir Nigel's latest masterpieces. I assumed eventually our paths would cross again." Mr. Brooks looked from the ruins of the church to the burned-out vicarage. "Vicar, I would guess you are the best one to bring me up-to-date on this tragedy. If you have the time, that is…"

"Of course, Mr. Brooks," her brother said.

Mr. Brooks motioned for Gregory to walk with him away from the others. When Lord Ashland made to follow, Mr. Brooks gave him a stern look that stopped him in midstep.

The viscount scowled, then stamped toward the carriage. "Coming, Meriweather?" he called over his shoulder.

"In a few minutes."

Vera was grateful that she stood far enough away from the viscount so she could not discern the words he growled under his breath.

Lord Meriweather watched Lord Ashland for a moment, then shook his head and sighed. He clasped his hands behind his back. "Miss Fenwick, who is Brooks?"

"Cuthbert Brooks is the local justice of the peace."

"That man is the justice of the peace?"

Vera kept her voice low. "Do not let his self-effacing image fool you. He is a brilliant man when it comes to keeping the peace in the Sanctuary Bay parish."

"He has been of little use with stopping the smugglers."

"But there has been less violence than in other places along the shore."

"Possibly because the smugglers know better than to upset their well-placed leader."

"That is something I cannot forget," she whispered.

"Nor I."

Vera was astonished when Lord Meriweather glanced at where Lord Ashland was climbing into the carriage. Did the baron have suspicions about the viscount's involvement with the smugglers?

She had heard enough whispers to know that the smugglers took their orders from someone of wealth and prestige. The viscount fit that description, as did

Sir Nigel. Mr. Brooks was not as plump in the pockets as the other two, but he held much sway in the parish as the justice of the peace.

"As a good host," Lord Meriweather said with a sigh, "I should escort Ashland back to Meriweather Hall. I have no idea why he wanted to come here." He glanced at the baptismal font.

"With the recovery of the font," she said, "the parishioners are going to be even more eager to have the church rebuilt."

"I agree."

"We need to start making plans for the interior. I can meet with you tomorrow whenever you wish. Or the next day if that is better."

"If you think that is the best time…"

Vera kept her face serene, so he could not discern how sympathy welled up within her. The poor man could not make a single decision. Facing each one seemed to scourge him.

"Let's not set a definite time now. I will make a list of what I think we need to do," she said, "and, when I'm done, I will bring it to you for review. Your expertise will be invaluable."

He nodded and turned to leave; then he paused. Facing her, he said, "One question, Miss Fenwick, if I may."

"Of course. Any time."

Again his smile came and went like lightning on a hot summer night. "It is a difficult question to ask. It has come to my attention that it is being said that you and your brother have offered assistance to the smugglers. Is there any truth in that rumor?"

"None!" Both anger and pain riveted her. Anger

that he would give that rumor any credence. Pain that such a lie could lead to her brother losing the living in Sanctuary Bay.

"I'm glad to hear that." He tipped his hat toward her. "I will see you at Meriweather Hall, Miss Fenwick. If you need anything, don't hesitate to ask."

She nodded, but she knew she would never be able to ask for what she needed most now: answers. She wanted to know who was spreading spurious tales about her and Gregory. She ached to discover if, upon first hearing them, Lord Meriweather had contemplated sending them away from Sanctuary Bay. And, as much, she longed to find out how she could halt herself from feeling the warmth of his touch, a warmth that could lead her into ruining everything…again.

Chapter Four

Vera stifled a yawn as she walked into her brother's room the next morning. The room Gregory was using was as masculine in style as hers was feminine. Dark furniture and rugs contrasted with the green velvet draperies. Friezes along the ceiling served as a frame for a mural of a hunting scene. Foxhounds bounded past hedges while riders on horseback jumped over them, suspended forever in midflight. The bright red coats matched the silk on the upper half of the walls above richly stained moldings.

She called his name, and he poked his head past the door that led to the room where his valet would sleep if he had one.

"Good," he said. "I had hoped you would get here before I left."

"Left?" She noticed he carried a stack of clothing. "Where are you going? We need you here now while we make plans for the new church."

He opened a bag on the bed that already held a few items, including several books that must have come from Lord Meriweather's book room. "I must seek the bishop's counsel on dealing with the smugglers. As well, I want to share our plans for rebuilding the church."

"The plans to move the church closer to the village?" She walked to the other side of the bed and watched as he deftly packed the bag. If she did not know better, she would have guessed he had done that many times before.

"Yes, but it is not only the building. There is the churchyard to consider. If we move to another location, do we build a wall around it to protect the graves? The parishioners will not want to be separated in death from their loved ones by starting a new churchyard with the new building."

She sat on a chair near the foot of the tester bed. "Perhaps we could move the new church a bit closer to the old foundation, so we can still incorporate the graves within the churchyard."

"A good idea, Vera. I shall share it with the bishop." He put the last of the clothing in the bag. "Thank goodness that Lord Meriweather and I are close enough in size so I don't have to call on the bishop wearing dirty and torn clothing." He closed the top of the worn leather bag and stepped away from the bed.

"I cannot imagine the bishop would judge your ability to lead our parish through this crisis with the smugglers because of what you are wearing." She smoothed her hands over her lap and the fine gown that was Cat's. It was even more elegant than the one she had worn to her friend's wedding, but for the daughter of a baron, it would be considered an everyday morning gown.

"True. Mr. Hamilton has agreed to lead the services on Sunday. I trust you will help him as you do me."

"Of course." She would write a simple sermon for Mr. Hamilton to read. He was a fisherman like many in the village, but he helped often at the church and tended the churchyard.

"And if you are away longer than that?"

"I will worry about that if I must."

Vera bit back frustrated words. Her brother allowed her to assist in his work, but nothing more. How could he not see that she longed to do more to serve God? Many times, she had dreamed of being the one standing at the pulpit preaching the words she had written. Her brother could not imagine a woman having such an ambition.

Gregory glanced toward her. "Something is bothering you, Vera. What is it?"

"Lord Meriweather asked me an unsettling question yesterday." That it was rumored she and Gregory had abetted the smugglers had kept her awake most of the night.

"About what?" He reached into the cupboard for a coat that, like the rest of his clothing, must belong to the baron.

"The silliest thing." She should have said nothing. Gregory had been pleased to have the old Lord Meriweather's complete confidence in him. That the new one might not would upset him more.

"What did he ask?" He folded the coat over his arm and looked at her.

"He asked if we had ever helped the smugglers, and I told him that we hadn't."

Gregory placed the coat on top of the bag. "That is not completely true."

"What?" She jumped to her feet. "Gregory, you cannot be serious!"

"I am." He motioned toward the door. "Let's find Lord Meriweather. I might as well explain to both of you at the same time."

She fought the sickness clawing at her stomach. Her brother had helped the smugglers? *Lord, how can I face Lord Meriweather knowing that my brother assisted the men who threatened the baron's cousins?* Both Sophia and Cat had escaped alive, but the situation could easily have gone the other way. And Gregory had helped them....

Somehow her feet carried her alongside her brother. She gripped the banister as they descended the stairs. She heard Gregory ask someone where the baron was but could not focus on whom he spoke with nor the answer. She realized where they were going only when she saw four suits of armor that held swords and lances at the ready lining either side of the corridor.

Gregory knocked on the door of the book room and called, "Lord Meriweather, may we speak with you for a moment?"

"Come in," the baron called.

Vera walked with her brother into the room that was lined with overflowing bookshelves. More books were stacked in front of them. A rosewood desk was set in front of a large double window. Chairs faced the white marble fireplace.

"Good morning," Lord Meriweather said with a smile as he stood from one of the chairs.

That smile wavered when Gregory said, "I understand you have asked Vera about our connections with the smugglers, and you need to know that the answer she gave you was not the truth."

She tried to keep from lowering her eyes when Lord Meriweather looked from her brother to her. Accusation burned in his eyes.

"Are you saying, vicar, that Miss Fenwick lied?"

"No." Gregory shook his head calmly. "She told you the truth as she knows it. However, it is not the true as I know it."

"I see. Perhaps," Lord Meriweather said, "we should sit and discuss this. Miss Fenwick, if you please..."

Both men waited while Vera selected a chair farthest from where the baron had been sitting. She stared down at her clasped hands. It might be futile, but she wanted to prevent him from having a good view of her face. If Gregory had been honest with her, they would not be in this uncomfortable situation.

No, a small voice whispered from her heart, *you would have had to spill the truth when Lord Meriweather asked you yesterday. You could have been the cause of Gregory being dismissed again.*

At that thought, her throat threatened to close and halt her breathing. The vicarage was gone, and they could be soon, too. Lord Meriweather might believe, upon hearing what Gregory had to say, that a vicar who consorted with criminals did not deserve to preach at the Sanctuary Bay church.

"Very well, Mr. Fenwick," Lord Meriweather said coolly. "I am waiting for you to explain that extraordinary comment which leads me to believe you have assisted the smugglers."

She closed her eyes, praying that Gregory knew

what he was doing. She did not open them as her brother spoke.

"It was not as you think, my lord," Gregory said in a quiet, calm voice. "The incident happened several years ago. It was one evening after I had visited a member of the congregation in the village. A man appeared out of the shadows. He wore cloth over his mouth and nose, and his hat hid his eyes. He did not say much, but it was enough to know that there had been a terrible accident and I was needed. A man was dying. I am not a judge. I leave that to God. What I could do was pray with him and offer his family comfort when he died."

She bit her lower lip to keep it from trembling as tears pressed against her eyelids. How could she have doubted her brother's integrity? One of the smugglers' greatest crimes might be making them suspicious of each other.

Lord Meriweather did not reply right away. When he did, his voice was strained. "I cannot fault you for doing your duty, vicar. I would never speak badly of any man who did that. But I do have a question."

"Certainly."

"Did you tell my predecessor of these events?"

"No."

"Why?"

Vera raised her head at the sudden sharpness in Lord Meriweather's voice. She was surprised to see that the baron sat on the chair beside hers and Gregory stood next to the hearth.

Her brother's face appeared as serene as if he stood at the pulpit to read his sermon until she noticed a tic near his left eye. "Because he would have asked me the question that you want to ask, too. He would have asked me the dead man's name."

"Yes," the baron said, "that is what I want to ask."

"I cannot tell you his name. His widow and children no longer live in the village, but other relatives do. Other relatives who have never been involved with the smugglers."

"But if his name directed us to the man leading them, more people could be kept from harm."

Gregory's eyes grew almost as sad as they had been the day they had left his last living. "If I believed that, I would have told the old Lord Meriweather straight-away. I hope you believe that, my lord."

The baron stood and offered his hand to her brother. When Gregory grasped it, neither man spoke, but she could not miss the mutual respect in their stances.

Vera released a breath she had not guessed she was holding. For how long? As the fresh air swirled into her lungs, she wondered if she had last drawn a breath when they walked into the book room. She rose as her brother explained that he was traveling to meet with the bishop.

"Have a safe trip," Lord Meriweather said, "and I hope that Miss Fenwick and I will have made some progress by the time you return."

A smile tugged at her brother's mouth as he said, "I know my sister well, and I have no doubts that you will have made significant progress. Vera can make amazing things happen when she sets her mind on it."

His compliment shocked her into silence, for Gregory was not a gushing man. He gave her a kiss on the cheek, wished her well then walked out of the room.

Leaving her alone with Lord Meriweather, she re-

alized with a pulse of something that was not dismay
and was not excited anticipation but a bit of both. All
words fled from her mind.

She needed not to worry because Lord Meriweather
said, "I am sorry that my question caused such up-
heaval."

"Once you heard the rumor, you owed everyone in
Sanctuary Bay an obligation to find the truth." She
stared down at her feet. "I hope you don't believe that
I misled you on purpose."

"That thought never entered my head." He put a
single finger under her chin and tipped her head back
so she looked up into his eyes, which revealed much
and hid even more. "I have seen your fervor in halting
the smugglers. I have seen your pain when they made
threats against this house or its residents or against
anyone in Sanctuary Bay."

"I wish they could be stopped." She should move
away, but his hand shifted until he cupped her chin, his
fingers splaying along her cheek. She drew in a slow
breath that was flavored by a hint of sunshine and the
lemon used to whiten his shirt and cravat. "They have
destroyed so much."

"Especially for you and the vicar."

She stepped back and shook her head. "Those were
things. We will miss them, but they can be replaced.
What if someone had been in the church when they lit
the brandy? And the man who died that Gregory went
to… What about his family? How do his children fare
without him?"

"As any child does who has lost a parent." He locked
his hands together behind his back and turned toward

the fire crackling on the hearth. "With sadness and regret."

"I know. My parents died when Gregory was still studying at Cambridge, and he took responsibility for me."

"As you now take responsibility for him?" He looked back over his shoulder at her when she gasped. "Don't look so surprised, Miss Fenwick. It doesn't take any great insight to be aware of how solicitous you are for his well-being. You want him to be happy, even when you wish you could gainsay him from his plans. Like now."

"What?"

"You think he should remain here to begin work on rebuilding the church rather than go to meet with the bishop."

"You are mistaken."

"Am I?"

Vera was about to assert that of course he was wrong, but she could not. She *did* think a call on the bishop now was premature. It would have been better to wait until after they had more information to share with him.

"No, you are right," she said.

He smiled, and she did, too, for the first time since he had asked her about the smugglers. "Not many people would own to that." He walked back to where she stood. His expression was lighter than it had been yesterday at the church with Lord Ashland or even when she and Gregory had come into the book room.

Lines vanished from his face as he smiled easily again. The darkness had disappeared from his eyes, which twinkled. His shoulders no longer seemed bowed beneath an invisible weight. He had the responsibilities of the estate, but she never guessed what a burden it must be. He bore it with good humor and dedication, even though he had not been raised to expect such a life.

He's a hero, she remembered her dear friend Cat saying about her cousin. *All three of these men who served together are heroes who don't flinch from doing the hard tasks. They not only rush in "where angels fear to tread," but stay to clean up the damage left behind afterward.*

"You were worried there was something behind the rumor, weren't you?" she asked, surprising herself with her audacity. A vicar's sister should not question a baron.

"I was not worried exactly. I know how worthless most gossip is, but the fact the rumor exists could make the situation more difficult for you and the vicar. Now that I know the truth, I can divert some of the talk with the facts."

"Thank you." She put her hand on his arm as she had others at church and in the village. But none of those other friendly touches had set her fingers to quivering as if she tried to hold on to a butterfly. No, a honeybee, because along with the buzz was the undeniable sense that she had made a mistake, but still she could not release the bee before it stung her.

Strong and startled emotions flickered through his volatile eyes as he slid his hand over hers on his arm. She could not speak, not wanting to shatter this lovely moment. He was silent, too. Could he hear the frantic beat of her heart?

He shifted his arm slightly, drawing it and her a single step closer to him, so she had to tilt her head back. His other hand rose toward her cheek. She closed her eyes, awaiting its touch.

It did not come. Instead, he released her hand and stepped away. Only then did she hear footsteps hurrying toward the book room. She barely had time to compose herself before Ogden, Meriweather Hall's butler, paused in the doorway.

The silver-haired butler, who always stood as straight as cliffs edging the bay, nodded toward her before saying, "My lord, forgive me for interrupting your conversation with Miss Fenwick, but there is a matter that requires your attention."

Something that resembled dread flickered through Lord Meriweather's eyes. Ogden looked away. She knew he did not want the baron to see the sympathy he felt for a lord who could not make decisions.

She made one herself and asked, "Where is Lord Meriweather needed?"

The butler's eyes widened at her inappropriate question, but when the baron motioned for him to answer, Ogden said, "In the stables, my lord. The matter of repairs to the smaller carriage."

"May I come with you?" Vera asked. "I don't think I have seen the smaller carriage."

"If you wish," Lord Meriweather said and sent for their coats.

As soon as the outer wraps arrived, Lord Meriweather assisted her with hers. His hands lingered for only the length of a single heartbeat on her shoulders, but that sweet sensation, stronger each time he touched her, swept over her again. She tied her simple straw bonnet under her chin as he pulled on his own coat.

The ever-present wind off the sea sliced through Vera's dark blue wool spencer before they had taken more than a few steps outside. She hurried with Lord Meriweather to the stables. As they stepped inside, the thick scent of dried hay and animals and men who lived too closely in a small space filled every breath.

A small, wiry man appeared out of the dusty shadows and put his fingers to his forelock. "Good morning, m'lord," he said in a thick Yorkshire accent.

"Good morning, Griffin," Lord Meriweather replied. "Do you know Miss Fenwick?"

"Aye." He bobbed his head toward her. "She and the vicar came to pray when my mother was sickly."

"How is Mrs. Griffin?" Vera asked.

"Much better, Miss Fenwick. She had hoped to come to church for the Easter services." His thin face lengthened. "Now there is no church for her to come to."

"There will be," she reassured him. "Maybe not this year, but certainly by next." She glanced at the baron. "Lord Meriweather has promised that."

"Aye, 'tis good. M'lord, if you will come with me..." The coachman motioned for them to follow him.

A great black bulk transformed into a carriage that was about half the size of the one Vera had ridden in on the way back from Norwich. The odor of fresh lacquer wafted from it.

"'Tis all finished, m'lord," Griffin said, "save for the upholstery inside. What do you want for it?"

Lord Meriweather said in a clipped tone, "I told you to put whatever was readily available."

"That is just it, m'lord. We've got enough red velvet and enough black to cover the seats."

Vera held her breath when the baron drew in a deep

one as if he were about to face the French army again. To him, his inability to make a decision was an enemy even more brutal than Napoleon's troops.

"If I may make a suggestion," she said with a smile, "go with the red. It will show dirt from the roads and sand from the shore far less than the black would."

"Trust a woman to know such things." Lord Meriweather chuckled, but she heard relief in the sound. "Griffin, make it the red."

"Aye, m'lord." He waved his hands at the stablemen. "Go on, the lot of you, and get to your work." He nodded toward the baron again. "It should take only a few days to finish the work, m'lord."

"Excellent." Lord Meriweather walked toward the stable door. He paused at the line where the shadows surrendered to the sunshine. He took her hand and bowed over it. "Thank you," he said so softly she almost missed it as her heartbeat thundered within her. He released her hand and walked away.

She rested her shoulder against the stable door and cradled the hand he had held in her other one. "You are welcome."

Edmund stared at the blank piece of paper in front of him. No doubt, by now four days after the vicar had left to call on the bishop, Miss Fenwick had several pages filled with ideas for the new church. He had nothing. For once, he was frozen not because he could not make up his mind what to do, but because he simply needed to figure out where to start.

When he had worked on houses in London, there had always been a customer with definite ideas. He would talk with that customer and then develop a plan out of that conversation. He needed to speak with Mr. Fenwick. To come up with a list of essentials for a church without the pastor sharing his needs and expectations felt like an impossible task.

Pushing himself to his feet, he strode to the book room window and gazed out at the sea. Would he ever tire of watching the waves tease the shore? He could not imagine a time, but he wished he was able to look at the sea without thinking of the smugglers.

There had been no sign of them since the fire. He hoped that the attack upon the village's church had sliced a divisive line among them. There must be some smugglers as horrified by what had happened as he and the Fenwicks were. Even though Ashland, Sir Nigel and the justice of the peace had shared their outrage, one of them—at least—had to be pretending.

"There is no one else along Sanctuary Bay but those three, who could be described by the smugglers as *his qualityship*," he said aloud.

"There is you."

At the quiet voice behind him, Edmund whirled to discover Miss Fenwick in the doorway. A twinkle brightened her bright blue eyes, something he had not seen since she had stood by his cousin's side while Cat had spoken her vows with his friend Bradby. He realized, only now, how dull her eyes had been since the news came of the fire at the church.

And how much he had missed that sight.

"Are you accusing me of being the leader of the smugglers?" he asked, grinning. He did not want to see her eyes lose that luster again.

"You could be described as *his qualityship*." She walked slowly into the room.

"True."

"This estate has the best view of the whole of Sanctuary Bay of any manor house in North Yorkshire." She paused by a chair about halfway between the door and where he stood.

"That is also true." He held up a finger as her smile widened. "But there is the small detail that the smugglers were busy in Sanctuary Bay before I arrived here."

"Yes, that is a small detail, but a resourceful man could arrange for his messages to be delivered to the smugglers, even from as far away as London."

"True yet again." He was enjoying this teasing game more than he had guessed he would. The dismals that had settled on his shoulders only moments ago were lifting. "But I also spent several years on the Continent."

"The smugglers ply the waters between here and the Continent."

"I must own that you are right about that." He stepped forward and put one knee on the chair she stood beside. Folding his arms on the back, he gazed into her lively eyes. "But I have one fact that proves without a doubt that I am innocent of collaborating with the smugglers. They have been swarming around Sanctuary Bay since before my father was born."

"Or his father."

He nodded. "I daresay there has been smuggling on these waters even before William the Conqueror came to claim the English throne."

Her brows arched as her smile faded. "That is true, and it is true as well that, while some of the members of the quality living close to Sanctuary Bay are older than you and Lord Ashland, none are quite that old."

"I am glad that you do not believe me to be the scurrilous leader of the smugglers, though I must say your arguments are worthy of a barrister. I hope I never have to face you across a courtroom, for I suspect I might be much the worse for the experience. You have a rare skill for following a bizarre thought to its most illogical conclusion in an effort to prove I am the smugglers' leader."

Suddenly her face turned bright red in the moment before all color faded from it. Her fingers trembled as she held out several pages. "Here are the ideas you asked for, my lord. If you will excuse me, I shall leave you to read through them to see if any of them have merit."

As she turned to leave—or was it to flee?—he spoke her name.

"Yes?" She turned, but stared at the toes of his boots.

He cleared his throat. "Thank you for your work on this."

"I am glad to help."

Placing the pages on the desk, he asked, "Have you heard the latest news from the fire?"

"That the vicarage must be razed?" She nodded, the last of the light snuffed out of her eyes. "I expected it, but, even so, it has been hard to hear."

"There was no choice. One of the walls collapsed and nearly killed a couple of the men working there."

"Was anyone hurt?"

"Not badly. Some bruises and one twisted ankle when they raced away to avoid the toppling wall." He hesitated, then added, "I wanted to let you know that Mme. Dupont will be arriving later today."

"The seamstress?"

"Lady Meriweather thought, as you will be out of your home for far longer than we had hoped, that you would need clothes of your own."

"That is not necessary."

"No?"

She glanced down at her borrowed gown, and he did, too. The rich blue suited her, making her eyes a richer shade and flattering her coloring. He preferred this blue to the dark gowns she usually wore. He knew what she would say if he spoke his thoughts aloud, but he could not agree. Simply because she was the vicar's sister should not mean that she always wore drab colors.

"Perhaps that is a good idea," she said. "Cat will want her own clothing back when she returns from her honeymoon. But you don't need to send for a seamstress. I can make my own clothing."

"When? You are going to be busy with rebuilding the church." He glanced at the desk. "This is only the beginning of the process. We will need plans and supplies and skilled laborers and someone to oversee those laborers. Each of those steps will require time. A lot of time, and I assume you want to be involved in each step."

"Yes. I am looking forward to seeing every bit of the progress, and I feel blessed that we have your knowledge to guide us." Her smile returned, sweeping away the lost expression she had been wearing as she started to rush out of the room. It was as if spring had come to banish the winter cold.

He wanted to bask in that warmth which promised everything was possible. Everything? Even him being able to make a decision? A good decision? As he gazed at her glowing eyes, he wanted to be the man she believed him to be.

That thought startled him. When had Miss Fenwick's opinion of him become so important? That was easy to answer. From the moment they had stood by the ruins of the church and she had asked him to play an instrumental part in bringing it back. She had so much faith in him that she dared him to have faith in himself. Too bad he was doomed to disappoint her and the rest of the parish.

"Thank you, my lord," Miss Fenwick said, her soft voice slipping through his dreary thoughts.

"For?"

"Anticipating both my and your cousin's needs." She glanced down at her gown.

"As I said, it was Lady Meriweather's idea."

"Which you agreed with, which is why I am thanking you now. I will thank the baroness, as well."

"When you do, she said she had some fabric that would be available for your use."

"That is wonderful." She took a step back. "If Mme. Dupont is coming soon, I should speak to Lady Meriweather straightaway."

"And pick which fabrics you want for your gowns."

Her smile widened. "I trust none of them are smuggled silk."

Edmund laughed at her saucy comment. He really laughed, as he had not in longer than he wished to remember. It was a remarkable release of the tension that he had been amassing since the night his worst decision almost cost him his sanity. He did not dwell on that, instead enjoying his amusement and the scintillating good humor in her eyes. Her agile and unexpected wit kept him off balance, for he realized he had his own assumptions about her.

As she gave him a wave and hurried out of the room, he kept chuckling. He walked over to the desk and picked up the pages Miss Fenwick had brought him. He sat to read them. Soon, he discovered that her wit was not the only aspect of her that would keep him on his toes. Her ideas for rebuilding the church were precise and insightful. She knew exactly what her brother and the parishioners would want.

He lowered the pages to his lap. There clearly was much more to Miss Fenwick than he had guessed. He looked forward to learning more about her.

Chapter Five

Vera rushed down the stairs, glad to have escaped yet another session with the chatty Mme. Dupont. Her ears rang with the seamstress's fractured French. Now, after her third session with Mme. Dupont, she understood Cat's complaints about the woman, who pretended she was French because she seemed to think that would make her work more desirable. Vera was tempted to tell her that such efforts were wasted on her, for she had never understood the *ton*'s fascination with French fashions and customs while England was at war with Napoleon.

She bumped into someone and almost dropped to sit on a riser. Strong hands grasping her elbows kept her on her feet.

"Lord Meriweather!" she gasped, knowing instantly he was the one holding her because of how her heart beat faster. "Excuse me. I wasn't watching where I was going."

"You looked as if you were the fox fleeing the hounds."

"Only from Mme. Dupont."

He laughed, the sound ringing through the stairwell. In the past few days since she had teased him in the book room when she had brought him her ideas for the new church, she had heard his hearty laugh often. But she must be cautious. Why had she let herself get caught up in the silliness that day? She had wanted to bring a smile to his face, but again she had spoken before she had thought. She had *accused* him of being the leader of the smugglers. He had treated her words as a jest at first, but then he had said, *You have a rare skill of following a bizarre thought to its most illogical conclusion in an effort to prove I am the smugglers' leader.*

Hadn't she learned her lesson about controlling her emotions around the peerage? Apparently not. She could not imagine Lord Meriweather taking Gregory's living away as Lord Hedgcoe had, but she had thought their lives secure then, too. She was relieved that Lord Meriweather had laughed at her sallies that day. Lord Hedgcoe would not have found such a jest amusing. If Lord Meriweather had not, either, she could have ruined everything for Gregory…again.

She had asked God to help her learn to think before speaking, but she had not succeeded in listening to His guidance yet.

"Then," the baron said, "I shall not stand in your way of eluding Mme. Dupont."

"Thank you."

He lowered his hands slowly to his sides, but did not move aside. Instead, he stood there, smiling. His eyes were level with hers because he stood on a lower step, and she was fascinated by the golden specks in his eyes. She had never noticed them before. They burned like miniature fires within his dark eyes.

Only the sound of the doorway in the entry hall below tore Vera's gaze from Lord Meriweather's. She looked down to where Jessup was stepping back to allow someone in.

"My lord?" Jessup called. "Miss Kightly has arrived."

Vera saw her own surprise on Lord Meriweather's face before he turned to walk down the stairs. Miss Kightly came into the entry hall, her clothing, as always, elegant and fashionable. The blonde greeted Lord Meriweather with a cool smile, then looked up the stairs to where Vera stood.

"Miss Fenwick, I am pleased to see you looking well." Miss Kightly's smile warmed as Vera joined her and Lord Meriweather. "I hope on this visit, we will have a chance to talk and become better acquainted."

"That would be very nice." With both Cat and Sophia planning to live elsewhere, she would appreciate having a new friend near Sanctuary Bay.

"I thought so, too." Miss Kightly turned back to Lord Meriweather. "Forgive me arriving without an invitation."

"You know you are always welcome at Meriweather Hall," he replied.

"That is good, because Uncle Nigel has been called away on some business, and he believes I would be bored at his house, though I am not sure why he thinks that. There are many parts of the house that I haven't seen yet. But he did not want me to be alone there."

Vera resisted the urge to lift her eyebrows in an incredulous look. If Sir Nigel's house was anything like Meriweather Hall, Miss Kightly could never be alone there. At least a score of servants worked in the house, and more people were in the stables and other outbuildings.

"A wise thought," Lord Meriweather said with a strained smile.

Miss Kightly must have seen only the smile, not the tension, because she said, "His business should take only a few days."

"You are welcome to stay as long as you need to." He looked at the footman. "Jessup, let Lady Meriweather know that Miss Kightly will be staying with us."

"Yes, my lord." He bowed his head, then hurried up the stairs.

After Lord Meriweather sent another footman to get Miss Kightly's bags from her carriage, he invited her into the small parlor. Vera could not keep from noticing what a handsome couple they made. Miss Kightly seemed to light up when the baron spoke to her, and, in spite of his taut smile, he clearly enjoyed the blonde's company. It would be an excellent match.

The thought created a cramp in her chest, as if she could not quite catch her breath. When a hand settled on her shoulder, she flinched.

"Why are you standing here alone in the entry hall?" asked Lady Meriweather with a kind smile. "Why aren't you going with the others?"

"I was unsure if they wanted…" She bit back the words she should not speak. To suggest that Miss Kightly wanted to be alone with Lord Meriweather would be a horrible mistake. Even a single wrong word, overheard and repeated, could sully a young woman's reputation.

"Of course, they wanted to have you join them." The baroness swept past her. "Come with me."

Vera had no choice but to comply. She could not speak of the sensations that had rushed through her on the stairs when she had first seen the golden flames in Lord Meriweather's eyes. Nor could she say how unsettled she had felt when she had thought of the baron and Miss Kightly making a match. She decided the best thing to do was to sit quietly and let the others talk. That way she would not betray that she found Lord Meriweather too tantalizing for her own good.

It was not how he had planned to spend his day, and Edmund wished he could find a way to excuse himself from the conversation the ladies were having. It had started with Lady Meriweather and Miss Fenwick's arrival, and it had continued through the midday meal, and now it was almost time for tea. He had hoped to finish his list of initial ideas for the church so he could share it with Miss Fenwick.

He glanced at her. She sat primly a little bit away from the rest of them. Now that he thought about it, he could not recall her saying very much while Lady Meriweather and Miss Kightly chatted.

Her eyes caught his. A slight tilt of her left eyebrow spoke volumes, and he had to turn his laugh into coughs before he embarrassed himself.

"Are you all right?" Miss Kightly asked when he managed to regain control of himself.

"Quite all right. Pardon me for interrupting." He avoided looking at Miss Fenwick again as the other ladies continued their conversation.

Suddenly a commotion came from beyond the room. As the ladies turned to look toward the door, he came to his feet.

A woman dressed like a tulip of fashion stood in the doorway. Her gown was a vivacious green that belonged on someone of his cousins' ages, not a woman of her advanced years. Sparkling silver hair edged her full face. Her brown eyes widened when she saw him.

"Eddie, my dear, dear nephew!" she cried out, rushing toward him.

Edmund closed his eyes as pudgy arms were flung around him. He stepped out of his aunt's embrace as quickly as he could without offending her.

"Oh, I forget. You are called Edmund now, aren't you?" Aunt Belinda chuckled, her double chins bouncing with her enthusiasm. "Now that you are a fine lord." She pinched his cheek. "But you still care enough about your auntie that…" Her voice faded away as she stared at the other women.

"Lady Meriweather, may I present my aunt Belinda Uppington?" he asked.

Aunt Belinda whirled to face the baroness, and he held his breath until he heard her say graciously, "Lady Meriweather, I am sorry for your loss. I have been informed that you and your daughters have been very, very good to my nephew since he assumed your late husband's title." She looked past the lady to Miss Fenwick and Miss Kightly. With a broad smile, she asked, "Are you Sophia and Catherine? Aren't you lovely? Edmund, you would do well to choose one of your cousins to be your wife."

Before his aunt could say something more to embarrass him and the others, he introduced her to the younger women and explained they were guests in the great house. Those were the last words he managed to insert into the conversation. He did not even have a chance to explain that both of his cousins now were married to his two best friends. When a maid brought in a tray with both tea and hot chocolate, as well as an assortment of sweets, Aunt Belinda barely paused to take a breath. She talked about herself and how excited she was to visit her favorite nephew and how she looked forward to bouncing his heir on her knee. Even as she babbled on, she still managed to correct him on how he passed a cup of tea to the baroness.

Edmund was relieved when he could excuse himself. He nodded when his aunt chided him for hurrying away without making sure a room was properly prepared for her. Aunt Belinda did not seem to notice the shock on the other women's faces.

"That is why I ask you to allow me to withdraw," he replied.

"Thank you, Lord Meriweather." Miss Fenwick's eyes twinkled like a pair of sunlit ponds, and her lips twitched. "I know we *all* appreciate your efforts on our behalf."

He resisted smiling back. That would bring another dressing-down from his aunt, and Aunt Belinda would realize he found her endless stream of advice bothersome. He bid the ladies a good afternoon and left.

Outside in the hallway, he surrendered to that smile. Miss Fenwick's words had defused the tension in the room. He must thank her later. For now, he needed to figure out how to keep his aunt from arranging his marriage before supper.

Rain splattered the window in the book room before wind rattled the glass. Vera looked up from the book she had been reading. It was a history of nearby

Scarborough. Since her journey from Sanctuary Bay to Norwich, she had been curious about the towns and cities she had passed through. The story of the Scarborough lifeboat service, started less than twenty years ago, should have intrigued her, but she could not stop thinking about Lord Meriweather.

He had not joined them for dinner, and she envied him because he had avoided listening to Mrs. Uppington's unending prattle. Instantly she chided herself. Lord Meriweather's aunt was excited to be in the manor house that her nephew had inherited along with his title.

As if she had called Lord Meriweather to her side, the baron strode through the door, muttering, "Maybe I am insane. If I am not, Aunt Belinda is sure to send me around the bend."

"Talking to oneself is a sign of being ready for Bedlam," she said to let him know that he was not alone.

He stared at her, astonished, then laughed. "Just what I was telling myself." He shrugged off his greatcoat and hung it over a chair before going to where she sat near the hearth. He started to sit, then paused. "Am I disturbing you?"

"No. Of course not. I was enjoying some quiet time for reading." She motioned for him to sit.

Lord Meriweather clearly needed an ear right now. If she wanted to do God's work beyond writing some of Gregory's sermons, she must accept each opportunity that came her way. After all, comforting others was something she found easier than Gregory did. He was a good counselor, but sometimes too ready with a solution when the person who came to him simply wanted to be listened to.

"I owe you and the others an apology," Lord Meriweather said, startling her.

"For what?"

"Aunt Belinda."

"Why would you apologize for your aunt?"

"As you may have noticed, she is very assured of her own opinions and delights in airing her vocabulary."

"Does she live alone?"

He looked baffled. "Yes. Her late husband was my mother's brother. Why do you ask?"

"So she has no one to talk with at home?"

"Only her servants, and I daresay, though Aunt Belinda has not noticed, her *major domo* is half-deaf and her housekeeper lost her hearing years ago." He raised his hands to forestall her response. "Not from her chattering. I did not mean to suggest that."

Vera hid her smile. Poor man! His aunt's appearance had left him on edge.

"I know you didn't. You are overwhelmed. We all are in the wake of the fire."

As if she had not spoken, he went on, "You have no idea how much trouble my aunt can cause." His tone was so grim that this time Vera could not keep from chuckling.

"She cannot be as bad as you suggest," she said.

"I could regale you with stories that would send you shrieking into the night." He tapped his chin. "Maybe that isn't such a bad idea. We could run away and…" He gave her a wry grin. "But it would do no good. After coming all this way from her home near Coventry, Aunt Belinda will not be waylaid from her plans to visit Meriweather Hall. She would not miss this chance to acquaint her nephew with each of his shortcomings."

"I am sure she means well."

He shook his head, then cradled it in his hands. "God above save me from well-meaning aunts."

"He will if that is His will." Vera reached out to put her hand on his arm, then drew it back. To touch him might be the worst thing she could do. After she had reacted to his touch, meant only to keep her from falling on the stairs, she must keep firm control on herself and her tendency to act before she considered the consequences.

"I wish I could be as accepting of God's will as you are." A smile tugged at his lips. "Of course, *you* don't have an aunt like mine."

"Actually I have a half dozen."

"What?" He sat straighter. "The vicar told me that you were without any other family."

"All right," she conceded with a smile. "These aunts are not blood relatives, but there are at least six ladies in the church who seem to believe God gave them the task of making sure I do exactly as I should."

"Which is to do exactly as they want you to."

Vera stared at him, surprised. "Yes. How did you know?"

"Because that is what Aunt Belinda has done my whole life." He drew up his knee and clasped his hands around it, more relaxed than she had ever seen him. "On one hand, I never have to worry about how I will be perceived. She is eager to inform me of the least misstep."

"Sometimes it feels as if it would be easier to be compliant."

He nodded, grinning. "Exactly. Miss Fenwick, I had

no idea that you endured the same from some of your brother's parishioners."

"I would not use the word endure, but I have learned when it is wise to keep my mouth closed."

Laughing, he said, "Maybe you could teach me then. Learning such a lesson could make Aunt Belinda's stay infinitely more enjoyable."

"It is quite simple." She leaned toward him. "I remind myself that God brought them into my life for all of us to discover how each of us can become a better person."

"Aunt Belinda and I must have a long road to that discovery then."

When he smiled, her heart did a flip-flop. That surprised her, because she had seen him smile many times since he first came to Sanctuary Bay last autumn. But this time, she knew his smile was solely for her.

Don't be a silly goose! she warned herself. He was a charming man. As he spoke to her easily, she understood why his friends liked and trusted him. But he saw her solely as his cousins' friend and the vicar's sister, someone he could speak honestly with and not worry about her repeating his words. She should expect nothing else from him, and she would be a fool to wish for more.

Knowing she needed to reply before he caught her musing about him, she forced a smile. "Should I pray that the road to discovery is short for the two of you?"

"A lovely thought, but I suspect it will be long and convoluted and filled with plenty of bumps and chuckholes." He laughed. "Miss Fenwick, if I may say so, you are a breath of fresh air and have given me a second wind in dealing with my aunt. I know she loves me, and she knows I love her, but…" He shook his head with an ironic grin. "But I must say thank you for listening to me being a sniveling fellow."

"No, I must thank you."

Startled, he put his foot down with a thump. "Thank me? For what?"

"Helping me keep my mind off what the bishop may say to Gregory. If the rumor you spoke of us aiding the smugglers has reached the bishop's ear, too, it may not go well."

"Don't look for trouble where there may not be any. During my time in the army, I too often heard men sitting around a fire in the hours before a battle talk about all the what-ifs, including what if we lost the battle. I reminded them that an army that believes it can be defeated will be defeated." He put his hand on the arm of her chair. "The advice works for situations like this, as well."

She sensed the warmth off his skin but did not move her hand closer or farther from his. She left it where it was and savored the connection between them. "That is good advice. All too soon, I will know what has happened."

"And that should be better than the worst we can imagine." His chocolate-brown eyes warmed.

She looked away…as she had not on the stairs. Then his eyes had glittered with even stronger emotions. She had to forget that, but knew she could not. No man had ever looked at her like that.

He took her hand in his, and her eyes cut back to him. Again she was caught by his gaze. In it, she saw compassion and honesty…and other things she would be wise not to examine too closely. He slanted toward her, and she held her breath, waiting to hear what he had to say.

"Ah, here you are, my boy." The voice was not his, but his aunt's. Mrs. Uppington strode in like a victorious general surveying the field of battle. Her nose wrinkled as she squinted at Vera. "Aren't you the vicar's sister?"

"Yes, Mrs. Uppington." She hastily pulled her hand out of Lord Meriweather's and laced her fingers together in her lap.

"Where is Miss Kightly?" she asked, dismissing Vera out of hand.

Lord Meriweather shrugged. "In bed and asleep, I assume. She mentioned that she rose early to come to Meriweather Hall."

"Miss Kightly is someone you should get to know better, Eddie." She grimaced. "I mean, Edmund. But my suggestion remains the same. Miss Kightly is a well-polished young lady from an impeccable family, and her great-uncle lives near you. A pursuit in that direction would be looked on kindly by both families, I assume."

Vera flinched at Mrs. Uppington's words that said quite blatantly that her nephew was wasting his time talking with a vicar's sister when he could be courting a viscount's daughter. Setting herself on her feet, she bid Lord Meriweather and his aunt a good-night. She left but wondered if either of them noticed her departure because Mrs. Uppington continued to lecture him on his obligations now that he was a baron.

Sympathy billowed through Vera, muting her vexation with Mrs. Uppington's assumption that she could speak without concern for Vera's feelings. As she rushed up the stairs to her room, she said a prayer for

Lord Meriweather. He was going to need plenty of strength to deal with his aunt.

And so was everyone else.

Chapter Six

After looking for Lord Meriweather in the book room, in the dining room and in the great hall, Vera sought the help of a maid who suggested she try a small room in a wing of the house that was seldom used. Vera took the drawing she wanted to show him and hurried in that direction.

The corridor was sparsely furnished but as immaculate as the rest of Meriweather Hall. Past half-open doors on either side, she saw beds that could be readied for guests. Portraits of somber people in their best finery were hung between the doors.

She paused to look at a woman who closely resembled her friend Cat. The woman had dark eyes and hair so ebony that the highlights were almost blue. Dressed in an elaborate gown with lace high around her throat, the woman must have lived during the reign of Queen Elizabeth or her successor King James I.

With that sense she could not define, she knew Lord Meriweather had come to stand behind her. She turned. "How do you do that?"

"Do what?"

"Sneak up on me without making a sound."

He smiled, but his eyes were filled with pain. From his memories, she knew, when he said, "It was a skill I honed during the war. Being able to slip past someone could mean the difference between life and death for me and my men." He leaned one hand beside the painting. "Does it bother you?"

"It is startling to discover someone close when you haven't heard him approaching."

"Shall I have a trumpeter announcing my passage?"

She laughed. "That might be helpful, though I suspect everyone in Meriweather Hall would soon tire of the blasts."

"Then, to avoid that, I shall try to sound like a herd of stampeding elephants wherever I go."

"That could work."

He pushed off the wall, and suddenly the broad corridor seemed smaller and more intimate. He did not touch her, but he might as well have, because she was as aware of him as if he held her close. Each breath he took and released seemed to set the pace of her own.

She tore her gaze from his. "Don't you think this woman looks like Cat?" Only a faint tremor in her voice hinted at her unsteady heartbeat.

"She does." He bent closer to the painting to examine it.

Vera took a steadying breath and had herself composed by the time he looked back at her.

"Her name is Antigone Meriweather." He shook his head. "Who would name their daughter Antigone?"

"Maybe they were fond of the ancient Greek play."

"I am impressed at your knowledge, Miss Fenwick."

She held the rolled page by her side in a calm pose,

but she was pleased at the admiration in his voice. "Reading and learning were valued in my family, so I was introduced to the classics at a very early age. After our parents died, Gregory insisted I continue to read challenging works."

Lord Meriweather stepped back from the portrait. "Why are you wandering along this corridor?"

"When I couldn't find you elsewhere, I was told I might find you here."

"Really?" He did not sound pleased. "Who told you that?"

"One of the maids. I'm not sure of her name."

"Or you would not say it to protect her from my wrath at having my solitary haven breached."

He was teasing, but she wondered if truth hid beneath the joke. "I did not mean to intrude, my lord. I can speak with you later."

"You have searched high and low for me, so the least I can do is invite you into my private sanctuary." He reached behind him and opened a door, one of only two that were closed. With a bow of his head, he indicated that she should precede him into the chamber.

Vera did not know what she expected to find on the other side of the door. It was a smaller version of the book room. Bookshelves flanked a black hearth and surrounded the tall window and the door. Like in the book room, leather-bound volumes filled every inch of shelf space and parts of the floor around a single wing chair and a table that looked as if it had been built in the Middle Ages. Heavy and blackened with age, it had what appeared to be a family crest on each leg.

"No question who commissioned this desk to be

built, is there?" Lord Meriweather said as he followed her into the room.

She examined it more closely. "So, this is where it went."

"You have seen this table before?"

"No, but I have heard about it." She straightened and smiled. "Once it was where the lord of the manor sat to collect his rents on quarter days."

He walked around the table. "That makes sense now. I thought it might have been built by someone with a bit too much pride."

"That probably is true, too."

As if she had not spoken, he went on. "I found this room shortly after Christmas. I would guess that my predecessor also used it when he wanted to be able to work uninterrupted."

"And I have interrupted you. I am sorry."

"You are no interruption. I am seeking refuge from my aunt and her matrimonial machinations. The good Lord save me from well-meaning aunts."

His tone was so grim that she could not help laughing. "I will keep your refuge a secret."

"Thank you." He came around the table again. "I see you are carrying a rolled sheet. Is it something for our project?"

She liked how he said *our* project. "I made this sketch after our previous discussions. I am no artist like your cousin Cat, but…"

"Why don't you show me what you have done? After that, I want to talk to you about some merchants in Whitby. You, having lived here longer than I, may know more about their reputations for service and honesty."

He took the page she held out to him. Setting it on the table, he placed a book on each corner to keep the page from curling. He leaned his elbows on the top and rested his chin in the palm of one hand while he appraised the drawing. It was a pose she guessed he had taken often when he had worked in London before the war. He ran a finger along the lines she had drawn. On one half of the page she had sketched a possible exterior for the new church with a square tower and simple windows. The interior was on the other half, and that had taken her many more hours than the outer view.

She watched his face, trying to discern what he thought of her efforts. Until this moment, she had not guessed how much she hoped the drawings would be able to convey what she had failed to with words.

"Miss Fenwick, this is excellent. I now understand what you want for the stone on the exterior walls."

"I know it is simple."

"Quite to the contrary. Each item on the page is in perfect proportion with the rest of the plan. I see that, unlike the high boxes around the pews in the previous church, you designed lower boxes."

"That's so the congregation can see each other as well as Gregory when he leads the service."

"From this raised pulpit." He tapped a small inset box which showed where the pulpit with its octagonal sounding board would be placed along with the repaired font and a lectern shaped like an eagle. "It says here that the lectern will be made of brass."

"I thought it would be simpler to obtain a brass one," she said. "I wouldn't know where we could find anyone with the skill to carve a wooden one like we had before."

"I may know someone." He straightened and smiled. "My predecessor ordered a billiards table, as you may recall."

She nodded. "Your cousins mentioned it to me."

"Come with me." Removing the books, he let the paper roll close before he picked it up. "Let's see if it points to an answer to your wooden lectern dilemma."

Vera regretted leaving the solitude of the wing to return to the main part of the house. For the past half hour, it had been as if she and Lord Meriweather were alone in the world, working toward a common goal. He had treated her as an equal. Not like Gregory, who gave her a perfunctory thanks when she handed him a finished sermon she had written for the next service. Her brother seemed to believe she was only doing her sisterly duty.

Lord Meriweather led her into a room she had never entered. It was close to the dining room, but it had been decorated as a place for gentlemen to withdraw while women chatted together in the drawing room. The walls were covered with dark green fabric and wood almost as dark as the table in his haven. The great billiards table, carved with the family crest and scenes from both the high moorlands and the curve of the bay, commanded the room.

"Look here," he said, squatting beside one of the thick, curved legs.

She knelt and ran her fingers along the carved leaves that looked like frozen vines climbing the wooden legs. "This is beautifully made."

"I agree." He offered his hand and waited for her to stand before he added, "If you would prefer a wooden lectern for the church, I can contact the artisan who made this and find out if he would carve a new lectern for us."

"That is wonderful! I know it would mean a lot to the congregation to have something else that looks familiar when they come into the new church for the first service." She halted herself. What was she thinking? She could suggest ideas for the church, but the ultimate decision was not hers. That belonged to her brother.

"Excellent! I will contact—"

"Not yet, please. I must check with Gregory first."

"On such a small matter?" His eyes widened.

She realized her voice had sounded a bit panicked. Before he could ask the questions she could see on his face, she took the rolled page that he had placed on the table. She opened it and began pointing out various design elements she had selected. She began talking about each. She was babbling, but that was better than having him ask questions she needed to avoid.

Lord Meriweather did not move for so long that she thought he was going to wait for her to explain herself; then he leaned on his hands on the edge of the table. He listened while she pointed out more details. When he asked a few thoughtful questions, she began to relax again while she answered him.

"Why did you put the pulpit in the front of the church?" he asked. "There seems to be a movement toward having them in the center of the sanctuary so that everyone can hear."

"We are traditional here in Sanctuary Bay, and there are enough other changes that I wanted to lessen them where I could. Gregory suggested a trio of pulpits like those in—" She gulped hard, and he stared at her. She pretended a cough and apologized.

"Go on," he urged. "A trio of pulpits like those in...?"

"A church not far outside York." She fingered the page he had spread out again on top of the billiards table, staring at her drawing. She almost had slipped and mentioned the church in the parish where Lord Hedgcoe controlled the living. "Gregory was invited to preach there, and he was fascinated by how they were used."

"I'm not familiar with them."

"Three pulpits are set one above the other with a set of stairs along one side."

"But what is the purpose?"

"It was explained to me that the lowest pulpit is for the clerk or the pastor to make announcements about the parish. The second pulpit, a bit closer to heaven, is for reading the Gospel. The topmost one with the sounding board above it is where the pastor stands to give the sermon."

Lord Meriweather laughed. "I think they have it out of order. I mean no insult to your brother or any man of the cloth, but I think God's word in the Gospel should be closer to heaven than man's word in a sermon."

"That was my thought, too, even though I did not speak that opinion in Gregory's hearing." Her shoulders eased from their stiff line. "And you can see, my lord, that I did not include a triple pulpit in my sketch."

"A wise decision." He winced as he spoke the word that he must hate. How must it be to have everyone around you making decisions all the time and be incapable of even the simplest ones yourself? "You have a clear eye for how a space should be arranged. Far more so than some of the so-called architects who make impossible demands on the men who actually construct their buildings." He let the page roll up again. "May I keep this?"

"If you think it will be of any value, of course."

"You should not be so self-effacing, Miss Fenwick. I can see you will prove to be a very valuable assistant in this undertaking."

Ice froze her heart in midbeat. *Assistant!* He saw her exactly as Gregory did. Someone who was there to listen and who was never expected to claim any ideas as her own.

"Ah, here you are, my boy!" Mrs. Uppington burst into the room with Miss Kightly in tow. "We have been looking for you. Miss Kightly has been telling me the most amusing stories about her great-uncle's art. You really must come and listen."

When he hesitated, Vera said, "Go ahead, for I have a fitting with Mme. Dupont in a short time." She eased past the other two women and headed out the door, relieved to have an excuse to escape before her frustration exploded.

Edmund wished Miss Fenwick had stayed at Meriweather Hall instead of coming to the church site, but maybe she had wanted to avoid his aunt as he did. He sighed. Aunt Belinda had once been his favorite aunt, because she had a generous heart and an honest concern about his future. But that concern had become obsession since she had arrived in Sanctuary Bay. He appreciated Miss Kightly's beauty and her obvious polish. He had no need for his aunt to point both out on every possible occasion. Even asking her to desist because she was embarrassing the young woman did nothing to change his aunt's eagerness for him to propose to the blonde.

A man who could not make up his mind about which waistcoat to wear each morning certainly was incapable of choosing a woman to marry. He had refrained from mentioning that in his aunt's hearing, however, because she would respond that he should leave everything to her.

Marriage was not as intimidating a prospect as it had been in the weeks after Lady Eloisa had tossed him aside for another suitor. After that had happened, he had put that part of his future out of his mind, even though he knew, as Lord Meriweather, he needed to marry and sire a male heir. Then he and his friends, Northbridge and Bradby, had come to Sanctuary Bay, and his friends had fallen in love and married. He could not fail to see their joy, and he began to envy them finding that connection with a special woman.

Lord, I will need Your guidance and assistance on this path I never expected to walk as a peer. Help my aunt understand that I want no less than what Northbridge and Bradby have found, and help me make the right decision if the time comes that such a love touches my heart.

A sense of peace filled him, and he realized he had been running around too much of late—often to avoid his matchmaking aunt—and he had not stopped to make a connection with God.

He walked to where Miss Fenwick stood to one side as two teams of oxen pulled down the last wall of the vicarage. Men scooped up the scorched flint with wide shovels or with their bare hands. The pieces were tossed into the back of a cart. When it was full, a team of horses drew it to where they could drop the stones into the cellar of the former church. The plan was to pack soil on top until there was no sign of where the church had once stood.

Several hundred yards away, more teams arrived with supplies from Whitby. After discussing the delivery with the merchants in the city north of Sanctuary Bay, it was decided that the slower overland route would be easier than bringing the lumber and stone up the steep streets of the village.

Edmund watched Miss Fenwick's face closely. It was one thing to know that the vicarage was being torn down. It was quite another thing to witness it. The flint cottage had been her home for ten years. He could not help wondering what thoughts filled her mind.

As if he had said that aloud, she mused, "I was thinking…"

"Thinking what?" he asked.

She looked at him. Her eyes were not filled with tears. Instead, the sturdy resolve that he admired burned in them. "It is a shame that all the stone from the vicarage is being dumped into the cellar. If several layers of the stone were laid along the walls in the new cellar, it might keep the smugglers from finding an easy route into our church as they did before."

"That is an excellent idea," he said, wondering why neither he nor the men working on the site had considered that. He had been so focused on making sure the old church's cellar did not collapse farther and jeopardize the graves closest to it that he had given no thought to protecting the new one from the smugglers. "Come with me."

"Where?"

"To count off the perimeter of the new church, so I can calculate the necessary amount of stone to line it thickly enough."

They went to where the foundation of the new church had been begun. The whole area was marked with pieces of wood and rope from fishing nets. Most of the brown grass had been stripped away, and in a few places, holes had been dug down a few feet. As he walked off the length of the sides, she kept track of the numbers. She gave him the total when he was finished, and he was not surprised that she had also added in the height of the future cellar.

"Assuming the cellar will be eight feet deep as the old one was," she added.

"That is a good assumption. Good enough for setting aside several runs of stone to make it more difficult for anyone to get through the walls." He excused himself and sought out Sims, who was in charge of the demolition of the vicarage.

Sims listened to Edmund's explanation, then said, "An excellent idea, m'lord. I am glad you thought of it because it will save us time in the long run."

"It is not my idea. Miss Fenwick came up with it."

Sims frowned. "'Tis a shame."

"That she had such a good idea?" he asked, baffled.

"No, but that a nice lady like Miss Fenwick has to have such thoughts in her pretty head. Riles me that the vicar's sister cannot think, as she should, only about keeping his house and the church clean and food on his table."

Edmund nodded, though he suspected she would be annoyed at Sims's comments. Any woman who could design a church with such skill and was able to find solutions to problems others had not even thought about must have done more for the parish than keep the church tidy. He was curious why she kept that fact to herself.

A shout came from closer to the cliffs where the wooden debris from the ruined church had been gathered. A flame flared among the charred rafters and floor joists, then almost died before leaping back to life. The breeze off the sea caught the flame and set it dancing. With each twist, it scattered more fire across the debris. The beams that had soaked up the brandy flared even more brightly.

Everyone watched the fire burn, but his eyes focused on Miss Fenwick who remained by the rope that marked the new foundation. Her face was composed; yet she must be sad to see all her brother's hard work being consumed by the flames.

Not only her brother's, but hers. Edmund was more sure of that all the time. Since the vicar had left Sanctuary Bay to confer with the bishop, Miss Fenwick had handled his work with a quiet and easy efficiency that bespoke much practice.

Drawn to her because she looked alone and yet brave, he gave her a sympathetic smile. Strands of ebony hair blew around her face, emphasizing the gentle planes that belied her inner strength.

"I would have insisted," he said, "that you remain at Meriweather Hall if I had known they intended to start burning the debris today."

"I know it has to be done," she said, "before our new church can rise like a phoenix from the ashes of the old one." She turned her back on the pyre and gazed across the cliffs toward the village. The red-and-gray roof tiles marked the uppermost houses along the steep street. "In a few years, all that will be left are our memories of these difficult days. We will be in our new church and the first weddings will have been celebrated and the first babies will have been baptized. Then we can look back and be relieved...." She glanced over her shoulder at him. "We shall be relieved that this time is past."

He chuckled under his breath. "I thought you were going to say something else."

"About how we grow stronger while overcoming challenges?" She shook her head. "If that were so, everyone returning from the war would be superior to the rest of us mere mortals."

"That definitely proves the inaccuracy of that adage."

"I am not so sure of that. You and Lord Northbridge and Mr. Bradby possess a strength that is admirable. You may have had it before you went to the Continent, but Sanctuary Bay is better for having you come here, my lord."

Her quiet praise, praise he knew he did not deserve, eased a few of the bands around his heart. Those strictures had tightened each time he was faced with a decision and could not make it. He wanted to believe that she saw something in him that he had failed to see himself. Maybe he was fooling himself again as he had when he had believed Lady Eloisa loved him, but he yearned to lose himself in the delusion while he stood beside Miss Fenwick.

"I don't know how to respond to that," he said with all honesty, "but I do know, as we are working together on this project to rebuild the church, it seems it might be simpler for you to call me Edmund."

He had shocked her, he could tell, because her eyes widened as she said, "Simpler, but not proper."

"Are you always the vicar's proper sister? My cousin mentioned once that you and she had a few adventures that turned heads."

She laughed. "Cat must have been talking about the time we dared each other to jump our horses over a low hedgerow. Neither of us stopped to ask ourselves if the horses we were riding had been trained to take a hedge."

"And they had not been?"

"No, and worse, the beasts were so insulted by the very idea that we would ask that of them that once they tossed us over their heads, they refused to let us remount." She laughed again. "It was a long walk back to Meriweather Hall with the bumps and scratches and bruises we received as a reward for our silliness."

"So if you could be silly then, can you be silly now and use my given name?" He grinned. "That did not come out as I meant it to."

"I know what you intended to say. All right. I will address you as Edmund."

"And may I use your given name?"

"Of course. The only thing more inappropriate than me calling you by your first name is for me to do so and you to continue to speak to me as 'Miss Fenwick.'"

He folded his arms in front of him as he watched sparks climb from the fire and flit like daylight fireflies on the sea wind. "Then that is settled. Would you settle something else for me?"

"If I can."

"Will you tell me now how and why I upset you before my aunt came into the billiards room?"

She opened her mouth, then closed it. Finally, she said, "Truly, my lord—"

"Edmund."

Nodding, she said, "Edmund, it is only me reacting to nothing. I have not been myself since learning about the fire at the church."

"I can understand that. I have not been myself for longer than I care to admit." His hands clenched in frustration at his side when deeper dismay flickered through her eyes. Now he had upset her by letting her know how his own words picked at the new scab over his war memories. "Forgive me. I should not have said something that makes you uncomfortable."

"I am uncomfortable only because I was unsure how to respond."

"You could have answered like my aunt and told me to do my duty and stop acting foolish."

Vera smiled. "I believe one woman giving you that scold is enough."

"Have I told you that you are, without question, a brilliant woman?"

"I don't recall you saying that."

He savored her light tone that floated like the sparks did. Being with her lifted the burden of his own flaws from his heart. For a single moment, but when he was with her, chatting easily as they were now, he could breathe deeply and relish each bit of air he drew in.

"I must," he said, "correct that oversight."

"If you fail to, I'm sure your aunt will point out your error."

His laugh exploded from him, and heads turned to discover what he found funny in the midst of the disaster the whole parish had suffered. Seeing Vera's eyes alight with amusement, he offered his arm. She put her hand on it, and he led her away from where the men were returning to their tasks.

They walked toward the cliffs where they would have a good view of the narrow beach at the base of the village that hugged the sheer wall. Upwind from the fire, the air was fresh and tasted of salt and recently caught fish.

He heard a shout and looked back to see Sims directing the few workers he had. "It is clear that we need more workers than can be spared from the estate farms and the village. With planting soon to start, even fewer men will be available to work here. I have already sent word to Whitby and Scarborough that there is a fair wage to be paid for hard work here on the church."

"You should get plenty of interested men," she said, becoming as somber as he was. "Many former soldiers have come home to discover there is no work for them."

He nodded. "And if there are not enough volunteers looking for work, I will look for more elsewhere."

"Where?"

"Both Sir Nigel and Ashland have expressed their desire to offer assistance. If I contact them, they might have some men they could spare on occasion."

Her eyes flashed. "Have you lost your mind?"

He struggled not to bristle at her vexed question. "Not that I am aware of, but it would seem that you have a differing opinion."

"Lord—"

"Edmund," he corrected in a sharper tone than he intended to use.

It did not matter, because she was now furious and

made no effort to conceal it. Her eyes snapped with anger.

"Of course, I have a differing opinion," she said. "Asking either man for help could be playing right into your enemies' hands. If one of them is leading the smugglers, as we believe, any man he sends from his estate to help may be a criminal." She stamped her foot against the ground in her frustration. "Don't you see the truth, Edmund? How could we trust them to rebuild the church and not create a place for the smugglers to stash their illicit goods in it? If—"

Her voice rose in a cry as her hand slipped off his arm. Her arms flew into the air in the moment before she vanished into the earth.

Chapter Seven

Edmund leaped to grab Vera's hands. His fingers missed hers by inches. He stepped back when the ground started to slip beneath him. Was the whole top of the cliff ready to give? If the earth collapsed more, it could bury her alive.

He heard running feet. The men must have heard her scream.

"Stay back," he ordered. "The ground isn't stable."

"Where is Miss Fenwick?" someone shouted.

"Down there." He pointed to the hole where dirt continued to trickle from its edges.

Sims yelled, "Get some timbers out of the fire. We're going to need them to shore up the ground so we can get her out."

"No time." Edmund dropped to his stomach and pushed himself forward with his toes. The buttons on his waistcoat caught, but he kept moving cautiously toward the hole. One of the buttons pinged as if it had been shot from a pistol.

He sensed rather than heard someone behind him.

Sims ordered whoever it was back. A low murmur of prayer came from the men.

Edmund concentrated on inching across the grass without disturbing the ground beneath him. When he was able to stretch out his hands and touch the edge of the hole, he shouted Vera's name.

A faint answer came from below the ground. She was alive!

"We are going to get you out!" he called back.

"Hurry! Hurry, please!" she shouted back, but paused between each word as if fighting for breath.

That spurred him forward. He heard her cry out as more dirt and small stones tumbled down.

"Go back!" she cried. "Get some of boards from the wagons. If you lay them on the ground, you may be able to get close enough so you can reach in and pull me up without bringing everything down on me."

He looked over his shoulder and repeated her orders. The men scrambled to obey. Only Sims remained by Edmund's feet. The man pulled off his coat and tossed it aside, then bent to yank off his boots.

"What are you doing?" Edmund asked, inching back and getting to his feet.

"I am the smallest and lightest," Sims answered. "I have the best chance of reaching her."

"You're right." He clapped the shorter man on the shoulder. "Good idea."

Edmund helped the men lay the wooden planks on the ground. He winced each time another clod fell into the gap. When Sims asked for someone to hold on to his legs, so if the ground gave out, he would not tumble on top of Vera, Edmund grasped one of his legs while a muscular man whose name he could not remember took the other as Sims crawled on his belly.

Edmund held his breath as Sims edged to the hole. When the man leaned over it, Edmund strained for any sound to reassure him that she was all right.

"Rope!" Sims called over his shoulder. "I need some rope to get her out. Dirt is filling in around her. She can't move."

Edmund looked toward the delivery wagons. The pieces of rope there were too short. "The rope marking the new foundation!"

Two men followed him as he raced across the cliff. He hoped none of them fell into another section of what had to have been the smugglers' tunnel. Unlashing the rope from a stick, he wound it around his arm. The men tore other sticks out and loosened the rope. A length of it trailed behind him as he ran back to where Sims had not moved. He tossed one end of the rope to the prone man. Sims lowered it with care into the hole.

Edmund motioned to the largest man. When the man came over, Edmund ordered him to tie the rope around his waist. He did and planted his feet while Edmund and several other men grabbed the rope, ready to pull when Sims gave the signal. Edmund tried to look toward the hole, but his view was blocked by the backs of the men in front of him.

"Steady," Sims called back before asking, "Miss Fenwick, can you get it tied around your waist?"

Edmund did not hear her answer, and his heart faltered. *God, keep her safe. Keep her safe. Please, keep her safe.*

The prayer kept repeating through his head as Sims yelled, "Pull. Slowly. Stop if I tell you to."

The rope grew taut in Edmund's hands as he and the other men edged back. A weight, greater than Vera's, warned that the dirt had clamped around her when she had fallen in. Maybe stones, as well. He tried not to think of how she might be crushed within the debris.

"Keep it up, lads," Sims bellowed. "She's coming loose. Slowly, slowly."

Edmund focused on moving his feet. Back on the ball of one foot, then down on his heel. Back with the other foot. Over and over.

Shouts raced along the line, Edmund ran to where Sims struggled to assist Vera out of the hole. Edmund grasped her under the arms and lifted her out. The dirt released her reluctantly; then she was free. He pulled her back. Sims jumped aside as the hole widened another yard.

"Are you hurt?" Edmund asked as he set her on her feet. When she winced, he scooped her up in his arms.

"My right knee," Vera replied with another grimace. "I twisted it when I fell. I guess this will teach me to hold on to my temper, won't it?"

He knew that, if she could make a joke, she was not hurt badly. But he did not feel like jesting. After giving her a chance to thank the men who had assisted in her rescue, he carried her to the carriage. Griffin, the coachman, rushed past them and opened the door so Vera could be placed on the seat.

Edmund stepped in and closed the door. The carriage jostled when Griffin climbed into the box. Seconds later, they lurched into motion.

Beside him, Vera made a soft sound halfway between a sigh of relief and a moan. When he asked her if she was in pain, she murmured, "Other than my knee, no."

"Thank God for that."

"Yes, thank God." She closed her eyes for a moment, and he had to wonder if her prayers of gratitude echoed his. She opened them and met his with her uncompromising gaze. "But no thanks to the smugglers." She leaned her head back against the seat and his arm that he had draped along it. "I saw broken timbers. Recently broken ones. I landed on a heap of stones, and the cavity was closed in both directions. I think I had the misfortune to stamp my foot on the one spot they failed to fill in before they set fire to the church." Her bonnet creaked against his arm as she turned her head toward him. "Thank you for saving me."

As he gazed down into her soft eyes and the faint smile on her lips that looked even softer, he could not imagine not being truthful. "I was only one of many who pulled you out."

"But you were the first one to try to reach me, and you directed the men."

"Following your commands." He looped a strand of her hair over his finger and tucked it behind her ear. His fingers splayed across her silken cheek.

She breathed out something that might have been his name, but he heard only an invitation to kiss her. As he leaned in closer, she flinched as his knee brushed her injured one.

He pulled back but kept his arm beneath her nape. What a bacon-brain he was! Kissing her was the first decision he had made in almost a year, and it was as half-witted as his last one.

"I am all right," she whispered.

She had no idea the course of his thoughts, and, for that, he was grateful. Telling her that her knee would be tended to as soon as they reached Meriweather Hall, he watched her eyes close. He looked out the window at the unending sea, wishing he knew how to heal the invisible wound he had brought home from the war.

Being bored was worse than being too busy. Vera sat in a chair with her foot propped on a high stool. Mrs. Uppington and Lady Meriweather had been insistent that she stay off her leg. That had been fine for the first thirty-six hours when her knee hurt. In the past two days, the pain had diminished to almost nothing. She had tried explaining that to both women, and both women had given her the same answer. Such an injury required her to remain off her feet for a week.

By that time, she would lose her mind. She had read two novels and paged through several other books. She knew little about needlework other than mending. There was none of that because her clothes were either new or borrowed. The same for Gregory.

Not that he had returned to Sanctuary Bay. She looked at the letter that had been delivered an hour ago. It had been simple and to the point. He had a meeting arranged with the bishop, but not until next week. Many Lenten responsibilities were occupying the bishop. Gregory stated that she should be hearing from a pastor from Scarborough who, though retired, was willing to come north to Sanctuary Bay for Sunday services until Gregory returned.

"But where will we hold those services?" she asked aloud.

After the most recent *al fresco* service led by Mr.

Hamilton, who had shivered so hard that none of the words she had written for him had been understandable, several parishioners had implored her to ask her brother to find a place indoors.

"Excuse me? What did you say?" asked Lord Meriweather as he came into the small parlor.

No, she needed to think of him as Edmund, as he had requested.

Maybe it would have been easier if he had not torn down that wall of formality. He had said nothing about their ride back to Meriweather Hall, but she could not forget the expression on his face as his hand had curled around her shoulder and his mouth had lowered toward hers. If he had not bumped her knee, would he have kissed her?

She would have been a willing participant to a kiss, but she must not let it happen again. That was how the trouble began. Nolan Hedgcoe had teased her into giving him a kiss, and she had believed it was because he was in love with her. What else was a naive girl of fifteen to think? She could not have imagined he was luring her into lying for him while he spent time with a woman his father had forbidden him to see. If she had been honest then, he might not have ended up fighting a duel and dying from his wounds.

"Vera?"

"Forgive me," she said, looking up at him for the first time.

He must have been outside because grass was stuck on his boots. His hair was damp and twisted on his forehead by the wind, and she thought of her fingers combing his hair back into place.

"For what?" He smiled while he crossed the room

and folded his arms on the back of a chair facing where she sat.

"For being so lost in thought that I started talking to myself."

"I recall someone stating that talking to oneself proves that person is ready to be banished to Bedlam." He glanced at the letter she held. "I trust that contains good tidings."

"Geoffrey is delayed because he will not be speaking with the bishop until next week." She folded the letter and put it beneath her glass of water on the table beside her chair. "He is sending a substitute for the service on Sunday, but the man is coming from Scarborough. I worry that few people will be willing to stand in the cold again."

"I might have a solution."

"Really?" Excited, she stood. A tiny twinge came from her right knee, but nothing more.

"Vera, shouldn't you remain sitting?" Concern darkened his eyes.

"Not you, too. Between your aunt and Lady Meriweather, you would think I am too feeble to do anything." She stepped carefully around the stool. "I am better, but they won't listen to me."

"I had thought Lady Meriweather would."

When his lips twitched, she rolled her eyes. "She is being as stubborn as your aunt." She did not pause before she asked, "What is your solution for the problem of having no church?"

"I was going to tell you, but now I think I will show you." He offered his arm.

She put her hand on his sleeve. Trying to pretend she did not like being near him was silly. Maybe the past two days had been boring and bleak because Edmund had been busy. The only time they had had together was during the evening meal, and his aunt had kept her from joining in the conversation by asking Miss Kightly a question each time Vera had opened her mouth.

As he led her out of the room, he made her promise to tell him the moment the journey became too much for her. Her knee would have to hurt as much as it had when they had pulled her out of the collapsed tunnel before she would call for a halt. It was too wonderful to escape from the chair in the small parlor.

"Has the hole been filled in?" she asked.

"Yes, but not before we examined it."

"Someone went down in it?"

He shook his head. "No, but we lowered a torch so we could see the broken timbers better. They looked like the ones in the cellar of the old church. I have told the men to be on their guard. If they feel the ground shifting beneath them, they should flee as fast as they can."

Vera let him change the subject to the progress on the new church. Now that the old cellar had been filled, the new one was being dug. It was slow work, because they had found a lot of stones that had to be lifted up and out. That was actually good news because it meant the smugglers had not dug underground in that area.

Edmund led her slowly along the hallway where they had worked together designing the church. He walked past his sanctuary, where the door was closed, and to the end of the corridor.

The door there was shut, as well. It was different from the other ones in the corridor, far older and a single panel of oak. The tree it had been hewn from must have been huge. No trees of that size grew around Sanctuary Bay any longer because they had been harvested to build ships.

"I was thinking we could use this for Sunday services until the new church is finished." He opened the door and stepped back to let her enter.

What she saw almost made her knees buckle beneath her. Not from pain, but from joy. The chamber was half the size of Meriweather Hall's dining room, but the ceiling soared more than forty feet above her head. The red-and-black floor tiles were hidden beneath deep dust and had been disturbed by only a few footprints. Simple benches were set in two rows, facing the simple pulpit. The sounding board leaned against the pulpit. Paint was peeling on the benches as well as the eagle lectern that had been made from black walnut. One wing was missing, and its beak broken, but it still gazed heavenward. A gallery was set high on the back wall. Its narrow stairs tilted away from the wall, and several steps were broken or missing.

She took in all that, before her eyes were caught by the resplendent altar screen beneath a large arched window that had been carelessly boarded over, allowing sunlight to slip past. The screen had been created by a master artisan. Cherubs held ribbons and trays of fruit along the top and down the sides of the screen that must have been more than twelve feet tall and almost as wide. Scenes from the Bible had been carved on the wood panels and painted such bright colors that even time had not faded them.

Walking to the closest bench, she discovered that it was as old as the rest of the woodwork. The tiles beneath her feet mixed with stones where memorial brasses were missing. Through the dust, she saw the shape of angels and animals as well as a man and a woman whose outline suggested they wore clothing with stiff neck ruffs of the same era as many of the portraits in the corridor.

"This is beautiful," she whispered, not wanting to disturb the silence. "Sophia and Cat never mentioned there was a chapel in Meriweather Hall."

"They may not have known. Few people come into this wing, and I had no idea the chapel was here until Lady Meriweather mentioned I might want to reopen it while the Sanctuary Bay church is being rebuilt."

"What a lovely space! It must be as old as the house."

"Perhaps older."

"Really?" She faced him and saw he was smiling as broadly as she was. "How is that possible?"

"Most of this house, save for the great hall and this chapel and possibly some parts of the kitchens, was built after the Norman keep was torn down four or five hundred years ago. It would appear that the oldest sections were updated in the mid-seventeenth century, which explains why much of the decoration here is in the baroque style." He gestured to the cherubs with ornate skies of pink-and-white clouds behind them. "The decoration is too embellished for my taste, but it has an impact when one enters the chapel. I suspect that may have been the intention of the Lord Meriweather of the time. He must have wanted the most magnificent chapel in North Yorkshire."

She regarded him in astonishment. "Did you find that information in one of the histories in the book room?"

"No need. I have seen many ancient houses razed in and around London. Some country houses had chapels like this, stuck on one corner of the house so nothing was between the chapel and heaven." He walked toward the pulpit, dust stealing the last of the shine from his boots. "It seems a crime to tear down such sacred places. They could be returned to their former glory with some structural support and soap and water."

"But you built new houses, didn't you?"

"At the beginning. Later, I opened an import company to obtain the marble and fine woods the wealthy want in their new homes. They care little about history. Instead, they want whatever is the rage." He ran his hand along the pulpit, paying no attention to the spider webs clinging to his sleeve. "Some, after hearing I had inherited this house, asked me how long I thought it would take to pull it down and build something suitable in its place." His mouth twisted. "Suitable! What could be more suitable for Sanctuary Bay than this house that has weathered time and storms and the vagaries of all who have passed through its doors?"

She stared at him, awed by his fervor. He seemed calm, seldom raising his voice and eager to please those around him. There were depths to him that she had not guessed existed. Depths that made him the best possible lord of the manor.

He flinched and said, "I'm sor—"

"Don't you dare say you are sorry for speaking from your heart, Edmund! If you want my opinion, and I'm going to offer it whether you do or not, you should speak from your heart more."

"Doing so has gotten me in trouble more often than not."

"But not doing so hides the man you truly are." Mischievousness crept into her voice. "And won't you shock your aunt?"

"Yes, she would be taken aback if I spoke so in her hearing. She comments how cold and drafty the house is. She thinks me quite the twit for wanting to live in what she deems the middle of beyond." He pushed away from the pulpit. "But enough of that. Is there enough room here for the whole congregation?"

She scanned the space again. "I'm not sure if that is anything to worry about. Many of the older parishioners will not be able to attend, because it is a long walk from the village to Meriweather Hall."

"Lady Meriweather suggested we arrange for wagons and carts to bring the parishioners here and back after the service."

"It sounds as if you have given this a lot of thought."

"Lady Meriweather has."

Vera turned slowly to take in every inch of the dusty space. The sounding board would not need to be put back into place, and a good scrubbing would bring both the floors and the wood back to a Sunday sheen.

"What do you think, Vera?"

"I think Lady Meriweather will enjoy welcoming the villagers here as her predecessors did. Will you?"

His brows lowered in a puzzled frown. "I'm not sure what you mean."

"Do you look forward to assuming the most important role of the lord of Meriweather Hall? Welcoming the people who work on your lands to worship with you?"

"The village, as you know, is not part of this estate."

She waved aside his words with a chuckle. "You

know what I mean. Back when this chapel was built, that baron held the land from this end of Sanctuary Bay to Whitby. Everyone who lived here was dependent upon Meriweather Hall for protection during war and for food during famines or when the fishing went bad."

"You know a lot about this house."

"I am interested in the history of the bay. When the previous Lord Meriweather told stories of the olden days, I listened eagerly." She paused, then said quietly, "You would have liked him, Edmund. I know you never had a chance to meet him, but you share many interests with him."

"I regret that we never met." He picked up a strip of fabric from a bench, and the material fell apart in his hands. "It will need some cleaning."

"I know the ladies from the church will be glad to help. If you send carts for them, we can get it cleaned before Sunday."

"We will be glad to help, too," said Mrs. Williams from the doorway. The tall housekeeper wiped her hands on her apron as she came into the chapel. Her black gown became hoary with dust from the floor. "It would be our pleasure, my lord. If I may say so, it's been too many years since this chapel was used. My granny told me how her granny was told by *her* granny about when the chapel was used for christenings and marriages for the Meriweather family back as far as anyone could recall."

Edmund hesitated, and Vera knew he could not make even this simple decision.

She hurried to say, "Mrs. Williams, that is generous of you. However, if you need help, please don't hesitate to ask. I know our church members would be glad to lend a hand."

"We will be happy for their help, Miss Fenwick." The housekeeper smiled broadly. "Imagine that! Services in the chapel. I never thought I would see the day. It is a true blessing."

Vera smiled at Edmund. "Yes, it truly is."

Walking toward the back of the chapel, Edmund left Vera to talk with the housekeeper. How easily they made decisions!

He turned to look at the boarded window. Mrs. Williams spoke to Vera about sending a couple of men up to remove the planks, and he imagined the colors and light that would fill the chapel. Lady Meriweather had mentioned to him that the stained-glass window would match the beauty of the altar screen.

"Or so I am told," she had said. "Not that I have ever seen the window uncovered."

He had chuckled with her, because it was impossible not to share Lady Meriweather's laughter. Now, as he looked around the chapel with its dust and webs and what might be bat droppings beneath the gallery, he vowed to take the time to check every room in the vast house from the cellars to the attics. From the day he had arrived at Meriweather Hall, he had wanted to do that, but events had distracted him.

Events with the smugglers and watching his friends fall in love and pledge to spend their lives with his cousins. They had begun to overcome the pain and unseen wounds they had brought back from the Continent.

While they had accomplished that, he still had not

taken a full tour of the manor house. He had not halted the smugglers. Getting past the changes the war had made on him seemed impossible. Nor had he trusted his heart as his friends had theirs.

His gaze went of its own volition to where Vera glowed with happiness as she and Mrs. Williams went over the tasks to be done before Sunday. She glanced in his direction, and her smile softened.

He wanted to shout that she needed to stop looking at him as if her heart ached to belong to him. It was true that, when she had fallen into the smugglers' tunnel, he had been more frightened than he had ever been on the battlefield. She would be a pea-goose to want more from him than his help in rebuilding her brother's church. He was not the man he had been, and, as each day passed, the hope dimmed that he would regain what had been lost.

"Here you are!" Miss Kightly's cheerful voice lilted through his grim thoughts.

"Come in," Vera called as Mrs. Williams excused herself to gather the necessary hands and supplies to begin cleaning the chapel.

Miss Kightly entered, holding her gown up so the hem did not brush the dirty floor. "Is this a chapel?"

"Yes, we will be using it for services for the parish." Vera smiled. "Isn't that wonderful? It has just been rediscovered."

"Oh, what fun!" Miss Kightly clapped her hands in delight. "I hoped to find some great treasure like this when I explored my uncle's house, but he keeps warning me to stop because parts of the house are not stable." Her eyes twinkled. "But I would risk it if I could find a special room like this one."

"Come. Let me show you around."

As Vera led Miss Kightly around the small space, Edmund watched them. Vera had a dark beauty while Miss Kightly was light and ethereal. He could not forget how much he had wanted to kiss Vera in the carriage. Yet, maybe his aunt was right. Instead of flirting with Vera, should he consider marrying a woman like Sir Nigel's great-niece? She knew much about the *ton,* and if he followed her lead, he might be able to hide his inability to make a decision. He almost laughed. To offer her marriage, he first had to *decide* to marry her.

"Mrs. Williams believes, with some help from the ladies in the village, the chapel will be ready for Sunday," Vera went on.

"Are you sure?" Miss Kightly's nose wrinkled. Her eyes widened when her gaze alighted on him, but she looked back at Vera who assured her that the chapel would be in good enough condition for Sunday.

"After all," Vera said, "our Savior was born in a stable where there must have been plenty of dust and spiders. Our prayers will not be deemed of lesser value because we are not sitting in a pristine chapel." Her laugh was filled with delight. "To be honest, we should be right at home here, because there were always webs in the corners of the church that I could not reach even with a broom."

"I hope you are right about having it ready," Miss Kightly said, holding her skirt close to keep it from touching the benches or pulpit. "I have my doubts." She looked at him again. "Don't you?"

Knowing he could not loiter in the shadows, Edmund walked along the single aisle. "Actually I do." He hurried on when he saw the joyful light in Vera's eyes dim. "But I am discovering that once Vera sets her mind on something, it comes to pass, no matter how many doubting Thomases surround her."

Miss Kightly gasped. "Vera?" She looked at Vera and grinned. "If he calls you by your given name, he must do the same for me." She laughed when Edmund started to protest. "Oh, bother! Do not offer me an etiquette lesson. We are not in London. Besides, you don't want to make Vera think you value her less because you address her by her Christian name?"

"I never—" he began.

Miss Kightly did not let him finish. "So it is set. You will call me Lillian, and I will call both of you by your first names. How much more companionable we will be!" She started to add more but sneezed once, then a second and a third time. "Oh, bother! 'Tis the dust. It always makes my nose itch. Excuse me!"

He stepped aside as she rushed out of the chapel, "Vera, it was never my intention to make you feel of lesser value by suggesting we call each by our given names."

"I know that." Vera smiled and tapped his nose as if he were a tot. "Couldn't you tell she was teasing with you? It was her method of getting her way without a long, drawn-out discussion."

"I never thought of it that way."

"Because all you were thinking of was how your aunt would see such casualness between you as a sure sign that you were ready to offer for Lillian."

"You know my aunt too well, it would seem."

"No, I have come to know you." Before he could reply to that unanticipated comment, she added,

"Thank you, Edmund, for making this chapel available to our parishioners."

"I told you. It was Lady Meriweather's suggestion."

"But you are the lord of Meriweather Hall. If you felt uncomfortable with the villagers coming here, nobody would gainsay you. I—and Gregory—appreciate this more than words can say."

He was amazed how difficult it was for him to accept a compliment from her. And how too easy it was for his attention to shift to her whenever she was nearby.

As they left the chapel, Edmund let Vera do most of the talking. She was making lists of what needed to be done and how to make sure it was completed. Her voice trailed away, and he saw a familiar silhouette walking toward them.

"They told me I would find you here, Meriweather." Sir Nigel's voice resounded through the hallway. "I thought I would find my niece with you." His eyes shot daggers at Vera who stood stiffly beside Edmund.

"Here I am!"

Lillian ran down the hallway, threw her arms around Edmund, rocking him back on his heels. Had she gone around the bend? Sudden insanity was the only reason he could imagine that she would act so *outré*. He raised his hands, but lowered them quickly. He could not push her aside. That would be ill-mannered. On the other hand, if he let her continue to cling to him, he might find himself in hot water with Sir Nigel. What to do…?

He looked over her head and toward Vera for help before he even realized what he was doing. In the moment before she drew an emotionless mask over her face, pain flashed in her eyes. Then Vera hurried away,

and he was left with Lillian hugging him and a broadly smiling Sir Nigel and the knowledge that he had hurt Vera because he had not been able to decide what to do.
   Again.

Chapter Eight

A fortnight later, Gregory had returned with good news from the bishop, who was pleased to hear that the parish had found a new home in the chapel at Meriweather Hall. Instead of working with Edmund as Vera had expected, her brother spent time writing to publishers and booksellers to find copies of the books burned in the fire. He seemed to receive a package at least every other day from Hatchard's or Lackington, Allen & Company's bookshops in London as well as others in York and Edinburgh. He focused on reading those and left the details of rebuilding the church to her and Edmund.

Vera made every effort to work with Edmund, though the memory of Lillian embracing him remained between them, an invisible wall that she had no idea how to climb over. He was trying to act as if nothing out of the ordinary had happened, too, but he had hosted both Lillian and Sir Nigel twice in the past fortnight, much to the delight of his aunt who had bluntly asked him last evening where he thought his and Lillian's wedding should be held. A flush had risen out of his collar before he had pardoned himself and left the table. Mrs. Uppington had continued to quiz Gregory about various churches in the area where banns could be read. Partway through the conversation, unable to listen to more, Vera had made her own excuses and withdrawn.

The match would be deemed an excellent one by the Beau Monde. A new lord marrying the daughter of a family that had been titled for generations, combining two prominent Yorkshire families. She should be happy for both of them.

She was not, because she could see that Edmund was not in love with Lillian. Yes, the *ton* married for other reasons than love, but Edmund was new to the highest realms of Society. Like her, he had a working-class view that love was necessary for a marriage. She kept reminding herself, Edmund's plans were none of her bread-and-butter. Their focus should be on the new church. That was why, at least every other day, they had gone to check on the progress.

Last week, the cellar for the new church building had been finished. It was lined with stone from the vicarage, as well as rocks brought from nearby fields. There had been some suggestion of taking rocks from the abandoned tunnel, but that could lead to more collapses. Nobody wanted to risk that.

More building supplies had arrived and were stacked near the site. They were guarded closely by men from Meriweather Hall. Vera admired Edmund's foresight, even though she was unsure if the smugglers would halt the new church from being built. There was no threat for them with the new building as there had been with the old. She wondered what might have happened if the tunnel had been discovered in the church cellar *before* the fire.

The breeze was, for a change, coming off the land as Vera and Edmund were driven toward the village. Warmth brought hopes of spring and an end to the winter that had been longer and colder and snowier than even the oldest residents of Sanctuary Bay could remember.

"May I ask you a question?" Edmund asked, cutting into her thoughts.

"Certainly." She tried to keep her voice from revealing how startled she was by the question. In the past two weeks, the trips to and from the church had been mostly in silence.

"You have known Sir Nigel longer than I have. Do his recent actions strike you as odd?" A smile pulled at his lips. "Maybe I should ask—do they strike you as odder than usual?"

"You would do better to ask my brother about that. I have spoken to Sir Nigel infrequently. Gregory has been at his house more often."

"So you don't usually attend his fall gala where he shows off his artwork?"

She shook her head. "A vicar and his sister are seldom invited to such social occasions."

"But you are good friends with the Meriweather family."

"The Meriweathers are unique in not judging one by one's social standing."

His light brown brows rose. "I never thought of it that way, though the whole family welcomed me without question."

"That is how they are. Why are you asking me about Sir Nigel?"

"He seems even a bit stranger than usual." He rubbed his chin with two fingers. "First, he sends Miss Kightly—Lillian—to Meriweather Hall, then he swoops in to take her to his estate as if she had run away. I have known him less than a year, but he did not act so out of hand before we went to Norwich for the wedding." He pulled his hand away from his face and stared at it. "And Lillian is acting even odder than her great-uncle. Have you noticed that?"

Yes! she wanted to shout, but she must never forget how her unbridled reactions had led to disaster before. She forced herself to ask calmly, "In what way?"

"If you have not noticed anything, then I should let it go. It may be nothing, and I don't want to besmirch her reputation by suggesting…by suggesting—"

"That she is as peculiar as Sir Nigel?"

He laughed, and she heard the carefree sound that had vanished weeks ago. "Right to the point as always, Vera. Thank you for reminding me that I should not look for trouble where there apparently is none."

She swallowed her frustration as he began talking about what he hoped they would see at the building site. She could not listen while she berated herself. She *had* seen how extraordinarily Lillian had acted. Instead of treating Edmund with warm friendliness as she had throughout her stay at Meriweather Hall, Lillian had appeared bereft at the idea of leaving him to go home with her great-uncle.

Why?

The question taunted her, but she could not ask Edmund now, not after hinting that she had seen no changes in Lillian. She had not wanted to upset the status quo and risk her brother's favor in his eyes. Instead, she had made Edmund question his own insights and left herself frustrated.

Vera was relieved when the carriage slowed to a stop by where the new church would stand. She doubted she had heard more than a word or two of what Edmund had said during the ride, and she felt guilty that she had been rude.

Bruse, the mason who had been overseeing building the foundation, hurried over to greet them. He was a squat man, as solid as the stones and bricks he used. Thick red curls matched his wiry beard, and he squinted. Whether it was because he could not see well or because he spent a lot of time working outside, she was unsure.

"I am glad to see you, my lord," Bruse said. "We are ready to set the first columns in place to support the main floor and the roof. I need to know if you are having aisles on either side of the center aisle or not."

"May I say something?" Vera asked when Edmund hesitated.

"Of course!" Color rose up Edmund's face at his overly enthusiastic response.

"Gregory would prefer a single aisle in the sanctuary," she said as if Bruse were not staring at Edmund in astonishment. "That will keep the congregation closer together so we have a true community when we worship. I think the parishioners would appreciate that, too, because it is what they are accustomed to."

Edmund nodded. "That makes sense." Looking at the mason, he said, "We will not have aisles on the sides, then."

Bruse nodded. "We will still put walls beneath the joists to support the floors, but only the outer walls will be tied into the roof."

Vera waited for Edmund's answer. He understood what the skilled laborers meant when their words often made little or no sense to her. How was she going to continue to help him? She prayed that God would show her a way. After all, she had put Edmund in this situation by not thinking how her request could lead to continuous embarrassment for him.

She sighed. No matter how much she had believed she had matured and changed, she had been as unthinking while standing beside the burned-out church as she had been before Lord Hedgcoe had sent them away. Would she never learn to consider the consequences of her words before she spoke them? She had injured Edmund when all she had wanted was to make sure the church was rebuilt so she and Gregory could continue to live and do their work in Sanctuary Bay.

Edmund tried not to make it obvious that he was watching Vera walk away after she excused herself abruptly. When he looked back at the mason as Bruse spoke about hiring a few more skilled masons, he realized he had not been successful. The mason kept his gaze on a button in the center of Edmund's waistcoat, and Bruse flinched when speaking Vera's name, clearly worried about what Edmund would do or say.

Why was nobody acting as they should? First, it had been Sir Nigel. Next, Lillian seemed to have two different women living underneath her skin—the one who treated him as a friend and the one who made no secret of the fact that she wished he would ask her to become his wife. Now, Vera, the one who always seemed the most stable and unchanging, the one he could depend on to be honest with him, was as unwilling to meet his eyes as the mason.

"You were told at the beginning to get all the men you need," Edmund said with what shreds of his dignity he could muster.

"I will send word to Meriweather Hall to let you know who I hire and at what wage, so they can be properly paid."

"Just make sure they are skilled."

"We are hiring men from Whitby and Scarborough and even as far west as Pickering." He glanced at the foundation, then tipped his cap. "I'll let the lads know that the church will have a single aisle like the old one."

Edmund nodded. It had been a simple decision. He should have been able to make it, but he could not halt the visions of the roof falling in if he chose unwisely. Men had already died because of his misguided decisions. He did not want to let that happen again. He was grateful—again!—for Vera's suggestion.

Vera stood near the old churchyard. As if he had called her name, she turned and met his gaze. She said nothing. What was she thinking about now?

Please, make it something that requires no decision, he prayed in desperation as he walked to where she stood. *I don't want to disappoint her.*

That thought drew him up short. Before, he had thought of himself and his embarrassment when he could not make a decision. Never before had he thought about *disappointing* Vera…as he may have disappointed her when he had drawn back in the carriage the day she hurt her knee. Or maybe she had been glad he had come to his senses and not kissed her. He had no idea, and she had given him no sign.

Unable to speak of his tangled thoughts, Edmund said as he reached Vera, "You appear perplexed."

"I am. I want to ask you about a matter that will be of greatest concern to the parishioners. Would it be possible for the lych-gate to be set so it can serve the old churchyard as well as the new?" She walked to a spot about fifteen yards away. "About here?" She returned to where he stood. "That way, those who wish to be buried with their loved ones in the old church-yard still can pass through a lych-gate on their way to the funeral service." She smiled. "Not that it matters as much to the deceased as it does to the pallbearers who may need some rest after coming up the steep hill in the village."

"That seems to make sense."

Her smile broadened, and he was sure the sun had popped through the clouds. Everything seemed brighter. "I'm glad you think so, Edmund. I cannot tell you how much this will mean to everyone."

"You know the parishioners better than I do."

"And I hope you don't mind when I make sugges-tions like this."

A suggestion that came with a solution already at-tached, a suggestion that did not require him to make a decision? He was grateful.

As they started back toward the carriage, she paused. "Look! Daffodils!"

A clump of yellow buds poked up out of the grass.

"Spring must finally be on its way to Sanctuary Bay," he said.

"We need a shovel."

"A shovel?" he repeated, confused.

"If we leave the daffodils here, they will be trampled by the workers. If you don't mind, I can transplant the bulbs to Meriweather Hall. Once a new vicarage is ready, I will move the bulbs there."

"Trust you to care about flowers as much as you do the church."

"The church is men's creation. Daffodils are God's."

He savored the happy glow on her face. He had last seen that expression when he had offered the chapel for the parish's services. Lost in his own uncertainty for the past few weeks, he had failed to notice her reticence. What a horrible host he had been! Worse, he had been a wretched friend.

Friend... Since their return from Norwich, while they had worked together, she had become his friend. Now, as he looked into her shimmering eyes, the word friend no longer seemed to fit. It felt too simple for the complex feelings tangled inside him.

"It will not take long to dig the daffodils up," Vera said. "The bulbs should be close to the surface here."

He nodded, glad that her words pushed aside his confusing thoughts. He enjoyed spending time with her, more than with any woman he had ever met. She accepted him for himself, not as the brave, damaged warrior or the very eligible baron in need of a wife. She would make any man a good wife, so he had to make sure he did not monopolize her time and prevent her from finding the one she could love. A curious sensation rushed through him, curious and altogether repellant.

He did not allow himself to examine it closely. He

gave a shout to one of the workers. The man picked up a shovel and brought it over to them.

"We'll need a box or bag to carry the bulbs in," Vera said after thanking the fellow.

He rushed away and came back with a small box that was about six inches on each side. "Will this do, Miss Fenwick?"

"It is perfect. Thank you."

He tipped his cap before returning to his work.

Vera held out her hand for the shovel, but Edmund shifted it out of her reach.

"You don't think I am going to let you dig them up, do you?" he asked.

"Actually I did."

"Why? Because such work is below a peer's dignity?"

"You do have gardeners at Meriweather Hall."

"I didn't always live at Meriweather Hall. Maybe I enjoyed digging in the dirt, too, before I inherited my title."

Her eyes widened. "I never thought of that. Did you?"

"Did I enjoy digging in the dirt?" When she nodded, he chuckled. "Only when it comes to raising a new building, I must admit. However, no lord of the realm would allow a young lady to dirty her pretty frock by digging up bulbs."

She swept out her hand. "I don't want to be the one who pulls out the underpinnings of the realm."

"And you have no desire to spend more time with Mme. Dupont being measured for a new gown to replace a dirty one."

"You said that. Not me." She laughed. "So, by all means, dig up the daffodils."

He pressed the tip of the shovel against the ground, then put his foot on it to drive it into the hard earth. He had been jesting with her; yet, he found doing something physical very satisfying. He had been accustomed to taking care of his own needs. Now he had a valet and a butler and a stableman and a coachman and a gardener and many others. He must not lose sight again of how pleasant it was to do a task himself.

As he worked, pushing aside stones and piling dirt to the left of the daffodils, Vera knelt by the flowers.

"It's said that the daffodils in North Yorkshire," she said, "come from those planted by the monks at Rievaulx Abbey out past the moors." She smiled at the buds where small slips of yellow were visible through the green. "Since then, they have spread throughout North Yorkshire and blossom each spring."

Her smile wavered as she glanced toward the ruins of her home. Nothing remained except the torn-up ground.

"Did you have daffodils by the vicarage?" he asked, aching that he could not ease her grief.

"There were lots of flowers." She drew the bulbs out of the ground and set them in the box.

"Let's rescue them."

Hope and gratitude blossomed in her eyes, as glorious as the first flowers of spring. "I can do that, Edmund."

He gave her a feigned frown. "Must I explain again how such a request could destroy nearly a thousand years of our country's society?"

"No. Please don't!" She picked up the small box

and stood. "I appreciate you helping me with this, Edmund."

"You have helped me often, so I am only returning the favor."

"We need not keep score." She motioned for him to lead the way. "That's not what a friend does."

There was that word again. Friend. He should be glad that she considered him a friend, but her saying so annoyed him in a way he could not explain.

He was glad that she kept talking about the flowers she had planted near the vicarage. Most of them must have been destroyed while the fire had been doused and when the vicarage had been torn down, but she had faith that some had survived.

After she pointed out where he should dig, Edmund went to work. The bulbs closest to the cottage were charred lumps, but a few had been protected by the cold ground. He kept digging, ignoring how sweat dripped off his forehead and trickled down his spine. It felt good to be doing something that required no thought, only hard work. Soon the small wooden box was filled to overflowing and a second was becoming full, too. The wind shifted and turned cold as it came off the bay. The sweat that had run down his back became a cold sheen, and he shivered in spite of himself.

"We have enough," Vera said.

"Let me finish this area, then we can return to Meriweather Hall." He pushed the shovel to break the ground and heard a clunk. "What…?"

"What is it?"

"Just a moment." Leaning down, he shoved the dirt aside. Something twinkled in the sunlight. He picked up a flask. "It is silver." He turned it over. "The only marks are the silversmith's ones." He tipped it to allow her to see the tiny indentations on the top. "The JB over the WW is for James Barber and William Whitwell, who work in York, as you can tell from the cross mark next to the lion mark. The tiny Y after it means it was made in the early part of this decade."

"You can tell all that from those tiny marks?"

"My business was importing exotic woods, but occasionally a client asked for fine metals or art. I had to educate myself so that neither I nor my client was cheated." He looked from it to her. "I assume it does not belong to you or the vicar."

"No. We never had anything of such fine quality."

"Yes, its *qualityship* is undeniable."

She gasped and pressed her hand over her mouth at the word his cousin had first heard one of the smugglers use to mean his leader.

"I need to examine this more closely," he said. "It may have something about it that will pinpoint the identity of the man giving the smugglers their orders. If he were here and ordered the fire set in the church, he may not have noticed that he dropped his flask."

"Or someone else could have dropped it."

"That is also a possibility." He put the flask under his coat before calling the man to come and get his shovel; then, taking the two boxes of bulbs, he led her back to the carriage.

As soon as they reached Meriweather Hall, Edmund went into the room near the chapel. Vera had paused only long enough to give the boxes of flowers to one of the footmen and then followed him.

"Close the door," he ordered over his shoulder as he

strode past the table where her sketches for the church were spread out across the top.

From a shelf near the window, he picked up a tortoiseshell case. He opened it and drew out an oval silver-edged magnifying glass. Setting the flask on the table, he aimed the glass at it.

"What do you see?" Vera asked as she leaned on her hands on the other side of the table.

"Actually it is what I don't see that is curious." He ran his finger over the plain area within engraved scrolling. "Usually there are initials within the scroll."

"But there are none here."

"Not any longer." He watched color wash from her face as he said, "They have been sanded away. It could have been by use, going in and out of a pocket, but I doubt that. The rest of the flask doesn't show the same amount of wear. Someone removed the initials to hide who owns it."

"Can you get any other information from it?"

"I am going to try." He stared down at the silver flask. "Trust me, Vera, I am going to try."

"I do trust you."

His head jerked up at her soft words, but she was already leaving the room. Because she had said too much or because he had?

Chapter Nine

The maid knocked as Vera was about to get ready for bed. It had been a busy day with making preparations for her brother's first service in Meriweather Hall's chapel. She had struggled to write his sermon, unsure which lesson to include. He had been busy tending to parishioners in the village and had asked her to take over the task which she knew he despised.

She had considered verses from the twelfth chapter of Luke: *"And this know, that if the goodman of the house had known what hour the thief would come, he would have watched, and not have suffered his house to be broken through. Be ye therefore ready also: for the Son of man cometh at an hour when ye think not."* But she guessed some people in the congregation would believe her brother spoke of the smugglers invading their village rather than of their Savior entering into their hearts.

She had prayed about using a passage from First Corinthians, third chapter: *"For we are laborers together with God: ye are God's husbandry, ye are God's building. According to the grace of God which is given unto me, as a wise master builder, I have laid the foundation, and another buildeth thereon. But let every man take heed how he buildeth thereupon. For other foundation can no man lay than that is laid, which is Jesus Christ."*

That seemed to be a lesson that would not infuriate the smugglers who sat with them like lions among the lambs. Usually, once she decided on the lesson, she could write the sermon easily. Not today.

Maybe because the day had been an unsettling one. She had hoped that when Edmund came to dinner that evening, he would have had something to share about what he had discovered about the flask. He had only glanced in her direction upon entering the dining room, and he had shaken his head slightly. She had never had a chance to speak with him because his aunt had spent the whole meal lamenting that Lillian had returned to Sir Nigel's house.

"Just when I thought you two were becoming much better acquainted," Mrs. Uppington had said with a look in Edmund's direction that would have quelled most men.

He had borne it with a smile. "I am sure we will see Miss Kightly soon."

"On Sunday in the chapel."

At that, Edmund had turned to Vera who had to shrug. She had had no idea why Mrs. Uppington had been certain that Lillian would be attending Sunday services at Meriweather Hall.

"It is Mothering Sunday, if you will recall," his aunt had said before smiling at Lady Meriweather, who, like Vera and Gregory, seldom had a chance to slip in a single word during the evening meal. "Our hostess has invited the parishioners to stay at Meriweather Hall for a celebration feast, as she does each year."

Vera wondered how Mothering Sunday had snuck up on them so quickly. It meant Easter was three weeks away. Time had sped past, unnoticed, while she had worked with Edmund. She'd had no time to prepare for Mothering Sunday.

"Miss Fenwick?" The maid's voice sounded as if she were repeating Vera's name for more than the second time.

Rushing to open the door, Vera swallowed her apology for keeping the maid waiting. The young woman relayed the message that Lord Meriweather wished to see her in his book room.

"As soon as possible," the maid added before walking away.

Vera paused only long enough to check her appearance in the cheval glass. Her hair was in its usual neat bun, though a few strands curled around her face. Her light green gown was wrinkled, and she was glad that she had insisted Mme. Dupont forgo the stylish rows of ruffles that would have sagged by this time of the day.

The house was quiet as Vera went down the stairs and to the corridor leading to the book room. Was it because of the fog that had come in from the sea late in the afternoon and cut off the house from everything else, even the nearby stables? She saw no one else, not even the shadow of a servant. She eyed the suits of armor when she passed them. They were empty, of course, but she could not shake her childish trepidation that one of them would come to life and swing his weapon at her. She preferred going past the stern portraits in the other wing.

As she reached the book room door, Edmund was coming to his feet. He had left his coat over a chair, and his dark brown waistcoat contrasted with the unblemished white of his sleeves and cravat. She would have liked to take a moment to enjoy the sight of him dressed casually, but that chance vanished when he handed her a piece of paper.

"What do you think of this?" he asked.

The page was thick and brown, like the paper used in a shop to wrap purchases. The edges were torn unevenly, and the writing on it had been done with what looked to be coal. The spelling was so bad that she had to read it aloud to figure out what the words were supposed to be.

The message was short. It asked that Lord Meriweather meet the writer on the shore tonight when the moon was new and the smugglers occupied with their heinous trade far beyond Meriweather Hall. The writer professed to have information about the smugglers and their leader he was sure Lord Meriweather wanted to know.

"What do you think?" Edmund asked.

"My first reaction is that it seems too good to be true," she said.

"That was my first inclination, as well."

"Is this someone's idea of a joke?"

"I don't think so." He took the paper, crumpled it and threw it on the fire. "I think it's more likely that it is an invitation to put my foot in a trap on a foggy night."

"Do you know who sent it?"

He nodded. "Here is a second page with the precise location I am supposed to meet him. Stanley Cadman's name is on the bottom."

"Stanley?" she gasped.

"You know him?" His mouth twisted with a reluctant grin. "Of course you do. You know everyone in Sanctuary Bay. What sort of man is he?"

"A good man, but are you sure that he truly wrote this message?"

"That is the question, isn't it?" He paced between the hearth and the rosewood desk, easily stepping around the stacks of books. "I can't trust such a boon falling into my lap."

"Many parishioners are furious that the church was burned by the smugglers. I believe Stanley would want to help if he can." She rubbed her hands together. "But to put such a request in writing is dangerous. He must trust whoever he gave it to would deliver without sharing it with someone else first."

Edmund halted his pacing and faced her. "That sounds as if you think someone in this house is working with the smugglers?"

She shook her head. "I haven't seen any sign of that, but if someone chanced to see him writing the note or coming here to deliver it, he could be risking his life and more."

"All the more reason to question the wisdom of arranging such a meeting."

"They feel they don't have any other choice, Edmund," she said softly.

"They? The smugglers or the law-abiding folk of Sanctuary Bay?"

"Both." She sat in one of the comfortable chairs facing the hearth and looked up at him. "It wasn't always like this. I remember when I first came to Sanctuary Bay that the smugglers kept to themselves, never interfering in anyone's lives. Then, there was an abrupt shift. The smugglers no longer seemed content to earn money by deceiving the excise men. They began to intimidate the honest villagers, something that Gregory heard about almost immediately."

"My cousin Sophia was sent to London, I know, when she came too close to unmasking the man who set the smugglers on that evil path."

Vera digested that tidbit of information. Why hadn't she been more curious why Edmund's predecessor had suddenly decided Sophia needed a London Season?

"You must be as careful, Edmund," she said, then felt her cheeks redden as she realized she was giving him an order.

"I will be."

"Not only with the smugglers, but with the fog. When it's this thick, it's easy to become disoriented and lose one's way."

"I know. This is not my first foggy night in Sanctuary Bay." He leaned forward and brushed his finger against her cheek. "I could say you don't need to worry, but I know you will. You care about those around you. To own the truth, I like that you are concerned about me because it shows that you have come to care about me, too."

"You have been kind to Gregory and me."

"I am not speaking of a 'Gregory and me' situation. I am saying that you, Vera, caring about me is wonderful. Too bad I had not met you before I joined the army. It would have been comforting during the war to know that you were thinking of me and praying for my safety." His fingers trailed down along her chin as he tipped it up toward him. "And I could have been thinking of you rather that what awaited me in the next encounter with the French."

Words filled her mind, but none that she could speak. How could she allow herself to forget, even for a moment, what he had endured on the Continent? Not that she knew exactly what had happened to him and his friends, but stories of the horrifying battles were still repeated almost two years after Napoleon had been defeated at Waterloo.

"And now…" He sighed as he drew away from her. "Now I must decide if I should meet Cadman or not."

She silenced her sigh of regret that he no longer was touching her; then she kept another from escaping as she realized the import of what he had said. He needed to make a decision, but it was an impossible task for him. Was he asking for her help? She had been making *suggestions* throughout the planning for the new church, and he had accepted them as such. Would he be as willing to listen to her thoughts on something that had no connection to the church?

She said quietly, "You should not go alone."

"It sounds as if you think I should go."

She could not miss the relief in his voice that he did not have to make the choice on his own. "If Stanley risked so much to get this message to you, he must have something vital to tell you."

"I agree." Going to the window, he looked out into the night where the land and the sea were both lost in the inky darkness. "I am not a man who turns away from risks."

"But you must not go alone." She came to her feet. "I will—"

"If you are going to say that you will go with me, don't bother." He faced her and put his hands on her shoulders. "You are right about it being a risky venture, and I will not endanger you by letting you come with me into what may be a trap."

"Edmund, I know Stanley. Gregory knows him even better than I do."

"But he did not ask to meet you or the vicar. He asked to meet me."

His hands gentled on her shoulders, and his eyes sparked as he held her gaze. The emotions flashing there were powerful. She could imagine the enemy quailing before him on the battlefield. But he was on her side, ready to defeat the smugglers who had taken too much from her. Not only her home, but her last remnants of security. She longed to lean against his broad chest and let his arms surround her.

She drew back and turned away. She must not make this bad situation worse by surrendering to her foolish desire to be in his arms. She must never forget—not even in the midst of a disaster—how her longing to be in a man's arms had almost ruined her brother's life.

"Take someone strong and smart with you," she whispered, unable to meet his eyes. If he looked as bereft as she felt after putting distance between them, she could not bear it. "Promise me that, please."

"I promise." He stroked her arm gently, then walked past her to the door. "And I will send a message to your room as soon as I return, because I know you will not sleep until you hear what Cadman has to say."

She had to smile. "You know me well."

"Not as well as I hope to." He winked and left.

As her knees grew weak, Vera sank to sit again. What had he meant by his bold wink? Her heart hammered within her, beating out a joyous melody. She longed to believe his words were an invitation to open her heart to him. She could not. She had made that mistake once already.

But Edmund isn't Nolan Hedgcoe, came the insistent voice in her mind. He would not try to twist her heart so he could pretend he was in love with her when he used visits to her as an excuse to pay secret calls on the woman he was truly interested in. A woman who lived near the parsonage on Lord Hedgcoe's estate, so he could leave his horse or carriage in front of the parsonage without drawing further notice. Why had she believed Nolan when he said, time after time, that he wanted to take a walk by himself through the wood that separated the parsonage from the other woman's cottage? She had been so in love with him that she would have believed him if he said the sun was going to shine at night.

She rose and went to the closest shelf. She selected a book with an interesting title. Turning the chair so she had a view of both the window and the door to the hallway, she sat and opened the book.

The words blurred. Closing her eyes, she prayed for Edmund's safety as he went out into the night where the smugglers roamed as if they were the lords of Sanctuary Bay. A place she had sent him when she could have agreed he would be wiser to remain beneath Meriweather Hall's roof. Why hadn't she thought through her own decision before making one for him? If she had made the wrong one again, the price could be higher than her brother's living. It could be Edmund's life.

Lights burned at many of the windows in the manor house. If the household staff believed the lamps could hold back what hid in the darkness, they were wrong. Evil stalked Sanctuary Bay.

Edmund tossed his greatcoat to a footman without even noticing which one it was. "Where is Miss Fenwick?"

"I c-c-an f-f-find out, m-m-my lord," stammered the footman that he now recognized as Foggin.

"Send a message to her room immediately," he ordered as he strode out of the entrance hall. "Ask her to accept my apologies if she is asleep, but let her know I need to see her without delay."

"Yes, m-m-my lord."

Edmund did not slow as he stormed through the house. He shot an order to a maid to have coffee brought to his book room. She acknowledged his bidding and curtseyed, but he only stepped around her and kept going.

Did he think he could flee from what had happened on the strand? No, he was not that foolish, but if he slowed, even for a moment, he would have to face the truth of how weak his position was now.

As he entered the book room, Vera came to her feet from where she had been sitting facing the door. He said nothing when he went to the window and pulled the draperies to shut out the view of the bay. Loosening his cravat that suddenly seemed as constricting as a hangman's noose, he looked at Vera.

She was the epitome of the brave, stalwart women

who lived in Sanctuary Bay. The women who waited ashore, tending to their households and families, while their men challenged the unforgiving sea and the predators both below the waves and atop them. Yet, in spite of her aura of strength, there was something fragile about her. Something that announced that her unrelenting resilience was partially a pose. Looking closer, he could see how her eyes glittered. With tears or fatigue?

"What happened?" she asked when he remained silent, not wanting to put the burden of pain on her slender shoulders. "Was Stanley there? Did he tell you anything that will help us uncover the identity of the smugglers' leader?"

His composure, strained already, almost cracked when she said *us*. That single word made him feel less alone, less lost because he could not find the man he once had been. He did not want to be lonely and uncertain any longer. He wanted to tug her into his arms, pull out the pins that held her hair in place and bury his face in those lush strands. Holding her close and shutting out the rest of the world was the sweetest balm he could imagine for his torment.

He did not move. She might be appalled if he drew her close. The tremulous connection they shared could be severed. He could not chance losing that. Vera had become an important part of his life.

"Edmund?" She put her hand on his arm. "What happened? Tell me, please."

He slid his arm out from under her gentle touch and put the desk between them. "Stanley Cadman is dead."

Vera moaned softly, then sank to the chair. Her fingers clenched the arm as if she held on to the side of a boat in a thrashing sea. "Are you sure?"

"Very." He spread his fingers across the desk, needing to steady himself when the world seemed unstable. "We discovered him at the base of the cliff below the garden. His neck was broken."

"Do you think…?" She choked on the words.

"Do I think it was murder? Yes."

Chapter Ten

Vera looked around the small parlor. Even though Edmund and her brother were also in the room and watching Mr. Brooks as closely as she was, not a sound could be heard beyond the crackle of the fire on the hearth and the clatter of cold rain against the windows. Her gaze shifted to Edmund whose face showed the strain of the night's events. She longed to kneel beside him while she told him how sorry she was that he had been the one to find Stanley Cadman's body on the sand. His gaze had turned inward, and she suspected he was thinking of the other deaths he had seen during the war.

Mr. Brooks had brought two thick volumes with him when he had arrived in less than an hour after Edmund had returned to Meriweather Hall. The justice of the peace turned the page in the slightly thinner book as he murmured to himself. She caught words like *during the reign of Edward III,* but was unsure what he was reading.

Looking up, Mr. Brooks said, "The law is quite clear, my lord. In circumstances such as these, there must be a coroner's inquest. What is discovered in that may lead to the cause of Cadman's death, though I would say it is quite obvious to me what happened."

"And what is that?" asked Edmund with a calmness that was belied by his fist clenched on the chair's arm. "Someone killed him to keep him from meeting with me tonight? Because that is quite obvious to me."

"I disagree. I believe it is far more likely that, in the foggy darkness, he misjudged how close he was to the edge of the cliff and stepped over it. However, that is not for us to decide. I must contact Ashland."

"Ashland is the county's corner?"

Mr. Brooks stood. "Unlike a justice of the peace, a coroner must be of the peerage, my lord. I am surprised you do not know that."

"It appears I still have more to learn about the peerage and its obligations." Edmund's sarcasm lashed through his voice, and, for once, he did not apologize for such a sharp tone.

As Edmund and Mr. Brooks glared at each other, Gregory said, "I assume Lord Ashland will want to see the body to assure himself that the man is dead."

"He has that right for the next fortnight."

"Fortnight?" Edmund shook his head. "Do you really expect Cadman's family will delay burying him for two weeks?"

Mr. Brooks sighed. "They can bury him whenever they wish, but the coroner can order the body disinterred anytime within a fortnight."

"That is barbaric," Vera said, then lowered her eyes when all three men glanced at her.

"It is," the justice of the peace replied, "but it is also the law. May I impose on you, my lord, to send someone to alert the viscount that he must gather men to assist him in the investigation?"

Edmund nodded, and Mr. Brooks bid them a good night before taking his leave. Gregory followed without a word. He had his hands clasped behind his back and stared at the floor, a sure sign he was deep in prayer that he would find the right words when he went to the village to inform Stanley's family of the tragedy.

"There is no need for you to remain here," Edmund said as Vera came to her feet. "Good night."

"No."

He faced her, startled. "I am not sure what you mean."

"I mean there is a need for me to remain here." She walked to where he stood by the hearth. "Something horrible happened to a man who had the respect of the villagers, for he took a moderate stance in any discussion. He has no enemies I've heard of."

"He had one." He went to a side table where a pot of coffee had grown cold.

"Or you do."

Pouring himself a cup of coffee, he held it up to her. She shook her head, and he added cream to the cup. After he had taken a sip, he said, "It would be far easier to deal with this if you were not so blasted insightful."

"I haven't said anything you were not already thinking."

"True." He sighed. "And I think it's true that Cadman may have been less a target than a message to me." His shoulders sagged, and he groped for a chair. "I had thought no more men would die because of me."

Vera gave in to her yearning and knelt by where he sat. Putting her hand on his that gripped the arm of the chair, she said, "Stanley did not die because of you, Edmund. He died because the leader of the smugglers ordered his death."

"You sound sure of that."

"I am."

He put his other hand over hers. "I hope you are right, but if you are, then that means someone learned about Cadman's message to me and alerted the smugglers' leader."

"His qualityship."

"Yes." Edmund looked toward the door. "If they were referring to Brooks, why would he call for a coroner's inquest?" He answered his own question. "Because it is the law, and he wants no suspicion to alight on him."

"But Mr. Brooks may not be the leader."

"No. One of my neighboring gentlemen could have ordered Cadman's death."

She flinched, in spite of her resolve to remain serene.

He lifted her hand off his and folded it between his rough palms. "Forgive me, Vera. I should not be speaking of such appalling matters with you."

"With whom should you speak of them?"

Again she could see that her blunt words discomfited him, but he recovered himself. Squeezing her fingers, he released her hand as he stood. He held out his to assist her to her feet. She took it and stood. Too close to him, but he did not back away. When she shifted slightly, he tightened his grip on her hand. Slowly, he raised it toward him. The warmth of his breath slid along her skin in the moment before he pressed his lips to the back of her hand. Her fingers curled over his as her knees shook. Slowly he raised his head until his eyes were even with hers.

"Know one thing," he said softly. "I appreciate your concern more than words can say, but I will not allow your well-meaning heart to lead you into danger."

She struggled to form words to reply, but her mind refused to focus. Even when he bid her good-night and left the small parlor, she could not move her still-outstretched hand.

In a few minutes, she would regain her perspective and recall the trouble she courted if she entangled her life with a member of the *ton*. For this special moment when she could believe that anything was possible, even not being made a fool of by another man, she was going to savor the sweetness of the memory of his kiss on her hand.

On Mothering Sunday, as the parishioners arrived at Meriweather Hall to attend morning services, Edmund had never felt less like playing the genial host. Many members of the congregation were equally grim. Vera had been correct when she had said Stanley Cadman was both well respected and well liked. The whole village was in mourning.

Not the whole village. He had no proof, but he was sure that Cadman had been killed by someone familiar who had been able to sneak up on him in the thick fog. If a stranger had been in the village, that news would have spread through Sanctuary Bay.

For once, he was very grateful for his aunt. Aunt Belinda was enjoying every minute of acting the chatelaine of Meriweather Hall. She stood by the chapel door and greeted the parishioners.

When he saw Lady Meriweather coming along the hallway, he went to meet her and offer his arm to escort her into the chapel. "I am sorry," he said low enough so nobody else could hear, "that my aunt has usurped your place."

"You need not apologize, Edmund." Lady Meriweather smiled. "Your aunt is having such a good time that I could not imagine putting a halt to it."

"That is kind of you."

"It is what families do."

"But she is my aunt on my mother's side. She is not related to your late husband."

"You are part of our family, Edmund, and she is related to you. That makes her family." She smiled, and the stress of the past few years of caring for her dying husband fell away to reveal the beautiful woman she was. "As you may have noticed, in Sanctuary Bay, we don't define family strictly. We all are God's children."

He had noticed that. In good ways, when one family helped one another without expecting anything in return. In bad ways, when the village families closed ranks to keep the identity of the smugglers a secret. Were they hiding the identity of a murderer who might be among them for the Mothering Sunday gathering?

Edmund scanned the chapel as they entered, not surprised to see it filled to capacity. Some of the youngsters had climbed to the gallery to find a place to sit. Not only was it a special Sunday, but the parishioners must hope—as he did—that the vicar's sermon would help them make sense of a senseless death.

Fingertips waved slightly to catch his eye, and he saw Lillian sitting by her great-uncle. On the other side, Ashland had a whole bench to himself. Maybe no one felt comfortable asking to sit next to the viscount. Brooks, his equally chubby wife and their dozen children had filled two benches closer to the back.

All the men who fit the description *his qualityship* were in the chapel and studiously ignoring each other. Did they suspect one of their fellows was the leader of the smugglers? Or did they care? Brooks seemed interested in not rocking the boat. Ashland acted as if being in their presence was an odious duty he had to perform, and Sir Nigel… Well, Edmund never guessed what the baronet might do or why.

As he escorted the widowed baroness to the front bench set aside for the lord and his family, he passed Vera who stood near the door instead of sitting in her usual spot across from the Meriweather family. He guessed she had offered her seat to someone else. She nodded politely to Lady Meriweather. A hint of color dusted her soft cheeks when her gaze met his.

"Do come and sit with us," Lady Meriweather said.

"Mrs. Uppington wants to share your bench," Vera answered. "But thank you."

He wished he could think of something to say, but words seemed mired in his mind. He wanted to tell her how lovely she looked in her simple gown that matched her blue eyes. Allowing even one of those words to pass his lips might free the rest as he spoke of how glad he was that she had come to stay at Meriweather Hall so he could get to know her better. Before he could find a way to control his own mouth, he and Lady Meriweather had walked past Vera.

The opportunity was lost. As many other opportunities had been because he could not trust himself to make the right choice after making too many disastrous ones.

Moments after he seated Lady Meriweather, his aunt hurried to join them. Aunt Belinda was as happy as a cat with a bowl of cream. She meant well, and he appreciated that. He simply wished he could interest her in something other than his future marital plans.

Mr. Fenwick stepped into the chapel, and the few whispers silenced. As the vicar led them through the service, Edmund heard some sniffling. Someone, maybe more than one person, was trying to keep from crying when Mr. Fenwick spoke of the sad events of the past week.

Wishing he had an excuse to stand and move where he had a good view of the whole chapel, Edmund sighed. Such a vantage point might give him a solid clue to who was involved in Cadman's death. He might as well have wished that the vicar would announce that the new church building was complete and the rest of the service would be held there.

Edmund forced down his frustration as the vicar began his sermon. He had expected a verse about honoring mothers, but the passage for the day's lesson was Proverbs 3:5-6. *"Trust in the Lord with all thine heart; and lean not unto thine own understanding. In all thy ways acknowledge Him, and He shall direct thy paths."* Had the vicar selected it to give hope to the parishioners toiling to rebuild the church? Or was it a warning for the villagers not to exact retribution for Cadman's death?

His gaze slipped to where Vera stood. His curiosity about what she thought of the verse her brother had chosen was replaced by astonishment. She had shifted so most of the chapel would not be able to see her face, but he had an excellent view of her lips forming each word the moment before Mr. Fenwick spoke it. His forehead furrowed. Even if she had listened to her brother practice his sermon, how would she know each word in advance of him saying it aloud? He could think of only one reason, but he could not confirm it until the service was over.

Sitting back, he listened to Mr. Fenwick and stole occasional glances at Vera whose face displayed every emotion in the sermon. He fought his yearning to put his arms around her when sadness filled her eyes as her brother reminded the congregation that while they might never know why Stanley Cadman died, God did, and even tragedy was part of His plan for all of them.

As soon as the service was over, Edmund stood. His hope of speaking with Vera vanished when she slipped out of the chapel ahead of even her brother. He guessed she had offered to help with the Mothering Sunday feast being held in the great hall. Once he bid the vicar a good morning, he intended to give chase.

That did not happen because his aunt looped her arm around his and kept him by the front bench until Sir Nigel and Lillian reached them. She took a half step into the aisle as if waiting for a break in the line of parishioners. She took Lillian's hand in her other one and drew her around the front of the benches.

She made sure that Sir Nigel stopped as well when she gushed, "My dear Sir Nigel, how kind of you to come to Meriweather Hall to join our Mothering Sunday celebration. It is always a pleasure to see your pretty face, Miss Kightly."

Somehow, she managed to jab her elbow into Edmund's side without letting go of his arm. A scowl at him was an unspoken order, and she was smiling again when she faced their guests.

"Good morning, Sir Nigel." Edmund nodded toward the baronet. "Lillian, I hope you enjoyed the service."

His aunt's eyes widened along with her smile. "It is wonderful to see that you two young people have journeyed along the path to friendship and beyond, far enough that you are enjoying the intimacy of using each other's given names."

He expected Lillian to roll her eyes and try not to laugh at his aunt's grandiose comment. When Lillian moved to wrap both arms around his other one, he was so shocked he could not speak.

"*Edmund* is such a dear man," she cooed in a tone he had never heard her use. Had a changeling taken over Lillian's body? He was accustomed to her treating him with the same warm friendship as she did Vera. Now she acted as if he already had made her promises of a future together.

Lillian stood on tiptoe and gave him a lingering kiss on the cheek before going to greet Lady Meriweather. Such a kiss offered more fuel to the speculative fire that he and Lillian were more than friends.

When he saw the expression on Sir Nigel's face, a predatory, satisfied smile that matched his aunt Belinda's, he had sudden sympathy for a fox being chased by the huntsmen and their pack of dogs.

"I cannot know the state of another man's heart," Sir Nigel said with a chuckle, "but I know my great-niece, Mrs. Uppington, and I can assure you that she has been raised well. She knows her place should be at the side of a fine lord, and she is welcome in the finest homes."

"She sounds like an excellent match, but my nephew is cautious in all his decisions," Aunt Belinda said, keeping her arm through Edmund's so he could not make an excuse to flee from the disconcerting conversation. "Do not fret, Sir Nigel. I can tell you that he is far from immune to your lovely niece's charms."

Edmund's face felt so hot, he feared it would blister. Why was his aunt prattling on as if he had confided his intentions to her? But, a small voice in the back of his mind asked, was she wrong? Sir Nigel had been right when he had said that Lillian Kightly would make Edmund an excellent wife. Lillian was beautiful and knew the exact thing to do as Meriweather Hall's lady. Far better than he knew how to be its lord.

But, as the justice of the peace had reminded him the night of Cadman's death, Edmund still had much to learn about being a peer. He wanted more from a marriage than a wife who would steer him through Society, but was holding on to the expectations of his earlier life the wrong decision?

As if to answer his question, though he could not guess what the answer was supposed to be, Vera appeared at his side.

She smiled. "If you will forgive me, Sir Nigel, Mrs. Uppington, I must steal Lord Meriweather from you for a moment."

His aunt started to protest, but Sir Nigel said, "Of course, Miss Fenwick. We must not be greedy when Lord Meriweather has many guests today."

"Thank you." She waited for Edmund to untangle himself from his aunt's clasp as well as Lillian's, then led him out of the chapel.

As soon as they were out of his aunt's earshot, he said, "I should be thanking you."

"You had the look of a man who wanted to be anywhere else but where he was."

"As I have said before, you have a gift of insight, Vera."

"I really had a reason to intrude."

"All the better."

"Lady Meriweather sent me to find you because she has some task for you."

He laughed. "I hope it will keep me busy for the rest of the afternoon."

"I can't promise that."

Before he could reply, he heard his name called in Ashland's arrogant voice. He stopped and said, "If I don't answer him, he will stalk me until I do."

"Go ahead. I can find someone else to help me."

"All right." He grimaced, then muttered, "There's no rest for the wicked."

"Or *from* the wicked," she said before she took his hand and squeezed it. "Be careful, Edmund."

She did not give him a chance to reply before she hurried away. As he turned to face Ashland, who was striding toward him, he appreciated her advice. He hoped he could follow it.

Chapter Eleven

Meriweather Hall's great hall harked back to the manor house's medieval origins. Thick rafters were stained with smoke from the large hearths where, once, meals were cooked. Iron chandeliers hung from the peak of the ceiling, and thick candles burned on them. The windows along each side of the room had been opened to allow in the breeze on a day that was both seasonably warm and sunny.

Tables were arranged in long lines, and the parishioners gathered around them, awaiting the rare treat of being served their food by the Meriweather Hall staff. Like all the traditions at the old estate, having the feast in the great hall was one that reached so far back in time that nobody knew how it had begun.

Not that it mattered, Vera thought, as she took her seat next to her brother halfway down the great hall from where Edmund sat with Lady Meriweather and his aunt as well as Lord Ashland and Sir Nigel. Lillian slid into an empty chair close to him and gave him such a warm smile that Vera could sense its heat from many feet away. She looked down at the plate in front of her before her expression betrayed her feelings.

A match between Edmund and Lillian would be an excellent one, combining two families who had lived on Sanctuary Bay for generations. Lillian made Edmund laugh, relieving the stress that too often lined his brow. She was beautiful, and, if Vera read her face correctly, Lillian had a *tendre* for him.

All that was true, but it was also true that the very thought of Edmund marrying Lillian sent a dagger of pain slicing through her heart. It was silly to imagine he might fall in love with her instead of Lillian. More than silly. It could lead to more trouble than she could handle. To be the cause of Gregory losing his living again would be devastating. No matter how many times she told herself that Edmund was a better and kinder man than Nolan Hedgcoe, letting her dreams wander in such a direction was dangerous. Better to relish their friendship and smile when he stood by his bride at the altar in front of Gregory who would pronounce them husband and wife.

A soft moan slipped past her lips, and her brother glanced at her before asking if something was amiss.

"No," she hurried to say.

"Then why are you groaning? You are not ill, are you?" He lowered his voice. "I'm going to need your assistance even more this week than usual after what happened on the beach."

"I know, and I am not ill." She forced a smile as she patted his hand. "Do not let me distract you from your duties."

"I never do." He stood and called out for grace to be said before the meal was served.

Vera did not listen to his words as she sent up a prayer of her own. She needed God to help her walk the path He had chosen for her and not let her stray where her own heart yearned to go.

Gregory smiled as a chorus of "Amen" followed his in the moment before dozens of conversations began, and the servants swarmed toward the tables to fill the plates. He sat and turned to answer a question from farther along the table.

Finishing her own prayer, Vera sampled the food placed in front of her. She was becoming accustomed to someone else cooking and serving their meals, but she missed her cozy kitchen. A sob bubbled up from the place where she had forced down her grief at losing her home and almost everything in it. Another loss to add to the others that had shaped her life.

She faked a cough when Gregory looked at her with curiosity. He had enough sorrow of his own, and she would not add to it by admitting she teetered on the edge of tears.

Quietly excusing herself, Vera walked with the kitchen maids out of the great hall. When they turned toward the kitchen stairs, she went in the opposite direction. She wanted to run, but that would draw attention to her. A single word or glance in her direction might shatter her.

Somehow, she found her way outside and into one of the smaller gardens. She sank on to a stone bench beneath an arbor that would, once summer arrived, be covered by a wild explosion of roses. The vines, like most of the plants in the garden, had only begun to green after the cold, snowy winter and the cool, rainy spring.

Her tears burned even more hotly against her lashes as she looked at the beds where the bulbs she had brought from the vicarage were planted. She had remained calm while Edmund had helped her dig them up and while she had pronounced that she would transplant them to this garden until a new vicarage was ready. When she had said that, she had been determined that not even a horrific fire would halt her from doing what she had promised to after she and Gregory came to Sanctuary Bay: make him a peaceful home where he could concentrate on the work he had been called to do.

A shadow crossed the ground in front of her, and she looked up to discover Edmund. She should have guessed he would notice her leaving. He seldom missed anything. Was it a skill he had honed during his time in the army?

"Your flowers will be sprouting soon," he said.

"I know." All her efforts to keep her sorrow out of her voice were in vain.

"Now I have distressed you."

"No, you haven't."

"If not me, then something or someone else has. Are you all right?" He ran a finger along her cheek, and she resisted the yearning to lean her face against his palm. "You have been crying."

"Only a stray tear or two."

"May I ask why?"

"Of course," she answered so he could not guess that her tears had welled up when she had seen Lillian flirting with him. "It is no secret that I always end up having a stray tear or two on Mothering Sunday."

"Because you miss your late mother?"

"Because I don't remember her." She stared at the ground. "Gregory has memories of her, but she died shortly after I was born."

He sat beside her without asking permission, startling her because his manners usually were perfect. She understood when he said, "I am sorry. I have few memories of my own mother, but the ones I have I treasure. When I was a child and someone remarked that one of my actions resembled my mother's, it was the finest compliment I could be given."

"When Gregory says something like that, it's often to remind me that our mother had a reputation as something of a saucy minx. He is certain to mention my resemblance to our mother if I speak without thinking."

"I think I would have liked your mother, then."

She raised her eyes to his earth-brown ones. "How can you know that?"

A smile curved along his lips. "Because I like when you speak without thinking. It shows me you are discerning and profound."

Vera smiled in spite of herself. "Profound? Nobody has ever described me that way."

"Maybe they would if you revealed that side of yourself more often." His words sounded as if he considered each one carefully before he spoke it. He grew serious, so serious she prayed that he was not about to impart more bad news.

"I think our parishioners prefer their vicar's sister to be in the background," she said. The words were bitter on her tongue and even more bitter in her heart. How she wished she could serve the parish and God in more ways than planning when the church should be cleaned and deciding which family would provide the

bread for communion! She understood it was important to have someone in charge of the annual calendar
of events and to make sure that no one felt left out or
overburdened. Still, she wished there was a way that
she could speak up in church and share her love for God
without having to remain half hidden behind Gregory.

"That is," Edmund said in the same deliberate voice,
"because they see you in no other way. If you were to
reveal the true Vera Fenwick, they might view you differently. As I do now."

She faltered, not sure how to reply. "What do you
mean?"

"Rather than answer that, let me ask you a question."

"All right."

"How long have you been writing your brother's
sermons?"

She pressed her hand over her heart that seemed to
have forgotten how to beat. Her breath burned in her
lungs, but she could not release it when she was not
certain she could draw another.

Somehow, Edmund had discovered she did that task.
He had come to get the truth. For him to leave the feast
as he had must mean that he was very displeased that
she had helped her brother. She stared at his face that
was as hard and unyielding as the stone bench. Frantic
thoughts exploded through her head, each gone before
she could grasp it, but one fact was frightfully clear.
Even though she had done only as Gregory asked, her
actions could cost him his living…again.

Edmund could not name a single emotion that
whipped across Vera's face, because he did not want

to believe he was seeing despair and fear. She gaped at him as if he had become a monster.

For a long moment, she was silent; then she whispered, "How did you know?"

"That you wrote today's sermon? The words your brother spoke sounded like ones you have used." He rested one shoulder against the side of the arbor, taking care not to get too close to the thorns. "And I saw you mouthing the words during the service before he uttered them. Either he had practiced his sermon in your presence so often you had memorized it—and that was unlikely with all that has happened this week—or you knew it because you had written each word."

"Please, don't think that Gregory is slacking in his duties."

He was taken aback by her response, because he had assumed her first question would be if he had enjoyed the sermon. His astonishment made him stumble over his words. "I—I did not m-m-mean to suggest that. I have seen how hard the vicar works, especially since the two of you have been staying here."

"Yes, he does." An odd urgency filled her words. "He works very hard, and when I can help, I do. The parishioners want the vicar to listen to their concerns. I cannot help with that. I cannot preside over marriages or baptisms. But I can write a sermon for him now and then. After all, I have learned much about faith and God from my brother."

"Vera—"

Her voice took on a hysterical note as she jumped to her feet. "Gregory has served this parish well for ten years, and he will continue to do so as long as you allow him to keep the living. If it concerns you that I am writing his sermons on occasion, I know Gregory will refocus his priorities."

He stood. "Vera—"

"I only wanted to help. Him and the parish. It was—"

He put his finger to her lips, shocking her into silence. "You are babbling."

"I want you to know that Gregory does so much that, if I help a bit, I don't want you to think he neglects his duties. He has not ignored them a single day of his time in Sanctuary Bay. He..." Her voice faded as he put his hands on her shoulders.

As he had suspected, she trembled with strong emotions she was trying futilely to control. He bent so that their eyes were level. He hated how the light had gone out in her eyes. Maybe he should have a talk with the vicar. If the man did not comprehend what a treasure he had in his sister, it was time that he did. "All I wanted to do is compliment you on how well-written today's sermon was. I know I was not the only one whose heart was touched."

"Oh."

He waited for her to add something more, something that would explain the haunted, hunted expression in her eyes.

"Vera, my dear—" Lillian paused at the edge of the terrace, her hand raised in a half wave. The wind that was blowing clouds in from the sea tugged at the ribbons on her stylish pink bonnet. "Pardon me. I did not realize you weren't alone. I hope I am not intruding."

"Not at all," Vera said with a smile and too much enthusiasm for Edmund's liking. She stepped away from him. "Do come and join Edmund. I must..." She left the rest of her excuse unspoken as she fled back into the house.

Lillian looked after her with a dismay Edmund guessed was mirrored on his face. He made sure his expression was bland by the time the blonde turned to him. After her outrageous flirting earlier, he did not want to be discovered alone with Lillian in the garden by her great-uncle or his aunt. That would guarantee the wedding banns would be read for the first time next Sunday.

Odd that he had not concerned himself with such matters when he had followed Vera into the garden. He had been thinking only of finding out what had upset her. He wanted to help her so she would offer him that smile that always made his pulse take off like a neck-or-nothing rider.

"I am sorry," Lillian said as she walked to where Edmund stood by the arbor. She kept a polite distance between them. "I know I interrupted something important."

He was astounded that she acted as if she had not been clinging to him earlier as tightly as the rose vines did to the arbor. Why was she acting differently each time she saw him? Her great-uncle was peculiar, but Lillian had seemed normal…until the past month.

"It is not an easy day for Vera," he said. "She feels the loss of her mother even more keenly on Mothering Sunday."

She nodded. "I can understand that." She tried to smile, but her lips trembled. "I miss my mother dreadfully. I understand that she wants time alone with her new husband, but I wish I could go home where I know every inch of our house."

"How is your exploration of Sir Nigel's house going? Have you found any secret passages or rooms filled with treasure?" He chuckled, though he never had felt less like laughing.

"Uncle Nigel has kept me busy with many small details for a gathering he wants to host later this summer, so that I have had no time to think of anything else."

"I thought his assembly was always in the autumn."

She shrugged. "He keeps saying that change is good, so he wants to hold the gathering shortly after the London Season is over." She looked out toward the sea. "It is splendid here."

"It is." Edmund glanced back at the house, hoping Vera would come back to the garden, knowing she would not. "And the view is never the same two days in a row."

"You are fortunate to live here. Uncle Nigel's house has a view of the sea, but the shoreline is straight. The crescent shape of Sanctuary Bay makes everything special. Oh, it's sprinkling." She hurried toward the house, then looked back. "Aren't you coming inside?"

"Of course. I know enough to come in out of the rain." As if his words were a signal, the sky opened and rain came down in a rush.

Edmund grasped Lillian's elbow and steered her toward the closest door. Even so, they were both wet by the time they reached the house. When he realized that they were close to the chapel, he led her along the corridor.

She paused by the door to his private office. It was ajar.

He frowned. He had closed the door, as he did every time he left the office. Who had opened it? There were a lot of people under Meriweather Hall's roof today, and he could not ask each one.

"Are those papers the plans for the new church?" Lillian asked as she walked into the office. She untied her bonnet and held it by its ribbons.

"Yes."

She examined the pages. "Did you draw these, Edmund?"

"No. Vera did."

"She has many special talents, doesn't she?" She smiled with warmth, but not coquettishly.

Maybe he would never understand women. Lady Eloisa had used him without a bit of guilt. Lillian was a chameleon, and he never knew what to expect with her. And Vera... His heart contracted in the midst of a beat. He had thought she possessed the strength he once had. When she had fallen apart in front of his eyes in the garden, he had been shocked; his first thought had been to bring her into his arms and soothe her.

But he had not acted quickly enough, being torn between the choice of comforting her and risking her reputation if anyone discovered them, unchaperoned, in the garden. He closed his eyes and sighed. If he could not make *that* decision, a choice so easy he once could have made it without even pausing to think, how could he ever hope to decide anything?

"Vera does everything well," Lillian continued as she walked back toward him, swinging her bonnet by its ribbons. "She is an extraordinary woman, and this parish is lucky to have her here to help with the rebuilding of the church. Without her— Oh!"

Something clattered to the floor. As she apologized, she bent to pick up the silver flask he had dug up at the vicarage. She turned it over in her hands, a perplexed look on her face.

"Don't worry," Edmund said. "You could not damage it more than it has been damaged already."

"Is it yours?"

"No. I found it, and I'm looking for the owner. Do you recognize it?"

"Maybe. I have seen one like it before."

"Where?" he asked, hope spiking in his chest.

She shrugged as she placed the flask back on the table. "Maybe at my great-uncle's house or maybe it was at my stepfather's house. Or maybe both. Such flasks are fairly common, aren't they?"

"Yes." His hope deflated, but he kept a polite smile in place. *Lord, I need Your help to unravel the puzzles in Sanctuary Bay.* He added another silent prayer that God would understand that he was seeking help in more than halting the smugglers. He never wanted to see such pain on Vera's face again.

Chapter Twelve

By the way others were devouring servings of bread pudding doused in caramel sauce, Vera guessed the dessert was another triumph from Mrs. Porter's kitchen. She had taken two bites and pushed it aside. Each spoonful had tasted like dust in her mouth. Hearing a lilting laugh, she looked across the great hall to see Lillian coming in with her hand on Edmund's arm. Her head leaned toward his, and Lillian gave that obviously happy laugh again.

Neither of them looked in her direction. Why should they? They were focused on each other, enjoying the day and the company. They were not lurking in a corner as she was, trying to still her frantic heartbeat at the same time she dressed herself down for blurting out too much to Edmund.

How could she have been so silly? Provoking Edmund when he wanted to praise her sermon. How many times had she longed to know if churchgoers were moved by her words? When he had sought her out to tell her what she had hoped to hear, she had reacted as if she had thought he was attacking her brother. She longed to apologize, but she could not when Lillian clung to him like a burr on a hem.

Vera instantly chided herself. Thinking of Lillian like that was inexcusable. The pretty blonde had done nothing but come to the garden looking for *her*. Vera had left her alone with Edmund because she could no longer bear to look at the bafflement on his face.

Edmund must think her half-mad. How could she explain that she had cost Gregory his previous living? Any respect Edmund had for her would be banished once she divulged her greatest shame. She could not bear the thought of that happening.

Suddenly, voices rose from the other side of the great hall. Heads swiveled as everyone strained to see who was disrupting the Mothering Sunday feast.

Her eyes widened when she saw Lord Ashland poking a finger at Mr. Brooks's waistcoat. The justice of the peace had his arms folded over his wide belly and a scowl on his face. Behind him, his wife pulled their younger children to her like a hen collecting her chicks. Sir Nigel edged to stand beside the viscount, clearly taking sides.

Everyone stopped talking, so Lord Ashland's words rang across the great hall.

"Brooks, if you would do your task as you vowed to, there would be no heaviness lingering over this day." Lord Ashland looked down his nose at the rotund justice of the peace.

"I am doing as I said I would the day I took my oath!" Mr. Brooks asserted as his wife began shooing their children out of the great hall so they did not witness the verbal attack on their father.

"Are you? You're making too much of a simple, albeit tragic, accident." The viscount exchanged a glance with Sir Nigel.

The baronet sneered. "Anyone with a bit of common sense knows that Cadman stumbled around in the fog, lost his bearings and fell over the cliff. Probably so deep in his cups that he didn't have the slightest idea where he was."

Gasps came from every direction at the slur heaped on the dead man. Vera jumped to her feet, ready to defend Stanley Cadman. A hand on her shoulder gave her pause, and she looked at her brother.

Gregory's emotionless face could have been carved from the thick beams over their heads. He stared at the three men and whispered a single word. *"Wait."*

She nodded, though every instinct told her to jump into the conversation to tell Sir Nigel he was wrong about Stanley. She gripped the table edge and bit her lower lip as she tried to see where Edmund was. Too many people stood between her and the far end of the great hall.

But the only one who spoke was Sir Nigel who said, "Brooks, be done with this inquest and let the matter rest as the dead man is."

"I will rest when all the facts are known," asserted Mr. Brooks.

Lord Ashland gave a terse laugh. "When have all the facts ever been known? Are you really that naive, Brooks?"

The justice of the peace turned a deep shade of puce. He opened his mouth to retort, but paused and looked past the viscount.

"Gentlemen, is there a good reason for raised

voices?" asked Edmund in a tone that suggested they would be want-witted not to heed him.

Vera drank in the sight of him, in command and calm amid the turmoil. While the other men were leaning toward each other, their fists clenched and their chins jutted, he stood with the easy assurance befitting a lord of the realm. She realized that, for the first time, she was seeing the man he had been before the war had stripped his confidence away.

"We are gathered here to celebrate Mothering Sunday," Edmund went on. "I think you forget yourself and the company you are in."

His simple, relaxed words eased some of the tension. Lord Ashland began to apologize, but his voice vanished beneath Mr. Brooks's furious one.

"My reputation has been sullied," Mr. Brooks said.

"Shall I arrange for my second to contact yours?" asked Lord Ashland, his arrogance once again in place.

The justice of the peace snarled, "Dueling is illegal."

"Only if one is caught," Sir Nigel said with a chuckle.

"Or one waits until the next day so cooler heads have time to prevail," Lord Ashland said. "I am sure you know that, Brooks."

"I know my duties as justice of the peace, and I know your duties as coroner. I am doing mine, and may I suggest that you do yours?"

Vera had heard enough. Already the smugglers had succeeded in disrupting too much of life around Sanctuary Bay. Allowing them to do so today through their vile deeds was too much. She slipped past her brother, sidestepping his hand that reached out to halt her. He caught her arm, and she whirled to him.

"Do something, Gregory!" she ordered in a sharp whisper, even though nobody was paying attention to them. Every eye and ear was focused on the men on the other side of the great hall.

"This is Lord Meriweather's battle. For me to intrude would be foolish, as you know all too well."

She flinched at his words meant to remind her of the muddle with Lord Hedgcoe, even though she could never forget it. She shook her head. "You are the vicar, Gregory. You would not be intruding. You would be reminding them that today is the Sabbath, and such accusations are inappropriate."

Gregory's eyes widened, then narrowed with an expression she had not seen on his face in many years. His mischievous smile suggested he was about to surprise everyone in the great hall.

"Thank you, Vera," he said, and he released her arm. "I needed to be reminded that I should minister not only to the sick of body." Turning, he strode toward the men.

She followed but paused by the end of the table where Lady Meriweather listened with a scowl. The lady glanced at her, then looked back at the men.

"I will say it again," Edmund said, his voice even. "This is neither the time nor the place for this discussion."

"I add my voice to Lord Meriweather's," Gregory said as he moved next to Edmund. "There are six days in each week for these matters. Can we not keep this day holy, even though a man is dead under what some deem suspicious circumstances?"

"What is suspicious?" demanded Sir Nigel. "You heard what Ashland said during the meal. A man got drunk and walked off a cliff after dark. It has happened before, and, sad to say, it will happen again. Lord Ashland has better things to do with his time than waste it continuing such a worthless pursuit."

Vera heard the baroness draw in a sharp breath at the baronet's heartless words.

"Is it worthless," Edmund asked, "if the investigation leads to answers that may put an end to the crimes around Sanctuary Bay?"

No sound was heard in the great hall, not even the footfall of a servant, as the meaning of his question sank into every mind.

"If we get the answer to that question," Mr. Brooks said, "it will be worth every minute. I think we are closer than we have ever been."

Lord Ashland's cocksure pose faltered at the quiet response. "Why would you say that?"

"*I* am still gathering facts, my lord," the justice of the peace said politely, but she sensed he was pleased he had pierced the viscount's arrogance. "I will not make any final judgment until I have as many as I can gather. However, I agree with Mr. Fenwick. Today is not the day to delve into that. I will contact you in your capacity as the county coroner, my lord, when I need further assistance."

Lord Ashland's face flushed, but Sir Nigel's turned an unhealthy red.

"That is ridiculous!" Sir Nigel argued. "Ashland is the coroner. He has—"

"To view the body and determine if he believes there has been foul play," Edmund said, clasping his hands behind his back. "Lord Ashland reported his findings to Mr. Brooks, even though I doubt any of us expected him to do so today. Therefore, he has discharged his duties, and the matter is back in Mr. Brooks's hands." He aimed a smile at the justice of peace. "As you can see, Mr. Brooks, I have taken your advice and learned more about the obligations each of us have to this parish and county."

Lord Ashland muttered something that Vera did not quite hear. Perhaps it was for the best, because the viscount stamped away, not even pausing to bid Lady Meriweather a good day or thank her for her hospitality. Sir Nigel motioned for Lillian but did not wait for her as he followed the viscount out of the great hall.

Lillian paused only long enough to express her apologies to Lady Meriweather for her abrupt departure. She glanced at Vera, but said nothing more before she ran to catch up with her great-uncle.

Nobody sat. The dessert was forgotten. Lady Meriweather sent footmen to have the wagons brought, so the villagers could return to their homes. Some did not wait, leaving immediately with their families. Others remained but drew together in hushed conversations in corners of the great hall.

"I must see to Mrs. Brooks and her children," Lady Meriweather said. "Will you let Edmund know where I have gone?"

"I could check on her if you wish, my lady," Vera said.

"No, but thank you." The baroness smiled and looked past Vera. "I think someone here needs you more."

As the lady walked away, calling to the footmen to assist her, Vera turned to look in the direction Lady Meriweather had. Mr. Brooks flung his hands about as he made a point to Edmund and Gregory. Which one did Lady Meriweather believe needed her? Surely, the baroness had been speaking of Gregory, but what if she had not?

Vera went to where the three men now talked in rapid, hushed voices. Hesitating, she wondered if she should say something so they did not think she was sneaking up on them.

Before she could find the right moment to interrupt, Edmund flung out his arm to make a point. It hit Vera's shoulder. Not hard, but enough to startle her.

He whirled. "Forgive me, Vera."

As she was caught by the mighty passions in his eyes, she realized he was apologizing for more than almost knocking her from her feet. New tears burned the back of her eyes as she said, "Most certainly, Edmund. You are forgiven."

She must be honest with him soon, but not now. Not when telling him the truth risked everything she had found in Sanctuary Bay…and with him.

Edmund had noticed Vera coming to join him, the vicar and the justice of the peace. He could never be unaware of her. It was not only the soft scent of the soap she used to wash her hair. It was as if they were connected in some invisible way that he could not describe. Brooks acknowledged her arrival with a glance in her direction, but looked at Mr. Fenwick.

The vicar said, "Perhaps this conversation could continue in a more private place, my lord. What Mr. Brooks is hinting at should not be discussed where many ears might overhear."

"Come with me," Edmund said.

"My family," began Brooks.

Vera interrupted, "Lady Meriweather asked me to let you know that she was going to spend time with your family."

As the justice of the peace nodded and thanked her for delivering the message, Edmund motioned for them to follow him as he headed toward the door where the villagers were leaving.

He opened the door to his private office and ushered them in. Vera chose the chair where she sat while they worked on the church plans, and Brooks took the chair Edmund used. Mr. Fenwick drew another one closer. Edmund leaned against the windowsill.

"Go ahead," he said to Brooks. "Explain to me why you have changed your mind. You discounted my theory that Cadman was murdered, but you defended it to Lord Ashland. I trust it was more than you wanting to vex him."

Brooks's chins jiggled as he chuckled. "Yes, though I have to admit that it was a pleasure to get a bit of my own back after dealing with his haughty ways." He grew serious and leaned forward, resting his elbows on his knees. "I have been asking a few questions as I know you have, too, my lord."

"Only a few, and only with people I trust."

"I have discovered how small the number is that I can say I trust without hesitation." The justice of the peace looked at each of them in turn. "What I discovered was, to say the least, very disturbing."

"That Cadman was murdered?"

"Yes, it would seem so. He was not a man with a reputation for drinking, and he was friends with many in the village. Some of those friendships included men rumored to be involved with the smugglers."

Mr. Fenwick sighed and bent his head. Vera reached out to stroke her brother's arm. Edmund wished she would offer him such comfort, too.

"So it would seem," the vicar said, shaking his head in frustration, "that Stanley Cadman really was on his way to share information on the smugglers. 'Tis unfortunate that the fog gave his enemy enough cover to ambush him."

"Whether that truly was Cadman's intention, we will never know," Edmund said. "It actually matters less than the fact that someone believed he was ready to tell me what he knew. Someone who had the power to order his death."

"We are fortunate that you are a soldier, my lord," Brooks said.

"I *was* a soldier."

He waved aside the words. "You have been trained how to protect yourself as well as those who depend on you, and we need those skills in Sanctuary Bay now."

Had his face gone deathly pale? His skin felt clammy. Vera started to rise but sat when he motioned with his fingertips for her to stay where she was. He gulped, then squared his shoulders.

"I trust, Mr. Brooks," Mr. Fenwick said, "you are not suggesting we declare war on our neighbors."

Brooks shook his head. "Our faith teaches that we should love our neighbors, but I know, my lord, that you share my dismay at the sorry state of affairs in this parish since the smugglers have grown more brazen. When I accepted the post as the parish's justice of the peace, I had great hopes of seeing the criminals brought before my court, but then I realized that the only way to end these crimes was to find the leader and hand out the proper punishment."

"It may not be as simple as that." Edmund pushed away from the window and sat on the arm of Vera's chair. It took all his willpower not to reach down and lace his fingers through hers. "A peer charged with a felony must be tried in the House of Lords."

"A peer?" Brooks's eyes grew wide. "You are jesting me!"

"I wish I were." He explained what his cousins had overheard at Christmastime when the smugglers had grown bolder and more careless. "While the leader might not be of the peerage, he must be a man of property and prestige who lives within a reasonable distance of Sanctuary Bay. That gives us a very short list of possibilities."

The justice of the peace said nothing for several minutes as he pondered the information. When he finally spoke, his voice was slow, as if he could barely bring himself to say the words. "If we believe what was overheard and reported to you, my lord, then there can be only three men who fit that description. The leader must live close enough to Sanctuary Bay to see the smugglers obey his orders."

"Three?" asked Mr. Fenwick.

"Lord Ashland, Sir Nigel and, excuse me, my lord, but I must add your name to the list."

Edmund laughed tersely. "You would be remiss if you didn't, but you should add yours, as well, Brooks."

"Quite to the contrary," Brooks said. "I appreciate your esteem, my lord, but a country squire, even one who takes on the task of serving as justice of the peace, never would be considered quality in the same breath as a viscount, a baron and a baronet. If you doubt me, ask those in the village whom you trust. They will tell you the same as I do."

Edmund stood and went back to lean against the windowsill as Brooks and the vicar continued to discuss Stanley Cadman's murder and how it might lead them to the smugglers' leader. He appreciated their enthusiasm, but he could not believe that *his quality-ship* would be careless and leave a clue along with the body of a dead man. He was beginning to doubt that they would ever discover the truth.

Vera was relieved when one of the Brooks children came to the door, more than two hours later, to ask if Mrs. Brooks should accept Lady Meriweather's offer for the family to spend the night at Meriweather Hall. Without additional clues to lead them to the person giving orders to the smugglers, the conversation had been going around and around and getting nowhere.

The men must have realized that, as well, because Mr. Brooks asked them to excuse him while he saw his family home. Gregory went with him and Edmund, asking their opinions if there should be more than one bell in the church's tower when it was completed.

She stayed where she was, exhausted by the day's events. She could think of several things she should do, but she did not move. Staring out the window, she watched rain curve down the glass, blurring the view of the sea. She did not realize tears were sliding down her cheeks, as well, until a gentle finger swept them away. Raising her eyes, she saw Edmund beside her.

"If I am the cause of these tears, I am sorry," he said, his voice the low rumble of half-heard thunder.

"You do not need to apologize."

"But I do." He caressed her face, and his eyes were filled with sorrow. "I upset you in the garden. I am not sure how or why, but if you will tell me, I vow I will not again."

"Thank you."

He waited for her to go on, then asked, "Will you tell me what I did to distress you? Tell me how I can make it up to you."

She started to answer but feared as soon as she spoke the truth, everything would change between them. Everything had to change eventually. If he did not wed Lillian, he would marry another woman of the *ton.* After that, nothing could be the same for them. No more long evenings of sitting and planning the church and talking of many other things. They could continue to work together on the church, but she truly would be nothing more than an assistant. That role she had yearned to break out of, but she would gladly assume it again if she could recapture the special times they had shared.

Life was uncertain, as Stanley's death had shown. All that was inevitable was change, and if their relationship must change, then...

She slipped her hand up his sleeve. His eyes widened in astonishment when she stood so her hand could curve around his nape. Knowing what she risked, but willing to pay the price when she might never have another chance to make this precious dream come true, she lowered his head and brushed his lips with hers. Shock riveted her. Not just at her own outrageous behavior, but at how a sweet warmth rippled out from the kiss to her fingertips.

Stepping back, she could not meet his eyes. "I am sorry. I should not have done that."

"No, you should not have done that." His hands framed her face. "I should have done this."

His mouth caressed her damp cheeks with a gentleness that captivated her. Laughter, joyous laughter bubbled deep in her throat. When he found her lips again, he pulled her into a deep embrace. She slid her hands beneath his arms and across his back's strong muscles.

Voices coming along the corridor compelled her to step back, though she longed to remain in his arms. She looked up into his eyes and was lost anew in these precious, fragile sensations that bound them together.

His name was called, and, not shifting his gaze from her, he whispered, "I have to go, Vera."

She nodded, unable to speak, as she wished she could make the rest of the world stay away a little longer.

He started to say something more, but his name was called more insistently. He stroked her cheek before walking away.

Unable to turn to watch Edmund leave the room, Vera heard him answering whoever had called to him and listened as his voice faded along with the other one in the corridor as they walked away. Then, closer, she heard a throat clear.

She looked over her shoulder to where Gregory stood in the doorway. His face was colorless and his voice held no emotion as he said, "Not again, Vera."

He was gone before she could speak. But what could she have said? That she knew it appeared as if she were letting history repeat itself by possibly jeopardizing her brother's living by kissing Edmund? She knew that, and like before, she had tossed aside good sense and listened to her heart.

She sank to the chair and covered her face with her hands. She had known that the joy of the stolen moment of being in Edmund's arms would be short-lived. She simply had not guessed how short.

Chapter Thirteen

Everyone seemed to be busy with some task…except
Vera. The household staff did their regular daily chores,
and Lady Meriweather was conferring with her housekeeper and cook. Gregory had shut himself away in his
room to work on the next sermon. Or so she assumed,
because her brother had not spoken to her since those
three accusing words yesterday in Edmund's office.
Nor had she spoken to Edmund, who before breakfast had ridden into the village to speak to people he
trusted. He wanted to affirm Mr. Brooks's statement
that nobody in the village would ever think of him as
his qualityship.

Maybe she could concentrate if she had not chanced
to see her brother walking past the armor by the book
room yesterday and going in. She had thought he was
looking for a book, but, before the door closed, she
had heard him say, "Lord Meriweather, we must talk
about Vera."

She had been tempted to press her ear to the door to
hear what was said. She already knew what Gregory
would say as he revealed her great shame to Edmund.

How had Edmund reacted? With anger that she had kept the truth from him, letting him think he had done something wrong in the garden to upset her? Or had he been sorry he kissed her, thinking her free with her affections? Oh, how she ached to tell him that, when she had fallen in love with Nolan Hedgcoe, she had been only a foolish girl with air-dreams of first love. That young girl was long gone, destroyed along with her youthful fantasies. Now...

She wished she could state as emphatically how she felt now. She could easily fall in love with Edmund, but she knew that yearning was as doomed as her calf-love for Nolan. Saying that aloud would be more painful than anything else in her life, even more than disappointing her brother again.

Vera stopped in midstep as she saw someone walking toward her. Her heart skipped. Was it Edmund? The man strode through the house with the ease of familiarity. But the man was too tall, and, when he neared, his black hair was burnished by the sunshine with streaks of blue. A scar along his left cheek where a French blade had struck him instantly identified him.

"Lord Northbridge!" she exclaimed.

"Miss Fenwick!" he said, feigning an identical amount of shock. He became somber as he added, "Meriweather told me that you and the vicar were staying here. I was very sad to hear about the fire at the church. As you can guess, that church holds a special place in my heart and in Sophia's."

The earl and the late baron's older daughter had been the last ones married in the old church. She could remember how happy everyone had been that day when the Meriweather family had set aside their grief from the previous baron's death and celebrated.

"I had not heard you were visiting Sanctuary Bay," she said, trying to keep her own sorrow hidden. "Are Sophia and the children here, too?"

"I made this a lightning fast ride north, so I didn't bring the children. As well, we thought it for the best for Sophia not to travel now." A grin on his stern face betrayed what his words meant. Sophia must be in an interesting condition, for no woman would risk her unborn child by journeying on rutted roads.

Vera wanted to offer her congratulations, but until an official announcement was made, she had to wait. She guessed the truth shone from her eyes as she said, "I am sure you and your family will make many other trips to Sanctuary Bay." *And I hope I will be here to see you.* She tried to shake her dreary thoughts from her head, but they refused to be budged.

"I don't think the children would allow me not to." Lord Northbridge's smile broadened. "Michael is already clamoring to see the sea, as he says, but I believe he wants to come back to enjoy the nursery."

"Have you heard from the newlyweds?"

"Yes."

"Are they enjoying their travels through Italy?"

"Why don't you ask them yourself?" He grinned.

"They are here?"

"Surprise!" called a beloved voice from behind her.

Vera whirled. She threw her arms around Cat and hugged her; then she stepped back to appraise her dear friend. Cat's smile and her dancing brown eyes conveyed her happiness. Vera was glad her prayer for Cat to find love had been answered.

Cat held out her hand, and her tall, lanky husband came to take it. With his ginger hackles and easy smile, Mr. Bradby did not look like the solicitor he was. Her friend must already be having an effect on him because he was not wearing his usual garish jumble of clothing. Instead, he wore a simple light brown waistcoat beneath his sedate black coat.

"Mr. Bradby, how good to see you, too," she said.

"Jonathan," he corrected with a smile as he draped his arm over his wife's shoulders. "Cat has told me often that she thinks of you as a second sister, and it would not do for anyone in her family to be formal with me."

Vera could manage no more than a tremulous smile. With her emotions raw, Jonathan Bradby's kindness was almost more than she could take without erupting into sobs. She must not ruin Cat's homecoming by weeping.

"That gown looks familiar." Cat grinned.

"It should. It is yours. Your mother gave me *carte blanche* to use anything in your room." She put her fingers to her lips as inspiration struck. She had the excuse she needed to leave before she embarrassed herself with tears. "Oh, give me a few minutes, and I will move my things out so you can use your room."

"There is no need. Jonathan made it clear on our way here that being in that pink room for more than a few minutes might drive him crazy." She took Vera's hands in hers. "Besides, it is *your* room now. My home is in Norwich with my husband. I never had a chance to tell you how sorry I was to hear about the fire. You left the wedding before I could even say goodbye."

"Thank you, but we have begun to rebuild. With

Edmund's knowledge of building, we are making good progress."

She saw the looks exchanged when she used Edmund's given name. A hysterical laughter tickled the back of her throat. Whatever they imagined was wrong. She had ruined everything by kissing Edmund yesterday.

"Yes, we are," came Edmund's voice from behind her. He pulled off his greatcoat and handed it to a footman before coming to greet his friends and younger cousin.

Vera saw her opportunity to slip away, and she took it. She thought nobody had noticed until Edmund called after her. She was too close to pretend she had not heard him, so she stopped while he asked the others to excuse him.

His smile fell away as he walked toward her. "Vera, we need to talk."

A shudder raced down her spine, but she nodded. When he led the way to the book room, she wondered why they were not going to his private office. She was surprised to see her drawings for the church stacked on the rosewood desk. Why had he brought them from his office?

"Please, sit," he said, his voice as taut as her brother's had been yesterday.

When she did and clasped her hands in her lap, she struggled not to ask what Gregory had said to him during their conversation in the book room. She wished Edmund would draw her into his arms again and tell her that was where she should always be, but instead he leaned back on the edge of the desk.

"I wanted you to be the first to know, Vera. I confirmed what Brooks said. Nobody I talked to at the church or in the village would describe him as quality." He grimaced. "I have always hated that term, but never more than now when a member of the so-called quality is a thief and a murderer."

Relief coursed through her. Maybe he and Gregory had spoken of something other than her mistakes. She chided herself. Instead of thinking about her own concerns, she should be thinking, as Edmund was, about the vital task of halting the smugglers.

"Then Mr. Brooks probably isn't the smugglers' leader," she said.

"No, and I am glad to hear that. Brooks has a sense of integrity and morality that is better suited to a justice of the peace than a criminal. From what we have seen, the real leader cares nothing about God's gifts of life as long as he keeps a tight hand on his contraband."

"That leaves us with two suspects."

"Both highly intelligent men who will be difficult to trap." He folded his arms over his chest and raised his gaze to the ceiling. She recognized that pose. He knew a decision must be made, and he was wondering how he could possibly be expected to make it.

Lord, comfort Edmund, she prayed. *Only You and he know why he suffers so. Only You can guide him out of the darkness of indecision that he has created around himself. He wants Your help. I know he does. And I want him to be happy. Truly happy, even if that means he spends his life with Lillian. Let me understand and accept that.*

She unclasped her hands in her lap. She had not expected the prayer to take that direction when she had opened her heart to God. For a moment, she longed to take the last part back, to say she did not really mean it. Pain surged through her at the thought of him kissing another woman as sweetly as he had her.

Pushing the thoughts aside, she forced herself to think about how to capture the smuggler's leader. Ideas formed and were tossed aside. They needed to do something as devious as the leader would do himself. A flicker of another idea flashed through her mind. It was only the seed, but maybe it was enough to get started.

"Edmund, both Lord Ashland and Sir Nigel have more than their share of arrogance. If there were a way to use that against them, we could set a trap and capture the one leading the smugglers. We could put out the word that you are planning to meet someone else who has the information Stanley did—"

"I will not risk anyone else's life."

"You wouldn't, if that person was safely behind the walls of Meriweather Hall before the rumor is started."

He shook his head. "That is no guarantee the person would be safe."

Vera sighed. "You are right. Maybe you should ask Lord Northbridge and Jonathan. They might have some ideas."

"I will do that." He pushed himself away from the desk.

"I think that's the best decision at the moment."

He stopped and scowled. "The best decision? Because you made it?"

"I only made a suggestion," she replied, dumbfounded by the sudden anger in his voice. She knew he was upset about the smugglers. She was, too. He should know that.

"Suggestion?" He pointed to the drawings. "How

many *suggestions* have you made to steer me to do what you want me to do?"

She set herself on her feet. "I have never tried to manipulate you. Never, Edmund." She wanted to add that she was not like Nolan Hedgcoe who had manipulated *her*.

"Maybe you did not mean to, but you did." When pain poured out along with his words, she realized she had mistaken it for anger. "How can I expect to get better if you never give me a chance to make a decision?"

"I have given you every opportunity to make a decision." She took a step toward him, wanting to touch him as she assured him that she had been trying to help him.

"Have you? Really?"

"I thought I had."

He shook his head. "You always interject a comment before I can come to a decision. I would have appreciated you giving me the chance to make a decision."

"It breaks my heart when you look lost and as if you would rather be somewhere else whenever there is a decision to be made. All I want to do is help you by showing that I understand how hard this is for you."

"Understand?" he repeated. "You cannot understand."

"I can try."

He shook his head.

"Give me a chance to show you I can understand."

"It is a waste of time. You have lived a peaceful life. You will never understand a life of war."

"You aren't being fair." She blinked back hot tears.

"Fair? Is it fair that I am the way I am?"

"That is not my fault."

"Are you saying it is mine?"

How had this conversation gotten heated so swiftly? She reached out her hands to him, but he did not take them. For an endless moment, they hung in the air, an illustration of the abrupt chasm that had opened between them.

As she lowered her hands to her sides, she said, "Of course, I'm not saying it is your fault, Edmund. I am only saying that I understand how difficult it can be when—"

"You don't understand. I know you want to, but you can't ever completely understand because you never made a decision that sent more than a score of men to their deaths. They died because I made the wrong choice."

"What?" She choked on the single word as the depth of his pain lashed out at her. Swallowing hard, she said, "Edmund, it was a war. Men die. It's sad, but it's war."

"But these men didn't have to die. *I* decided that the foray was low risk. *I* decided which men should go, including several who were as green as the leaves on the trees. *I* made the decision that sent them to their deaths in an ambush."

"How were you to know that ahead of time? If you made the best decision you could—"

"Don't give me platitudes!"

She bit her lip and stretched her hand out again. She took his hand, but he slipped it out of her grip and stepped back.

"I know you want to help me, but I need to help myself!" he exclaimed. "I don't want your help any longer. Not ever again, Vera!" He walked out and slammed the door behind him.

The sound was still reverberating through the room as she sank into a chair and stared at the plans scattered across the desk. Her brother's voice echoed in her mind.

Not again, Vera.

But she had done it again. She had tried to solve a problem on her own instead of handing it over to God. When she had let Nolan Hedgcoe beguile her, she had not stopped to pray for guidance about listening to her heart or to her good sense that his sudden interest in her was uncharacteristic when he had paid her scant attention before that. Instead, she had gone forward, unstoppable and never thinking of the consequences, like a charging bull. She had thought she was doing the right thing then, not realizing that he was using her as an excuse to pay court to a married woman. When the woman's husband had found out about their affaire de coeur, he had challenged Nolan to the duel that left him wounded and dying. In his grief at his heir's death, Lord Hedgecoe had discovered Vera's unintended part in his son's lies. Lord Hedgecoe had, in his anguish, lashed out and taken away Gregory's living. She had been foolish to agree to believe Nolan's excuses for leaving his horse in front of the parsonage. She had only wanted to help him.

She had thought she was helping Edmund, too, but he had been blunt. He did not want her help.

Not ever again, Vera!

All she had done was make everything worse.

Edmund could not sit, and he paced between where his friends sat and the window in his suite of rooms. He had asked Northbridge and Bradby to come there, because he knew these rooms were one place where he could be certain they would be undisturbed by anyone else.

So why was he finding it impossible to think of anything but the horrible conversation he'd had with Vera? He had tried to hold his frustration at his inability to make a decision when they needed to find a murderer, but it had burst out at her. He did appreciate all her help with the church, but he needed to relearn how to make decisions himself. Quick and good decisions that would lead to capturing the man who had ordered the death of Stanley Cadman. He likely would not have time to hesitate or to seek her help. He would have to make decisions himself.

And what if you never can? You told Vera you no longer want her help. What happens when you need one of her suggestions? Will your pride keep you from bringing a killer to justice? His fears taunted him with each step he took.

Bradby shifted in his chair. "If you bid us to come here to watch you walk back and forth, I would say you have achieved your goal."

"I need your advice," he replied.

"About the smugglers or about women?" Northbridge smiled when Edmund stopped and stared at him. "From your expression, it is clear that you need advice on women. Or did you ask us here to tell us you plan to marry Lillian Kightly as rumor says you will?"

"Rumor? What rumor?" Edmund frowned as he looked from one of his friends to the other.

"The rumor that you were going to come to Town to get her mother and stepfather's blessing before you offered for Miss Kightly."

Bradby chuckled. "Sometimes, the groom-to-be is

the last one to know. Marrying mamas like to start talk that may make hopes a reality."

"I don't plan to offer for Lillian."

"If it's not Miss Kightly on your mind," Bradby said with a wink in Northbridge's direction, "then I would guess it must be the vicar's lovely sister. You courting her will make a lot of tongues wag, but if you love her, that should mean nothing to you."

"Will you stop prattling like two old toughs and listen?" Edmund locked his fingers together behind his back and hurried to explain what had happened in the book room less than an hour ago. It was not easy to concentrate on that when Northbridge's words careened through his head. Courting Vera? He hardly allowed himself to imagine that in his most private thoughts. He enjoyed the time they had together, save for earlier, but how could he ask her to marry when her kind heart would keep him from finding a way to get past his debilitating inability to decide even the simplest things?

His stomach clenched as he recalled his conversation with her brother yesterday. The vicar had expressed his concern about Edmund showing interest in his sister. His account of what had happened with another young lord before the vicar left his previous living had been difficult to hear. Vera's gentle heart had betrayed her, and now Edmund was adding to her pain with his unpardonable accusation that she would never understand *his* unseen wound from the war.

"She has done nothing different from what Bradby or I have done on your behalf," Northbridge said, pulling Edmund out of the vicious circle of frustration and guilt, "and you have been grateful for our assistance since the war."

He agreed, though he did not want to. "True, but we were comrades-in-arms. We had to depend on each other."

"And she is your comrade in rebuilding the Sanctuary Bay church," Bradby said. "How is that different?"

Wishing he had never broached the topic of the quarrel, he shook his head. "If I had the answer to that, I wouldn't be miserable now."

Northbridge settled back in his chair and rested one foot on his knee. "Women have that effect on us, especially women in Sanctuary Bay. They make us see parts of ourselves that we would rather not look at, but the light of their love and faith shines too brightly for us to hide the truth from ourselves or them."

"And, in spite of what they illuminate in our heart's darkest recesses," Bradby said, with an ironic smile, "they love us still."

"Until we push them away." Edmund stood again. "I would not blame Vera if she never spoke to me again."

"But that is not your decision, Meriweather." Bradby clapped Edmund on the shoulder. "It is Miss Fenwick's. Your only decision is what you will do if she cares enough about you to forgive you."

Trust Bradby with his concise logic to get to the crux of the problem. Edmund wished his friend would have such a clear answer to it, as well, but that was a decision he must make himself. If only he had some idea how.

Chapter Fourteen

Vera arranged the flowers in a clear vase on the altar cloth, taking care not to splatter any water on the fine linen. She appreciated Lady Meriweather opening the trunks in the attic and allowing them to use the embroidered altar cloth, but she worried that she would do something to damage it.

As she had damaged everything with Edmund. How could her good intentions have gone terribly wrong? She had thought she was doing the right thing, helping him make decisions, so the new church could be finished as soon as possible. Now he was furious.

She shivered. Edmund had been as irate as Lord Hedgcoe had been when he had taken Gregory's living away. She still recalled the loud voices that had come through the door while she had sat out in the hallway on a bench, trying not to meet the eyes of anyone who walked past. Even though Edmund had seemed to be more willing to listen to sense than Lord Hedgcoe ever was, he had been very, very angry when they had quarreled two nights ago. She had not seen him since then, not even at meals.

"How lovely," Lady Meriweather said as she came into the chapel.

"Thank you." She tried to smile but failed.

"Come here, my dear." Seating Vera on the first bench, the lady said, "You look forlorn. I had hoped that, by now, you and Edmund would have smoothed over your differences."

"You know about that?"

"Nothing stays a secret in Meriweather Hall very long. Surely, you have been here long enough to know that."

"I hoped in this situation, it would be different."

Lady Meriweather pushed Vera's hair back behind her ear. "If you will forgive a meddling woman—"

"You have never been a meddler!"

"Apparently I am about to change, because I want you to know that I believe, in this case, you did the right thing."

"But I could have ruined Edmund's recovery!" she cried, unable to halt the words that came from the center of her heart.

The baroness nodded, a smile barely touching the corners of her lips. "It pleases me to hear you say that."

Vera gasped. Why would the lady be happy that Vera might have hurt Edmund's chances to put the anguish of the war behind him?

"It pleases me," Lady Meriweather went on, "because it shows how much you care for him. Maybe that will help you understand when I say that I believe that he also was right in what he said."

"I have come to realize that. Lady Meriweather, after others have made heartless comments in his hearing, I wanted to spare him that humiliation."

She patted Vera's cheek as she stood. "I suspect Edmund may have come to understand that you are his ally in this."

"Should I seek him out and apologize?"

"Apologize for what? Caring too much about both him and your brother's longing for a new church?" Lady Meriweather shook her head. "You appear to be a docile lamb, Vera, but you have a lion's heart. For you, it is a constant battle between fixing what you deem is wrong right away and pausing long enough to listen to the opinions of others who may have a different way of handling the problem."

"You mean I am stubborn and single-minded?"

Laughing, Lady Meriweather said, "I would not go that far, but I can tell you that I know there is One who has blessed my path through life. If you heed that One, you may find your path easier." Without waiting for an answer, she left the chapel and Vera to her own thoughts.

How many times had Vera heard Lady Meriweather speak with the same gentle compassion to her daughters? She never lectured. Instead, she spoke of her own experiences, using both her mistakes and her triumphs as examples. It had been Sophia and Cat's responsibility to learn from the stories. Lady Meriweather had offered her the same kind counsel, and Vera would be wise to consider her words.

She folded her hands in her lap and gazed at the flowers on the altar and the cherubs on the screen behind them. The chapel was a place of peace. She had sensed that the first time she had entered it.

When Edmund brought her here.

She closed her eyes and saw the hope that had been

on his face when he had offered it for services. He had opened the chapel to the parish at the same time he had been opening himself to her. She had seen his unhappiness with what he saw as utter failure. Instead of accepting him as he was, she had pushed her way in and made the decisions for him. She had mistakenly believed that was the way to heal his pain, rather than accepting the truth. Healing came from the One who knew all their hearts. As Lady Meriweather said, letting God lead the way on the path He had chosen for her would ease her way.

I will try to hear Your counsel, Lord, instead of doing what I guess You want me to do. I will follow where You lead me.

Vera sat for a while longer in the chapel, then walked out into the hallway. She was not ready to encounter Edmund, so she went to her own room. When she reached it, she kept going to the door to her brother's room a short distance away. She and Gregory had been caught up in the aftermath of the fire, and the time they were accustomed to spending with each other had been taken up with other matters. She missed that, and she missed how they prayed together when one of them felt overburdened and lost, as she did now.

Knocking on the door, she called, "Gregory, can I come in?"

She waited for an answer, but got none.

She knocked again. When there was no response, she opened the door enough so she could peek around it. She expected to see Gregory sitting on the chair by the window where he could read as long as the sunshine poured through it.

The chair was empty.

Pushing the door open farther, she called her brother's name again. Only silence answered her.

Maybe he had gone for a walk along the shore or ridden over to check on the work on the new church. He might be anywhere in the many corridors and rooms of Meriweather Hall. She would find Ogden. The butler kept close track of everyone's comings and goings.

Vera was torn between hoping she would see Edmund and hoping she would not. No, she would not give in to anxiety. She would trust God was leading her to where she needed to be. She could not wait to talk to Gregory and share with him what Lady Meriweather had told her.

"The vicar wants to have a trio of bells in the tower," Edmund said, pointing to the plans spread across the desk in his book room. His friends and his cousin peered down at the sketch.

Cat shifted back from the desk and sat on the window bench. "I had no idea Vera could draw so well."

"No wonder the two of you are bosom-bows," Bradby said. "You both have tried to hide your artistic skill."

Edmund looked away from the smiles the new husband and wife shared because it seemed almost too intimate to be seen by anyone else. Would that closeness elude him forever? He would marry. That was his duty. Marry and give the title a legitimate heir. But would he find what his friends had with his cousins? That special knowing that one person was always on their side.

You had that with Vera, his conscience reminded him. *You had it, and you tossed it aside because you were angry she was trying to help you. What sort of man treats a woman he cares about that way?*

The door crashed open, and, as if conjured out of his thoughts, Vera burst in. Her usually neat hair was tumbling down her back. Her blue eyes were large in her distraught face.

Cat jumped to her feet, but Edmund reached Vera before his cousin did. Putting his hand on her quaking arm, he asked, "What is it? What is wrong?"

"Gregory is missing." Her voice was no more than a whisper.

"Missing?" asked Northbridge as he came to stand next to Cat.

She nodded, but her gaze focused on Edmund. "I don't know where he is. I have looked everywhere."

"Come and sit," Cat said, putting her hands out to Vera.

Backing away as she kneaded her fingers together, Vera cried, "We have to find him before something happens to him like it did to Stanley."

Edmund's jaw clenched so hard he could hear his teeth gnash. Vera was not easily frightened. She had been ready to set a trap for the smugglers, even though it might have been foolhardy.

He reached for the bell on a shelf by the door, but Ogden appeared before he could ring it.

The butler did not look at anyone but Vera as he said, "We can't find him, Miss Fenwick. I have sent a lad riding at top speed for the village in case he went there."

"But Gregory would never leave without telling me where he was going," she said, her voice threatening to break on each word. "We have always let each other know where we were in case of an emergency. If he had been called to the village, he would have left a note for me."

Edmund clasped her hands between his before she wrung them so hard that she hurt herself. "Vera, if that is the case, then I'm sure he is somewhere in the house or nearby." He looked past her to Northbridge and Bradby. "Let us look for him."

"I have already looked for him everywhere I can think of," she said. "The last time he was seen was when he was in the garden several hours ago. One of the maids saw him out there, but when she looked later, he was gone."

"Maybe he walked down to the shore," Bradby suggested.

"I asked Ogden to send Foggin there."

The butler's face was taut. "Foggin reported back to me that he didn't find any footprints or any other sign that anyone had been there since the last high tide."

Northbridge said, "Maybe he went to the church—"

"He did not take a horse or cart." Her voice was growing higher with dismay. "I checked with Griffin in the stable, and, as I told you, if he had left of his own free will, he would have left a message for me."

"Maybe—"

Vera interrupted Bradby. "Maybe the smugglers took him."

Silence gripped the book room. Every face became as pale as Vera's.

Edmund looked at Northbridge. The habit had been ingrained during their years of fighting, side by side. Once, Edmund had made suggestions and waited for his commanding officer to decide.

Like Vera had done for him, he realized with a pinch of remorse.

Northbridge did not hesitate. "We will mount an organized and thorough search of the house and the grounds and the shore below the headland before we make any assumptions about where he might be or why. It is possible that he is in a place that has already been searched."

While the others rushed out of the room, Ogden calling for the footmen and maids to report to the entry hall, Edmund kept Vera from following by taking her hands again. He half expected her to yank them away. She did not, and he knew she was heartsick with fear for her brother.

"Do you think something terrible has happened to him?" Her voice shook.

He forced a smile. "Other than he has lost track of time wherever he is, no. He was in the gardens, Vera. Not even the smugglers are bold or foolish enough to come here in the sunlight. They could not slip in and out without being seen."

"I wish I could be as sure as you are."

"You will be when Northbridge and I bring him back, quite chagrined that he has upset his sister." He brushed her hair from her ashen face. "And then maybe you will let me apologize to you."

"Not now, Edmund."

Her soft answer would not have hurt more if a cannon ball had been driven into his gut. It was what he deserved after he had spewed his frustration on her. He clamped his lips shut, not wanting to chance hurting her further when she was fraught with fear for her brother.

Even though there was much he longed to say, he only nodded as he left her standing in the book room. He caught up with the others in the entry hall and thanked Lady Meriweather who offered to sit with Vera while the house and grounds were searched.

"Find him," Cat said, blinking back tears. "He is all Vera has left."

The words pummeled Edmund anew. Once, Vera might have counted him among the most important people in her life. Now...

"Let's go," Bradby said, tugging on his sleeve. "We can't waste a second." His face was as set and determined as Northbridge's. "Ogden, we need to search each room. When it has been searched, the door must be locked so nobody can go in."

It was a good plan, but by the time they finished searching the house, the stable, the outbuildings and even the cottages on the estate, there was no sign of Mr. Fenwick. Nobody spoke again of the smugglers, but Edmund had seen the many glances toward the sea. He wanted to kick himself for putting false hope in Vera's heart.

Lord, help me find the right words to hold her up and help her know that she and the vicar are both within Your care.

"Meriweather," Northbridge said as they walked through the front gate again, "I think we need more help. You already have the villagers going through the village and along the beach. We need others who can help us look in the wood. It may be that the smugglers are involved, and they have used the wood before to conceal their dirty work."

"That makes sense, but there are a few more places that I want to check along the shore."

"Do you want me to go with you?" Northbridge asked. "I thought I could ride for Sir Nigel's estate while Bradby went to Ashland's. Both of them should send help."

"Go ahead. Let me check those places on the other side of the cliffs along the headland."

"How long do you think it will take?" Bradby asked.

"An hour. Two at the most."

"Good. Make sure you are back within two hours. Not a minute longer. And take care, Meriweather! Your family doesn't need another baron to die without an heir."

Chapter Fifteen

Vera rushed down the kitchen stairs at an unseemly pace. What did propriety matter when her brother was missing? Her hopes had risen when a couple of hours ago, Lillian had arrived with Sir Nigel and the men he had brought to help search for Gregory. Then a half-dozen men had come from Lord Ashland's estate, though the viscount did not join them.

She listened while the men were given their areas to search. Lord Ashland's men were to check the woods with men from Meriweather Hall while Sir Nigel's men concentrated on the areas around the church and the village. She heard Sir Nigel tell his men that if they did not find Gregory, they were supposed to check in both directions along the shore. Lady Meriweather had invited Vera to join her and the other women in the withdrawing room. The baroness was being a gracious hostess, as she always was, but Vera could not stand the idea of quiet conversation and speculation. She had to do something.

With extra people in Meriweather Hall, there would be need for more food. She missed working in her kitchen in the vicarage, so she decided to join Mrs. Porter and her staff. That would keep both her hands and her mind busy.

Long tables filled the kitchen's main room. Doors opened on both sides to the various pantries and still-rooms. Both hearths had fires blazing, and sweat popped out on Vera's forehead.

She looked around in amazement. The kitchen was empty. Where were the maids who should be working in it?

As if in answer to her unspoken question, she heard giggles near the back door. She walked down a short corridor to discover the door was open. The kitchen maids were gathered inside and beyond the door. More laughter resounded along the passage.

Deeper voices came from beyond the door. She looked out a window. From the flirtatious sound of the maids, she had expected to see a man or two. Anger burst within her. All of Sir Nigel's men loitered by the door, flirting with the maids. If they had finished their search in the woods, they should be looking elsewhere. Sir Nigel had told them to keep looking until they scoured every inch of Sanctuary Bay.

She opened her mouth to ask them why they had given up, but she did not get the chance. Mrs. Porter must have noticed the maids were missing, too. The cook stormed out of the kitchen. The maids scattered with apologies. Vera leaped out of the way as the cook shooed the men away by waving her apron at them.

Only then did the cook seem to notice Vera. "Miss Fenwick, can I do something for you?"

"I thought I could offer an extra pair of hands. I

know you must be busy with all these people here today."

"We *should* be busy." She aimed a glower at the maids. "That is kind of you, Miss Fenwick, but you are a guest in this house, and it would not do for you to work with these lazy maids." She raised her voice on the last three words, and the young women moved even more quickly.

"Mrs. Porter, I am not a fine lady. I am used to cooking and cleaning. Please let me help. I cannot sit and do nothing."

The cook's face softened into a sympathetic smile. "Of course, Miss Fenwick. What was I thinking? You are accustomed to full days like we are." Pulling an apron off a nearby peg, she handed it to Vera. "Would you mind rolling out crusts for the meat pies we will be serving the searchers?"

"Thank you!" She gave Mrs. Porter a hug, then hurried to one of the tables while the startled cook looked after her with a widening smile.

Vera could not put her fears for her brother out of her mind, but she did not have to focus on them while she worked. The maids talked to her shyly, then with more friendliness. She appreciated their efforts to make her feel at home in their kitchen. When she whispered yet another prayer for her brother's return and the searchers' safety, murmurs of "Amen" came from around the table.

After the pies were in the oven, Vera offered to help with other tasks. It became apparent that she was hindering rather than helping Mrs. Porter, who did not have time to direct her. Also, the cook was frustrated at not being able to order her staff around as she usually did. More than once, Mrs. Porter had started to yell at a maid, then, glancing toward Vera, lowered her voice. Even though Vera would have liked to remain, she thanked the cook and left. She was halfway up the stairs when she heard Mrs. Porter loudly reprimanding a maid for ruining a dish by adding the wrong ingredients.

Vera walked toward the front of the house but paused when she heard the unmistakable sound of weeping. She turned down a hallway in time to hear someone cry out, "He was supposed to be back more than an hour ago!"

"Who?" she asked as she walked into the withdrawing room. She had avoided the elegant pale gold room with its damask draperies and thick carpets because she would never be comfortable sitting on the shimmering settees edged by tables with fine Meissen china sculptures on top.

"Edmund," Lillian answered, trying to wipe away her tears with a sodden handkerchief.

"Edmund is missing, too?" She grasped the back of the closest chair before her legs failed her.

A gentle hand cupped her elbow and lowered her into the chair. She looked up at Lord Northbridge's stern face, but saw the kindness in his eyes. Only then did she realize Jonathan was also there along with Lillian and the Meriweather women.

"What has happened?" she asked, forcing the words past the clump of unshed tears in her throat.

"Nothing may have happened," Jonathan replied. "Meriweather simply is late returning from his search."

"He may have found something interesting that delayed him," Lord Northbridge added.

"But you don't believe that." She did not make it a question.

"We don't have enough information to believe one thing or another." Lord Northbridge moved so he could look at her and the others. "Jumping to conclusions would be the worst thing we can do now. I have sent several men from the stables to follow the route Meriweather told me that he intended to take."

"But what if they don't find him?" choked out Lillian.

"Find who?" demanded Sir Nigel as he strode into the room. "Lillian, why are you a watering-pot?"

Lillian jumped to her feet and ran to her uncle. "Edmund is missing, Uncle Nigel."

A flurry of emotions flew across the baronet's face before it hardened. "Northbridge, is this true?"

"Meriweather failed to report in as he had planned. As we were telling the ladies, that might mean only that he has found some clue to the vicar's disappearance and is following it."

Sir Nigel's mouth worked, then he ground out, "Come along, Lillian. We are leaving. Now." He stuck out his chin as if daring them to counter his order.

"Uncle Nigel, how can we leave? The vicar hasn't been found, and Lord Meriweather is overdue."

"*Those* are the reasons. It is no longer safe for you here."

"But Edmund may be on his way here now," Vera said.

Sir Nigel shot a withering glare in her direction, but she did not quell before it. "Let Meriweather deal with his own problems." His sharp laugh tore at her ears. "If the want-witted fool can. He probably is standing on the strand, unable to decide which direction to walk in."

"Sir Nigel," Lady Meriweather began, but Vera interrupted with, "For a man who professes to have an artist's soul, Sir Nigel, you show a shocking disregard for others' feelings."

His gaze flitted from one face to another, except for Vera's. He ignored her as he said, "Forgive me, Lady Meriweather. My anxiety for my great-niece's safety has put me on edge." He took Lillian's arm and tugged. "Come along. Now!"

"Let me get my coat and bonnet. I cannot go bareheaded."

Vera thought he would insist Lillian come without delay, but Sir Nigel relented enough to say, "Hurry!"

"I shall." She glanced at Lady Meriweather who rang a bell to summon a maid.

Lillian's garments were brought, and she pulled them on. After she tied her bonnet under her chin, she rushed to Vera. "Stay safe, my dear Vera." Hugging Vera, she whispered, "Check the public house at the lower end of the village. I heard Lord Ashland speak of meeting people there."

Vera murmured, "Thank you," before she released Lillian. The young woman gave her an intense look, and Vera nodded. Lillian shared her suspicion that the viscount was the leader of the smugglers. If so, it was possible the people he met there were smugglers. Others would be there, too. Someone who was upset about the vicar's disappearance might be willing to give her information.

"Where have you been?" Cat asked as she came over to stand beside Vera.

"Keeping busy."

"You haven't done something risky, have you?"

"No!" *Not yet.*

She walked with the others to the entrance hall. After she bid Sir Nigel and Lillian a farewell and left the rest to do the same, she hurried up the stairs and to her rooms. She forced her eyes not to look down the hallway toward her brother's room.

Instead, she went into Cat's beautiful bedroom. If Vera were the daughter of a peer, she could not go to the village by herself. No one would think twice about seeing Vera alone on the steep streets, because she often went to call on parishioners when Gregory was busy. Even though she had never been inside The Scuppers, as the vicar's sister, she could enter the public house without worrying about her reputation.

She opened her cupboard and pulled out her dark gray gown. She had worn it on her way to Cat's wedding. Since her return, she had not been able to put on the grim garment. Not when she had a rainbow of gowns at her fingertips.

Undoing the buttons down the back of her borrowed gown was difficult, but she refused to call a maid to assist her. That could raise questions she did not want to answer. Finally she got enough undone so she could squeeze out of the gown. The sound of threads snapping urged her to go slow, but the moment she wasted unbuttoning the gown farther might be the very moment that she waited too long to begin her search at The Scuppers.

Smoothing her hair into a simple bun, she grabbed her funereal cloak and straw bonnet. She tied the ribbons under her chin and took a deep breath before looking in the glass. The face reflected back to her had not a single hint of color. She turned away, reminding herself that she must not give in to the panic uncurling in her stomach. She hoped someone at The Scuppers could help her. If they could not, she had no idea where to turn.

Edmund's coat ripped again, but he kept his shoulders pressed to the rough face of the cliffs. With the sun setting, deep shadows gathered around him. The large rocks that had tumbled to the shore offered some cover, but he stayed against the sharp cliffs as he inched north toward the village.

His search on the southern side of the headland had turned up nothing. All he had found were clumps of seaweed that stank and swarmed with flies and other insects. Strands still stuck to his boots. He had come around the headland and almost reached the path up to the gardens when he saw men gathered on the shore.

They did not see him, because they were staring at the ground. Their voices carried to him on the capricious sea breeze. He heard one say, "His qualityship sends his regards."

As the men laughed, Edmund dropped behind one of the huge boulders that had fallen from the cliffs. Smugglers! So close to Meriweather Hall. He gauged the distance between him and the men. They stood close to where water rolled down from a stream to the sea. There, the cliffs had worn back to create a deep cut into the stone wall. Bradby and Cat had found the piece of a brandy crate nearby. It had no excise stamps and must have been discarded by the smugglers.

Was the vicar with the men? Even if he had been

closer, Edmund could not have identified any of them. They wore their hats low over their brows, and kerchiefs pulled up on to their noses. Exactly as the vicar had described the smuggler he had met.

If Mr. Fenwick had come down to the strand for a walk and run into the smugglers... He tried to keep Vera's distraught visage from appearing in his mind, but failed. He wanted to be with her, holding her in his arms, kissing away her tears.

No, he must keep focused on the task at hand. He pressed against the cliff, his gaze focused on the men. They never looked in his direction. A couple bent down, but he could not see what they did.

Then they went up the stream between the two sections of cliff. Their voices were muted as they drifted toward him. He did not move, knowing they would have a good view of his hiding place from the top. Slowly he squatted where the shadows were deepest.

As he heard his coat rip another time, Edmund watched the cliff. The smugglers appeared one after another. Caught by the last rays of the setting sun, they were easy to see against the sky. They must have realized that, too, because they turned as one and headed toward the wood to the north of Meriweather Hall. He guessed from there, they would wend their way back to the village or to their lair somewhere else, like the snakes they were.

He waited a few more minutes, then stood. He slipped along the cliffs. He was late returning to Meriweather Hall, but he needed to see if the smugglers had left a clue behind. Close to where the men had been, he saw a long piece of wood that must have been tossed onto the shore by a storm.

The light thinned as he approached the spot. He squinted through the dusk and gasped. That was not driftwood. It was a man.

He gulped. For the past three hours, he had refused to let the idea that the vicar might be dead slip into his mind. Now, seeing the motionless form on the beach, his hopes faded.

He started to step out of shadows, then paused to look in every direction, including up. During the war, he had learned not to trust what he *thought* he saw. He might not be on the Continent, but the smugglers had declared war on the law-abiding residents of Sanctuary Bay. He could not forget that.

He pushed away from the wall. One step. Another step.

The waves splashed against the dark shape on the sand. A groan came from it.

The man was alive!

Rushing forward, Edmund carefully turned the man over on his back. Blood covered the man's face, but it was a face Edmund recognized immediately.

"Ashland!"

The viscount groaned, then cursed as he tried to sit.

"Easy. Let me help you." Edmund put his arm beneath the other man's shoulders and slowly tipped him up. Dampness oozed through his sleeve. He did not need to look down to know the warm liquid was Ashland's blood.

He did not hesitate. On the beach, he and Ashland could be seen by anyone passing by on the top of the cliffs. He hooked his hands under the viscount's arms and dragged him into the shadows.

Ashland murmured a single protest, then subsided

when his attempt to get to his feet failed. He groaned
again as he tried to move his right leg. Giving up, he
dug his left boot heel into the sand and stones to help
Edmund move him to a safer location.

Edmund scanned the break in the cliff walls. He saw
what must be caves, but he rejected going there. Caves
this close to the sea would be used by the smugglers to
stash their illegal cargoes.

There! Where the stream fell over the cliffs. A tree
with a couple of logs leaning against it. He could conceal Ashland there while Edmund went to get help.

The viscount was barely conscious by the time Edmund tugged him between the thick logs and the tree.
Leaving him, Edmund worked to erase every sign of
their passage from the beach to the tree.

He cupped his hands by the stream and brought
Ashland some water. More of it spilled on the viscount's face than into his mouth, but it roused Ashland
enough so that he opened his eyes.

"Meriweather!" He coughed and wiped blood from
his forehead. "How did you find me?"

"God must have guided me here. I was on my way
back to Meriweather Hall to report that I had not found
any sign of the vicar, and I saw a group of men—"

Ashland grasped the front of Edmund's coat weakly.
"The vicar is missing?"

"Yes. Nobody's seen him since this morning."

"That may be whom they were talking about."

"The smugglers who attacked you?"

Ashland's scowl was a pale version of his usual one.
"How did you know they were smugglers?"

"First, because people normally don't go around
beating up other people in Sanctuary Bay. Second, be-

cause I overheard enough of what they said to know." He did not repeat the exact words because he wanted to be absolutely sure Ashland was not *his qualityship*. Infighting among criminals was not unheard of. "They spoke of the vicar?"

"Not by name." He released Edmund's coat and sagged back against the tree. "They were talking about spiriting away someone, so they could force you and your friends to look the other way when a big delivery comes at week's end. You have them scared because the three of you have the skills to defeat them." He tried to chuckle, but it came out as another groan. "I could have used your help this afternoon."

He began to check Ashland's wounds. In addition to the one at his hairline, he might have a broken arm and probably at least one broken bone in his leg. No ribs were broken, but he guessed they were tender by the way the viscount flinched. "What happened?"

"I was ambushed." He winced, then coughed and winced again. "I got careless. Even though I had two pistols with me, I never got a single shot off."

"So, you have the pistols still?"

"Yes." His voice was growing feeble again.

Edmund got more water from the stream. This time, Ashland was able to swallow most of it. Tearing fabric off the hems of his shirt and Ashland's, Edmund wrapped the linen around the viscount's head. It instantly stained red, but he was more concerned about the injuries he could not see.

"They might be worried about Northbridge, Bradby and me," he said, picking up a couple of sticks and binding them around Ashland's leg, "but they gave you quite the basting."

He pulled two more sticks toward him and handed them to Edmund. "I think they discovered who I am."

Edmund frowned. "You aren't Lord Ashland?"

"I am." He winced as he moved his right arm to let Edmund put a primitive splint on it. "But they must have discovered that I have been working on behalf of the government to put a halt to the smuggling in Sanctuary Bay." He muttered something under his breath as Edmund tied off the material.

"Why didn't you tell us that?"

"Because I was unsure which side you were on. There was talk in Whitehall of how the previous Lord Meriweather had asked a lot of questions about the smugglers' leader, but, when you assumed his place, there were no more questions. It was thought that you might have seen a way to increase your wealth by bringing the smugglers to heel under your boot."

Edmund sat back on his haunches. "Because I wasn't nobly born?"

"No." He shuddered but waved aside Edmund's hands when he reached to redo the bandage around his head. "Leave it. Meriweather, your station at birth had nothing to do with the suspicions. Your leadership qualities during the war drew attention to you." His voice grew more strained, but he pushed on. "A man who can make quick, good decisions in the midst of battle is a man who can also make good decisions about sneaking goods ashore, stashing them and then selling them for profit."

The irony that he was suspected because he once had been skilled at making decisions almost made him laugh, but it was not the time. Ashland was hurt, and

Edmund needed to get him somewhere where a physician could tend to his injuries.

"I'm confused," he said. "Why do the smugglers fear my friends and me but kidnapped the vicar? That would make us more determined to halt them."

"They are desperate, and their leader is even more so."

"Sir Nigel?"

"Yes, Tresting." Ashland's voice was scarcely more than a whisper. "I see that is no surprise for you."

"Not a surprise, but I had hoped I was wrong." He thought of Lillian and how her great-uncle's connection to the smugglers could tarnish her reputation. "But supposition won't be enough to have someone arrested. We must have proof."

"You may find it in the village." A smile flitted like a shadow across his pale lips. "Or, to be more accurate, under the village. You have heard about the tunnel built to divert the beck down to the sea?"

"Yes." His cousin Sophia had spoken of the tunnel on the very first trip he had made to the village. A small stream, which the locals called a beck, vanished under some houses midway down the steep hill and then emerged at the foot of the street where the fishermen drew their cobles up on the sand and hung their nets to dry.

Nets!

"The entrance is hidden behind the fishermen's nets, isn't it?" he asked.

"Yes, but it is well guarded." He shifted and moaned. Again he waved Edmund away. "It is easy for the smugglers to pretend to be doing work while they make sure nobody gets too close to the entrance.

If you bring others to overwhelm the guard, a fight would erupt. With the houses having a good view of the foot of the street, reinforcements would be upon you in seconds. You'd be waging a battle on two fronts with the sea to one side." His eyes narrowed. "But one man alone might sneak past the guard."

"Was that your plan, Ashland?"

"It was, and you see how well that turned out. Until you chanced by, I thought we would have to let the smugglers win this round." He drew out a pistol from beneath his coat and handed it to Edmund. "Now…"

"Is the time to strike." As he finished Ashland's sentence, he stood. "Will you be all right here for another hour or so?" He knew well what he was asking the viscount to endure, but Ashland was alive, and Edmund wanted to make sure the vicar was, too.

"I will with God's help."

"There isn't any better."

A faint smile tipped the viscount's lips. "I'll be praying that you succeed where I failed, Meriweather."

He nodded his thanks, then edged around the fallen log. No movement on the cliff top or along the beach was a good sign. He hurried into the shadows before he could think about what awaited him in the village.

Chapter Sixteen

The public house smelled, like many other buildings in the village, of fish and salt and the sea. The odor of ale and burned food wove through those smells when Vera opened the thick oak door. Overhead, a sign with a ship on a high sea swung in the wind. The white-washed plaster walls were dull in the dim light of a single lamp. She wondered how burly fishermen fit into the cramped entry. She pushed aside the door to the left and stepped into the tavern.

Thick rafters made the ceiling feel even lower. Battered chairs surrounded small tables. The tops of the tables were marked with rings from tankards, but the uneven floorboards, painted the same black as the rafters, glistened with care.

Through an arch, she saw the bar. It was simple, a counter where drinks could be served. A single person stood by it. When the person moved into the light from the lamp on one side of the bar, Vera sent up a prayer of gratitude.

"Jeannie," she said, weaving her way between the tables.

"Miss Fenwick!" The short brunette dropped a wet cloth on the bar and rushed to meet her. "What are you doing here? Ladies don't come in here."

"As the vicar's sister, I have been welcome in every building in the village. Why not here?"

"You would be welcome." She glanced toward the pair of windows overlooking the steep street. "Just not tonight."

"It must be tonight because I have to find Gregory."

"The vicar? Is *he* the one they grabbed?" She clapped her hand over her mouth.

"Where can we talk in private?" Vera could not risk Jeannie, who knew, all too well, what the smugglers were capable of. Stanley Cadman had been her nephew.

"Come with me, Miss Fenwick." She hurried Vera past the tavern and toward a narrow staircase that leaned drunkenly against the wall. Opening a short door, she led the way down a pair of brick steps to a room that appeared to be both a kitchen and a storage room. Casks were stacked against two walls. A few rusty, scorched pots sat in the dead embers on a smoke-stained hearth.

Vera started to speak, but Jeannie put her finger to her lips and tiptoed around one stack of casks. When a door opened and closed, Vera realized she was checking to make sure they were not overheard.

Jeannie slipped back around the barrels, her blue eyes glimmering with fear. "Miss Fenwick, you need to go back to Meriweather Hall. You will be safe there."

"Gregory wasn't." She hesitated, then said, "Neither was Stanley."

"I don't know anywhere that is truly safe since *he* took control of the owls."

Vera recognized the cant term for smugglers. "Who is he?"

"I cannot tell you that, Miss Fenwick, because Stanley never told me. He said it was too dangerous for me to know what he had chanced to learn while working on the new church. He thought he was safe because he waited almost a week before he contacted Lord Meriweather."

"But the smugglers must have realized he had overheard and they waited for him out on the cliffs."

"Yes! That is why you must go, Miss Fenwick. If they think you know, they will kill you, too. That you are the vicar's sister means nothing to them."

"I can't go without my brother."

"Miss Fenwick—"

Vera grasped Jeannie's hands. "Would you leave without doing everything you could?"

Staring at the floor, Jeannie sighed, then shook her head. "If I could have done something to protect Stanley, I would have gladly risked my own life." She drew her hands out of Vera's and motioned for her to follow.

The barmaid led Vera among the casks. She squatted and gestured for Vera to do the same. Close to the stone floor was the perfect hiding place. They could see if anyone approached, but, unless someone looked closely, they would be hidden.

"What I am about to show you," Jeannie said, "you cannot share with anyone. You must promise that."

Vera hesitated, knowing what Jeannie knew might offer Edmund the key to putting an end to the smugglers. Not to give him that information would be more difficult than anything she had ever done. For a moment, she was as indecisive as Edmund but knew, as much as he was determined to halt the smugglers, he would not want the victory to come at the cost of Gregory's life.

"I promise," she whispered.

"If the smugglers have the vicar, there is only one place he could be. Under the village."

"Under? In a cellar?"

Jeannie would not meet her eyes. "No, not a cellar."

"In a tunnel? The smugglers had a tunnel into the old church's cellar."

"These tunnels—"

"There are more than one?"

"Yes. I don't know how many, but at least one goes all the way to the sea."

Vera nodded. That no cargo had ever been found in the village or on the beach was a sure sign the smugglers had an efficient way to get it out of sight.

"And they open into a few buildings along the street," Jeannie said.

"What?" Her voice squeaked, and she lowered it. "The tunnels are connected to the houses?"

"Into the cellars. That allows for cargo to be moved if someone gets too close." She glanced out between the casks, then at Vera. "There is a way into the tunnels from The Scuppers. I found it a few months ago."

This time, she did not hesitate. "Take me there."

Stopping only to get two dark lanterns and lighting them, Jeannie led the way down into the public house's cellar. No cobwebs clung to the walls, and the dirt floor had grooves where heavy items had been dragged across it. Jeannie did not give her time to look around as she went to a stone wall that looked no different from the others.

Vera watched closely where Jeannie put her fingers. The way to reopen the door would require identical motions on the other side. When a stone slab swung back on silent leather hinges, rushing water sounded as loud as a shout.

"The beck?" she asked.

Jeannie nodded. "The rocks are slippery. Watch where you put your feet. Once you're through the door, turn left and climb the hill. If your brother is in the tunnels, he most likely will be in that direction."

"I don't know how to thank you."

Handing her a lantern, its door slid almost closed so only a narrow line of light emerged, Jeannie said, "Thank me when you and the vicar are safe. Whatever you do, don't come back here for at least three hours. The tavern will be busy soon, and someone may see you. There are places along the tunnels where you can hide in the shadows, and you may escape notice."

"All right." Her voice was small as her fear loomed larger with every passing second.

"Are you sure you want to go?"

"I have to go."

Jeannie nodded with a sad smile. "When you do come back, hide among the casks in the kitchen until I can sneak you out. God go with you."

"Thank you." Vera stepped through the door and onto a stone slab. She edged down a step, and the door closed behind her.

Fear gripped her for a second, then she told her frantic heart to slow. She ran her toes to the edge of the stone and discovered it was another step. Cautiously she stepped down and grimaced as cold water washed over her shoes.

The beck was only a few inches deep, so she held up her gown with one hand as she began walking. She peered through the darkness, wishing she could open the panel on her lantern wide enough to let her see where she was putting her feet. She had to be grateful she had even this much light, because the tunnel was as black as Whitby jet. The beck flowed swiftly between large rocks. It would be too easy to twist her ankle on the uneven stones, so she edged around them. She had to be extra careful because years of water running over the rocks had dug out channels between them. Someone had built a low ridge on one side of the tunnel, but it appeared even more treacherous than the floor of the tunnel. Water oozed down the walls, puddling on the ridge before falling into the beck.

She heard nothing but the beck. The arched top of the tunnel was constructed of tightly packed bricks. None of them had shifted out of place, unlike the stones in the walls. Several had collapsed, bringing dirt down with them.

The late Lord Meriweather had known there was at least one tunnel. Cat had told her how he had searched but never found it. Had he known how big this tunnel was? Was this tunnel the one that connected to the old church, or was that a separate one? She wondered how many tunnels snaked through the cliffs.

Stop thinking about the tunnels. Find Gregory and get out of here!

She inched forward. Her left foot slammed into a rock she had not seen. Tears filled her eyes as pain surged from her big toe. She hoped she had not broken it. Not that it mattered. A broken toe was not going to keep her from finding her brother.

A hand settled on her shoulder. She drew in a breath to scream. A hand closed over her mouth, and she was tugged back against a firm chest. Another hand wrapped around her waist. She kicked back at her captor's legs and clawed his arms.

"Vera, it is me," came a whisper in her ear.

Edmund!

He was alive!

But what was he doing in the tunnel?

He spun her to face him. His arms encircled her. She threw hers around his shoulders as he lowered his mouth to hers in a kiss that offered healing for wounds left by angry and thoughtless words. She sank into him, savoring his rough mat of whiskers against her face.

Too soon, he drew back, but he leaned his forehead against hers. He whispered her name as if it were the sweetest prayer. Her fingers stroked his cheek, and she hoped her touch said what words could not. She heard him sigh when he released her.

"What are you doing in this tunnel?" he whispered.

"Gregory may be here. What are you doing here?" She gasped as she realized he was not carrying a lantern. "How can you see where you are going?"

"The smugglers use this tunnel. I figured if they could slip through without light, I could, too. I've been running my fingers along the wall to guide me."

She nodded, then realized he might not be able to see the motion. "I know about the smugglers, but Jeannie thought Gregory might be down here."

"Who is Jeannie?"

Vera hesitated, then realized her promise to Jeannie had been negated because Edmund already knew about the tunnels. "She is a maid at The Scuppers. Her full name is Jeannie Cadman."

His eyes widened, catching the faint light. "Stanley Cadman's wife?"

"His aunt, but she offered to help me when I told her that the smugglers might have taken Gregory."

"But that doesn't explain how you got into the tunnel."

"Tunnels," she corrected.

"There is more than one? How many are there?"

"I don't know, but several houses up the hill are connected by branches of the main tunnel."

Edmund took her hand as the current between the boulders tugged at their feet. She still was scared, but having him with her increased her chances of finding Gregory and returning alive to The Scuppers.

"But that doesn't tell me how you got in here," he said.

"One of the buildings connected to this tunnel is The Scuppers. I suspect the publican allows it in exchange for the smugglers providing him with inexpensive brandy. Jeannie didn't tell anyone else other than her nephew."

"Which may have been what he intended to tell me before he was murdered."

"No, she said he overheard something at the building site." She glanced at Edmund. "If anyone else finds out that she told me—"

He put his finger to her lips, and she wished he had silenced her with a kiss instead. "Don't worry, Vera. Assuming we make it out of these tunnels alive, I will arrange for Jeannie to come to work at Meriweather

Hall. That way, nobody will suspect she was the one who led you here."

"No, that would be the worst thing to do. If she leaves The Scuppers immediately, no one will doubt the position at Meriweather Hall is a reward for her help in finding Gregory."

She could tell his mouth twisted by how his words sounded. "Yes, yes, I should have known that, but we don't have time for this. You need to leave, Vera. Now."

Edmund watched her eyes grow wide in the light from her lantern. He tried to deflect the protest he knew was coming by saying, "This is no place for you."

When he had seen a light ahead of him in the tunnel, he had skulked as quietly as he could toward it. He had expected to find one or more smugglers, so he had drawn the pistol, ready to fire if necessary. He had hid it under his coat when he had seen Vera wading up the stream with the dark lantern to light her way.

"This no place for you, either," she retorted.

"At least I am armed. You are not. You should go back, Vera."

She shook her head, long strands of her black hair cascading around her shoulders. "Even if I were willing to stop looking for Gregory, which I'm not, I cannot go back the way I came. Not for three hours. The public house will be busy. I could be seen. I won't betray Jeannie. Her family has suffered too much already."

"You cannot go back the way I came in, either." He told her how he had bamboozled the man standing guard at the foot of the street. He had recognized the man from services at the chapel, and he had hoped that asking for his help in rescuing a fellow parishioner who had been hurt at the church would lure the man from his post. It had. The man had run up the steep street as if it were as flat as the top of the cliffs overlooking Sanctuary Bay.

"Good. That buys us some time."

"No. As I was ducking beneath the nets, I heard him call to one of his fellows to finish up his *work*. You can be certain someone is standing guard close to the nets now, though they cannot be certain I entered the tunnel."

"That gives us no choice. We have to go forward." She held up the lantern, and the moss on the walls looked like a green waterfall. "It will not take long for the word to reach Lord Ashland or—"

"Ashland isn't the smugglers' leader."

"How do you know?"

He let his frustration sift into his voice. "I found him bleeding on the beach. Beat by smugglers acting on Tresting's orders." He told her what the viscount had shared with him. "That is why you must get out of here. If Tresting is willing to order a viscount's death, he won't hesitate to see a vicar or his sister dead."

"Or a baron."

"That is why…" He paused when a distant sound reached his ears.

He grabbed the dark lantern from her hand and shut its door, leaving them in utter darkness. He strained to hear the sound again.

Splashing. Closer than before.

Voices resonated along the tunnel. Many voices.

The smugglers!

Chapter Seventeen

Vera grabbed Edmund's hand, and they ran as fast as they dared, jumping from rock to rock so no splashing called attention to them. She reopened the dark lantern, and a sliver of light flashed up and down the wall in time with their steps. He took it from her. Reaiming it at the water, he urged her forward. They had to slow because the tunnel began to slant steeply uphill, and the footing became precarious.

No shouts came from behind them, so it was possible the smugglers had not guessed they were in the tunnel. Or maybe they had gone into one of the cellars connected to it.

Her shoe slipped. She would have fallen in the icy water if Edmund's arm had not caught her at the waist and kept her on her feet. She leaned against him, trying to catch her breath which was not easy when each one was flavored with the scent of him.

"Which way?" he asked.

"What?" She raised her head.

He gestured with the dark lantern, and she saw the tunnel split a few feet in front of them.

"Do you know which way we should go?" he asked.

"I don't know!" Vera stepped cautiously forward. "Jeannie said there was more than one tunnel, but she never said where any of the tunnels went."

Raucous laughter came from behind them. They had to make a choice. With a shudder, Vera realized *she* had to make the choice. That Edmund had asked her opinion meant he could not decide which branch to take.

She closed her eyes and prayed she would not lead them straight to other smugglers. In the quiet while she sent up that prayer, she heard a faint sound from ahead of them.

"Listen," she whispered. "More voices."

"I hear them. They are coming from the right-hand tunnel."

"Then, let's go left," she said.

"Sounds like the best decision to me." He took her hand and waded with her into the tunnel to the left.

Even though danger stalked them in the darkness, Vera's heart danced at the light tone in Edmund's voice. He had not been angry when she had made the decision. Maybe there was a chance for them, after all, to remain friends. She longed for more, but she had to be realistic. Lillian would be a better wife for him, assisting him to learn when he must.

Those thoughts raced through her head in a heartbeat; then crushing fear returned. If they did not escape with their lives, the future was unimportant.

Edmund hissed something. His arm pressed her back against the slimy wall. He shuttered the lantern. An ache built in her chest, and she realized she was holding her breath. She let it sift out softly. Breathing normally was impossible when her heart beat as if trying to bang its way out of her chest.

The smugglers behind them came closer and closer. Their words became more distinct. They were boasting how much money they would make now that they had disposed of Lord Ashland. Her stomach threatened to erupt at how easily these men who were her neighbors spoke of murder.

"Day and night," one man said, "there has to be someone at the entrance by the shore. We cannot be sure if Ashland shared his knowledge with anyone else."

"He won't share anything else." A harsh laugh grated on her ears. "Dead men don't tell tales, as the saying goes."

Edmund's shoulders grew rigid with fury. She rubbed one gently, wanting to remind him that Lord Ashland had been alive when he had left him where the smugglers would not look for him.

"What about Meriweather?" a man asked. "He sent Curley on a fool's errand."

"And followed after him, Jeannie said. She saw him go up the street past The Scuppers."

Jeannie had helped them again!

Vera's relief vanished, and she put her hand over her mouth to silence her gasp when she heard one of them mention Gregory. She strained her ears but, other than speaking his name, they said nothing more about her brother. The men were too excited about their next rendezvous with a ship out at sea.

As soon as their voices grew distant again, Edmund let Vera edge away from the mossy wall. He opened the lantern to give them a splinter of light. Taking her hand as they walked along the left tunnel, he muttered to himself.

Vera noticed a faint easing of the darkness. At first, she thought her eyes were playing tricks on her. The gray grew stronger.

"There's something ahead of us," she whispered.

"I see it." His voice was grim. "Let me go first." He reached under his coat and pulled out something that flashed in the light from the lantern.

A pistol!

She gulped and edged behind him. She kept her hand on his coat as she tried to put her feet where he had his. More than once, she looked back. No signs of pursuit. She hoped more smugglers were not lying in wait ahead of them.

Edmund inched toward the soft twilight that, as he and Vera got closer, became no brighter. He held his pistol at the ready. It was a single shot, and it would not be enough. If they could have gone back the way they had come, he would have.

Be with us, Lord. Watch over us here in this dark place. He repeated the prayer over and over, setting a rhythm for his feet. Ice pumped through his veins. The only warmth was Vera's hand on his back.

He climbed on to the stone ridge at the side of the tunnel and assisted Vera up. She almost stumbled but caught herself. Her feet must have been even more frozen than his, because he wore boots. Here the stone was not crumbling, and he understood why when he saw the stones in the wall ahead protruded into the tunnel. A door. To a cellar or somewhere else?

With a signal he had used in the army, he told Vera

to remain where she was. Did she understand? He was relieved when she nodded. He edged to where he could peek past the door. In the twilight, he saw crates stacked haphazardly throughout the room. He did not see any lamp, so he guessed the light must be coming from beyond the room. He held up the lantern.

The light caught a pair of eyes close to the floor. Not a cat or a rat. A man's eyes! The vicar's eyes!

"He's here," Edmund whispered, "but it may be a trap."

"I know," she said as softly.

"I will go first. If I shout, run back the way we came. Promise me that."

"I will."

He handed her the lantern, then tipped her mouth up for a kiss. He tasted fear on her lips. Reluctantly, he stepped away and slipped into the room.

His eyes adjusted to the dusk as he scanned the space. There was nobody but the vicar, who lay on the dirt floor. Taking a chance, he reached out the door and crooked a finger to let Vera know she could come in.

She pressed the lantern into his hands and ran to where her brother lay trussed up on the floor. Dropping to her knees, she tried to pull the gag away.

"Let me." Edmund pulled out a knife and carefully cut the filthy fabric from around Gregory's head and sliced through the ropes binding his wrists and ankles, as well. "Are you injured, vicar?"

"No, other than from being forced to lie on this cold floor in one position for hours." He chafed his wrists, then held out his arms.

As she embraced her brother, she said, "Don't ever do anything that foolish again!"

"I didn't do anything foolish. They grabbed me while I was standing on the headland."

"But why?"

"They didn't say, but I got the idea they wanted to draw attention from themselves and put it on a search for me."

"Then they have succeeded," Edmund said. "Can you walk, vicar? We need to get out of here, collect Ashland and return to Meriweather Hall."

"I will do my best." He put his arm around his sister's shoulders.

"Tresting is there," Edmund said.

Vera shook her head, making her black curls bounce around her face. "He and Lillian left when they heard you were missing, too, Edmund."

"No doubt to put some heinous scheme into motion, but not having him there is good news."

Edmund took the lantern and slipped out with the Fenwicks following. Nobody spoke of how the vicar's escape could be discovered at any moment. When Vera turned her brother in the direction they had come, Edmund put the vicar's other arm over his shoulder.

Mr. Fenwick's steps grew more sure as they went to where the two branches combined into one tunnel. Every few minutes, Edmund stopped and listened. The only sound was the running water against the stones.

"They may have left," Vera said when they reached the main tunnel, "to prepare for whatever Sir Nigel has ordered."

"But they will leave at least one guard at the entrance beneath the fishing nets." Edmund moved forward. "From here, we must be silent."

The Fenwicks nodded. The occasional splash

seemed as loud as cannon fire to his ears, but he had learned during the war that nobody else would notice such a common sound. As the blackness eased, he closed the lantern and left it on a boulder.

Edmund stopped when he was near enough to touch the layers of nets hiding the tunnel entrance. Slowly he pulled one, then another aside until he could see past them. A lone man stood with his back to them. With Jeannie Cadman's lie, the smugglers had no reason to keep an eye on the inside of the tunnel.

But how to slip out, silence the guard and make their escape without alerting half the village?

As if he had asked that question aloud, Mr. Fenwick whispered, "I have an idea, my lord."

Edmund nodded, though he was unsure what the vicar planned. He had learned early in the war that if a man had an idea, a wise officer let him give it a try. If he had remembered that the night he had made his worst decision, many men might not have died.

"I will distract him," the vicar said. "If you can render him unconscious, my lord...."

"That I can do," he replied.

Mr. Fenwick smiled and squeezed his sister's hand before he crawled past Edmund. She slipped her fingers into Edmund's, such a caring, courageous motion that he was awed by her trust in her brother...and in him. If he had trusted her as much, he would have seen that she was not trying to undermine him with her suggestions. She wanted to spare him embarrassment and give him time to heal. His pride and self-pity had kept him from understanding.

His attention refocused on the vicar as Mr. Fenwick edged to the other side of the tunnel's entrance, so he had a chance of emerging without the guard seeing where he came from. As Edmund had, the vicar peeled back the corners of the nets. He dropped to his haunches and slipped out without causing the other nets to ripple.

Edmund arched his brows at Vera, who smiled. Pulling the pistol from beneath his coat, he held it by the barrel. He waited for the perfect moment to attack.

"Well, good evening," Mr. Fenwick said as if he appeared out of nowhere every day of the week.

The guard stared at him. "Vicar, what—?"

He never had a chance to finish as Edmund burst through the nets and struck the pistol against the man's skull. The weapon vibrated in his hand as the man collapsed into the water. He shoved the pistol under his coat and helped the vicar pull the unconscious man into a sitting position on the sand. When Vera stepped out of the tunnel, she picked up the man's floppy hat and put it on his head. Edmund drew the man's left leg up and propped the heel of his boot against a stone. He pulled the outermost net up and draped it across the man's lap.

He stepped back and appraised the scene they had created. Anyone looking quickly would think the senseless man was repairing a net. Turning, he saw Vera smoothing the others over the tunnel entrance so it looked as if they had not been disturbed.

She looked over her shoulder and smiled. He held out his hand to her. She slipped her fingers into it and urged, "Let's go."

Edmund smiled as they walked with her brother along the beach. He longed to hurry her out of danger, but his experience in the war told him that three people running along the sand would catch more notice than a trio out for a stroll. With the vicar's collar turned up against the wind and all three of them dirty and damp from their time in the tunnel, they looked as if they belonged on the shore. It might be the best disguise to let them reach Meriweather Hall alive.

Vera sat with her feet beneath her and a blanket draped over her shoulders. She was chilled to the very marrow, and she was grateful for the pot of hot chocolate that had been delivered to her room. She hoped some had been sent to her brother, too. He was with Lord Ashland and Lady Meriweather, praying for the viscount's recovery in another bedchamber. Sneaking the viscount into Meriweather Hall, so only a few people knew he was still alive, had been simpler than she had thought it would be. Edmund had alerted Ogden and Mrs. Williams. The butler and the housekeeper had sent the rest of the servants to another wing of the house while the injured man had been hidden in an unused bedroom. Gregory had stayed out of sight, too, because they must keep his escape a secret for as long as possible.

A light outside caught her eye. Were the smugglers heading out to sea? No, she realized as she stood and let the blanket fall off her shoulders. It was a carriage light. Who was coming to Meriweather Hall at such a late hour?

She pulled on dry shoes and tied her mussed hair back with a ribbon. She slipped out of her room and hurried to where she could look over the stairs, like an impish child, to see who was arriving.

Sir Nigel stepped into the entry hall, and she edged back so he did not catch her spying on him. Why was

he here? Her eyes widened when Edmund came into
the entry hall as the baronet was giving his coat and
hat to a footman. Edmund welcomed the baronet to
Meriweather Hall with a handshake as if nothing had
changed.

She wondered what game Edmund was playing
when he said, "I am glad you could come right away,
Sir Nigel."

"I would be remiss as a great-uncle if I did not come
here immediately on Lillian's behalf. She will be de-
lighted with the wonderful tidings."

Tidings? What wonderful tidings?

As the men disappeared from view, Vera tiptoed
down the stairs. The footman had taken Sir Nigel's
hat and coat away, so nobody saw her sneak after Edmund and Sir Nigel.

They entered the small parlor, and she heard the surprise in Sir Nigel's voice when Lord Northbridge and
Jonathan greeted him. Whatever he had come to talk
about with Edmund, he must have assumed it would
only be the two of them. She moved closer to the door.

A maid came along the corridor, carrying a tray
with refreshments for the meeting.

Vera put her finger to her lips, then glanced at the
small parlor.

The maid nodded and walked into the room without
acknowledging Vera. Maybe the servants were more
aware of what was going on than she had guessed.

Vera almost called the maid back when she saw a
flash of silver on the tray. Why did the maid have the
silver flask that had been dug out of the vicarage garden?

Suddenly Mrs. Uppington rushed past Vera who

backed up to avoid being run over. Edmund's aunt hurried into the room.

"Is it true, Eddie?" Mrs. Uppington asked, excitement heightening her voice. "Are you making an offer for a bride tonight?"

A bride? Vera leaned her head back against the wall and closed her eyes. Was that why Sir Nigel was at Meriweather Hall? To arrange the details for Lillian to marry Edmund?

No, something was not right. Even if Edmund did eventually offer for Lillian, he would not be meeting with Sir Nigel about that on the very night when the baronet had given orders to kidnap her brother and kill Lord Ashland.

"Aunt Belinda," Edmund was saying when she could hear past her thudding pulse, "I must ask your indulgence to allow us men to discuss this."

"Men! What do you know of weddings?" There was a pause, and Vera could envision Mrs. Uppington's face brightening with what she would deem a good idea. "There is one man who knows all about weddings. Let me get the vicar."

Edmund's voice grew taut. "The vicar is not available."

"But he is! I saw him on my way down here. He was—" Mrs. Uppington screamed.

The maid did, too.

Vera pushed closer to the doorway and stared at a horrifying tableau. Sir Nigel held Mrs. Uppington by the arm and was pressing a pistol to her temple. Lord Northbridge and Jonathan stared, clearly not daring to move a muscle. The maid had swooned, dropping the tray and its contents, including the silver flask, to the floor.

She saw all that in a single glance before her gaze focused on Edmund. He stood inches from his aunt's outstretched fingers. Fury, unlike any she had ever seen, twisted his mouth, but his eyes had that haunted expression she saw each time he was faced with a decision.

"There is no need for this," he said, and Vera wondered if everyone else sensed he was stalling for time.

"No?" Sir Nigel kicked the silver flask away and snapped a curse before snarling, "You thought you were clever by inviting me here on the pretense that you wanted to make an offer for my niece, didn't you, Meriweather? You and your friends. Bah! You think you're great heroes, but you haven't been able to see the truth under your own noses. You are no better than Ashland who pretended to be my ally before showing his true colors." He gave a maniacal laugh. "He learned his lesson. Now you will learn yours."

"Let my aunt go." Edmund spoke calmly. "There is no reason to frighten her. This is between us, Tresting. Let us handle it like gentlemen."

"Gentlemen?" he spat. "You are no gentleman, just a common laborer who has been raised above his station."

Lord Northbridge started to protest the insult, but Edmund silenced him with a single twitch of his finger. His friends exchanged a look she could not interpret. Some message had been passed between them. She thanked God that the men had learned to communicate without words in battle.

On the floor, the maid stirred. She opened her eyes

and shrieked, flinging out her hands and feet. One of them struck Sir Nigel's leg, knocking him off balance.

Edmund grabbed his aunt's hand and tugged her away, shoving her behind a chair. As the maid scrambled to get behind another, Sir Nigel grabbed her arm and jerked her to her feet.

"I may have been raised as a common laborer, but I know a gentleman does not hide behind an innocent woman," Edmund said with cool dignity. When Sir Nigel swung the pistol toward him, he added, "Nor does he kill an unarmed man. Or should I say try to kill? You do know that the Earl of Northbridge is an excellent shot, don't you?"

Vera glanced across the room. Like Sir Nigel, she had not noticed in the chaos when the maid regained her senses that Lord Northbridge had drawn a pistol of his own. It was as steady as the stones beneath the manor house and aimed at the baronet.

"Will he try to kill me, Meriweather, at the same time I shoot you dead?" Sir Nigel asked. "What say you, Northbridge?"

The earl lowered his weapon but held it at the ready.

"It seems our business for tonight is concluded." The baronet stepped back, pulling the struggling maid with him. He was not young, but his determination to escape with his life added strength to his grip on the girl.

No one else in the parlor moved as Sir Nigel edged toward the door. With a sudden motion, he spun, shoved the maid forward and ran out of the room. He did not look in Vera's direction as he fled toward the back of the house.

"Vera!"

She looked up at Edmund's drawn face as his friends ran past him. Questions filled his eyes.

"Go to your room," he ordered. "Lock the door and wait there until one of us comes to tell you it is safe."

He turned to follow his friends, then whirled to capture her by the shoulders and give her a swift, fiery kiss. He released her and was gone before she could urge him to stay safe himself.

Hearing a shriek from the parlor, Vera rushed in and helped Mrs. Uppington to her feet. Edmund's aunt was having a *crise de nerfs,* and Vera called the maid to help her get the older woman to her room where she could recover. Mrs. Uppington was staying in a different wing of the house, so Vera and the maid half carried her toward the closest staircase to her bedchamber.

Meriweather Hall was preternaturally silent, and every shadow seemed to hold a threat. Mrs. Uppington's sobs dissolved to soft whimpers. Still, she insisted on going to the book room to get something to read so she could relax enough to fall asleep.

"I can get you a book, madam," the maid said. "If you will tell me the title of the volume you want, I will bring it to you."

"How can I know which one I want when I don't know which books are there? Are you bird-witted, girl?"

Vera felt sorry for the maid who had suffered as much as Mrs. Uppington. She did not deserve to be dressed down. Asking the maid to make sure Mrs. Uppington had a hot drink in her room, Vera nodded when the young woman gave her a grateful smile and scurried away.

She strained her ears for some clue to tell her if Sir

Nigel had been caught. She heard nothing as she helped Mrs. Uppington toward the book room. As she opened the door, a shot resonated through the house.

Mrs. Uppington screamed.

"Go inside the book room," Vera said. "We can shut off the lamp, and we should be—"

Mrs. Uppington screamed again, this time pointing past Vera.

Spinning to look back, Vera saw Sir Nigel running toward her. Did he have a second pistol? She had to protect herself and Edmund's aunt. But how? He was almost to the suits of armor. His eyes glittered as they focused on the sword held by the first knight.

With a shout, she leaped forward and yanked the long lance from the gauntlet of the nearest suit of armor. It was heavier than she expected, but she held it up, ignoring her protesting shoulders. She had to halt the baronet before he could reach the armor and the weapons waiting there.

"Stay back," she ordered as she tried to see if anyone was following him. She doubted she could keep the baronet from pushing past her for more than a few seconds.

"Now, Miss Fenwick, this isn't how a vicar's sister should act. I assume you were the one who found my flask and gave it to Meriweather." He inched toward the lance's pointed end as he taunted, "Did you think it would make him fall in love with a mouse like you?"

As he put his hand out to grab the lance, she jabbed the sharp point toward him.

He jumped aside and cursed before ordering, "Put it down, Miss Fenwick. Now. Before I become angry.

I don't want to hurt a woman, but, if you don't move, I will make you very sorry."

She shouted over her shoulder, "Mrs. Uppington, go and get help." She did not dare to look back to see if Edmund's aunt did as she asked.

"Help won't come in time," Sir Nigel said. "I have led them on a merry chase. Put down the lance, and we will forget this happened."

"Forget that you ordered your smugglers to kill Lord Ashland and they nearly succeeded?"

"Nearly?" His arrogance cracked for a moment. "Ashland is alive?"

"Alive and sharing everything he knows about you and your smugglers. It's over, Sir Nigel."

"Not yet." He tried to sidestep the lance, but she countered.

The motion threw her off balance. As she teetered, trying to keep the tip of the lance from hitting the floor, he reached to grab it again. He miscalculated, and the sharp edge cut into his hand. He shrieked even more shrilly than Mrs. Uppington had. Blood dripped onto the floor as he yanked the lance from her hands.

She stepped back as he flipped the lance and pointed it at her heart. He moved toward her. She banged into the wall. Hearing a scream, she realized Mrs. Uppington had not gone for help. Sir Nigel's smile became savage as he drew back the lance to thrust it into her. She closed her eyes, knowing she had no escape.

Help Edmund, Lord, she prayed. He had suffered so much sorrow. Now...

There was a thump, but no pain. The lance clattered against the floor. Another thud. Louder than the first.

Opening her eyes, she saw Sir Nigel sprawled on the

floor. Behind him, Edmund held his pistol by the barrel as he had on the shore. "Maybe one of these days, I will actually fire this thing instead of using it as a cudgel."

She threw herself into his arms. They closed around her, and, for the first time since she had discovered Gregory was missing, she surrendered to tears.

Chapter Eighteen

Three days passed before Lord Ashland was well enough to return to his estate. Lady Meriweather had ordered a wagon lined with enough blankets to keep a fairy tale princess from feeling the bumps along the road. It waited outside the stable, because it had been simpler to bring the viscount down the back stairs than the front.

Edmund went to the side of the wagon to bid the viscount a good journey. "If there is anything we can do while you are recovering, let us know."

Ashland clasped Edmund's right hand with his left. "I owe you my life, Meriweather, and I will not forget that."

"You owe God your life, because He set my feet on the path that let me find you in time."

"I admire your faith, Meriweather." Lord Ashland smiled, but tightly. "And I wish I had realized earlier that you were on the side of good in this battle."

"What have you reported to your superiors?"

His smile broadened. "If I were ever to forget that you are a former army officer, questions like that would remind me." He grew serious. "I have reported the recent events."

"And their response?"

"What you would expect. They will send some extra excise officers to arrest any smugglers they can catch. With the tunnels no longer hidden, their activities will be curtailed at least for a while."

"And Sir Nigel?"

"Without clear proof that Tresting is the leader of the smugglers, they will not move against him. To accuse a baronet, even though he is not a member of the peerage, is a grave matter." He smiled coldly. "However, the charge of murdering Cadman is another thing, though that is still under investigation. The attempted murder of your aunt will be easier to prove because there are plenty of witnesses."

"Mr. Brooks has made arrangements for him to be held in the cell he keeps for that purpose. As soon as all the information is gathered and you are recovered, the trial will move forward."

"Good." He called for the driver to leave.

Edmund watched the wagon drive away, then smiled when he saw daffodils blooming by the stable door. Picking one, he went back toward the house. He knew someone who would be happy to see it.

Lillian put her teacup gracefully on her saucer, each motion perfection. Even in her unusually dark clothing, Lillian looked beautiful. The navy fabric made her blond hair glow.

"You don't have to look at me as if you expect me to shatter into a million pieces," Lillian said. "And you don't have to apologize, Vera. Not again and again and again. *You* did nothing wrong."

"But I *am* sorry that you have been dragged into this because Sir Nigel is your great-uncle." Vera set her own cup on the tray, but the china rattled in her unsteady hand.

"My mother should have given some thought to what the old fool was up to before she banished me here so she could enjoy an extended honeymoon with her new husband. Now she will have to spend plenty of time making sure none of this scandal attaches itself to me."

"Is that possible?"

Lillian smiled. "My dear Vera, anything is possible if my mother flatters the right people and my stepfather arranges a large enough dowry for me. Don't worry that I will be a pariah because of my great-uncle. He hasn't made an appearance in London for many years, so he has no allies there. Fortunately my mother has many."

"I'm sor—" Vera halted herself when Lillian frowned. "One thing I'm not sorry about is that I have gotten to know you, and having gotten to know you, I have to ask. You didn't know Sir Nigel was leading the smugglers, but you knew something wasn't right, didn't you?"

"Yes to both. I had hoped that Uncle Nigel wasn't involved, but I could no longer ignore the clues right in front of my face. He was acting stranger and stranger all the time. When I wanted to explore the house, he kept suggesting I come here for a visit instead."

"He didn't want you to find the smuggled goods he hid in his house after the church was burned."

Scores of crates had been discovered in the unused

wings of the great house. Some were marked for shipment to customers. The excise officers who had come from Whitby were already hunting down those customers to arrest them for dealing in illegal goods.

"Not only that. He hoped to distract Edmund by pushing me at him. I humored him so he would not guess that I suspected something was amiss. That is why I acted madly in love with Edmund whenever my great-uncle was near." Lillian smiled. "Go ahead. You might as well tell me what you thought. I must have appeared to be touched in the head."

"I did wonder. Edmund was totally left at sixes and sevens, or so my brother told me." She did not add that she had been baffled, as well, and hurt.

"The poor, dear man. I must apologize to him." Wrapping her arms around herself, she sighed. "He has endured too much from my family. I hope he doesn't believe my betrayal was worse than my great-uncle's."

"You are worrying needlessly. Edmund is a fair man. He will listen to you and forgive you."

"Good." Lillian stood and lifted her chin. "When I decide to marry, it will be because I have fallen in love. Not because my great-uncle wants to arrange for another shipment of illegal brandy and silk into Sanctuary Bay."

Vera struggled to keep her voice serene as she rose, too. "So, you have no interest in marrying Edmund?"

"He is a nice man, but not one who touches my heart. He likes living out here in daisyville. I want to live in London. I want the excitement of the Season, and the chance to choose my husband from among the many who will be vying for me." Her nose wrinkled. "To own the truth, Vera, I would go out of my head if

I stayed here for the rest of my life." As her eyes widened, she hurried to add, "Please don't take offense at my words, because I know this is your home."

"I'm not offended. You want to go to London, and I would have to be bound and gagged to go there." Vera smiled. "God made every one of us differently."

"And what about you, Vera? Are you happy?"

She hesitated. How could she explain what she felt to Lillian? She was relieved that the smugglers had been halted, at least for now. She could not say that to the blonde, because, no matter what he had done, Sir Nigel was part of Lillian's family.

She could say that she was happy that Gregory was writing his sermon for Sunday himself. His close call with death had brought back his fervor for preaching as well as tending to his flock. He was revitalized and reinspired and thankful to be alive to do God's work.

But was *she* happy?

"Good afternoon, ladies," Edmund said as he entered the room, saving her from having to answer. "If I had known there were two lovely ladies here, I would have brought two flowers." He held out the daffodil.

When Lillian took it, Vera's heart cramped. It pounded harder when Lillian handed her the flower and said, "This is for you, I am sure." She picked up her gloves, smiled at Edmund and left.

"It really was for you," Edmund said as he walked to her. "I know how you love daffodils. It'll be some time before you can replant your daffodils by a new vicarage."

She forced her smile not to waver as he spoke easily of her leaving Meriweather Hall. What had she thought he would do? Draw her into his arms and profess his undying love?

Mrs. Uppington stormed into the room. She pointed an angry finger at her nephew. "Why are you here with the vicar's sister when Miss Kightly is leaving?"

"We were having a pleasant conversation, Aunt Belinda," he said as he turned to face her. "You are welcome to join us for a *pleasant* conversation. If you wish any other sort, I must ask you to excuse us."

"You have made a complete muddle of this!" Aunt Belinda scowled.

"I have? I thought I had—with the help of my allies—done a very good job of ridding Sanctuary Bay of a band of reprehensible smugglers."

His aunt leveled her trembling finger right at his nose. "Don't give me back-answers, boy! You have made a higgledy-piggledy mess of everything! Letting Lillian Kightly slip away! The match would have been a grand coup for our family. Since her mother remarried and is now a viscountess, Miss Kightly's worth as a potential wife has risen."

"Her great-uncle—"

"Bah! And who cares about him? He has been one oar short for years. He will be sent away to where they keep addled people like him. By this time next year, when you and Miss Kightly could be happily married, he will be forgotten. If you know what is good for you, my boy, you will chase after her and ask her to marry you before someone else asks her."

Vera hated the weak tears that seared her eyes. In a whisper, she said, "If you will excuse me…"

"Please stay," Edmund said, taking her hand. He looked at his aunt. "First of all, Aunt Belinda, I am no longer your boy. I am a man, and I have the responsibility of overseeing Meriweather Hall."

"I meant—"

He did not let her finish. "Second, I am not marrying Lillian Kightly. My reason for that has nothing to do with her great-uncle."

"But Miss Kightly spent all that time flirting with you," his aunt insisted. "She must have some affection for you, Edmund."

"One thing I have learned in the past weeks is that I don't have to settle for *some*. I can ask for more from the Lord and from myself." His expression gentled as he looked at Vera. His warm smile touched her heart, setting it to dancing like starlight on the sea. "Would you remind my aunt of the verse from Proverbs that your brother shared with us on Mothering Sunday, Vera?"

"'Trust in the Lord with all thine heart; and lean not unto thine own understanding. In all thy ways acknowledge Him, and He shall direct thy paths,'" she said softly.

"And that is what I am doing," Edmund said. "I am trusting God, and I am trying to walk the path He set out for me. That path does not include marrying Lillian. I cannot marry Lillian because I hope I will be marrying Vera, if she will have me."

"Me?" The single word came out of her in a squeak.

At the same time, his aunt gasped. "Are you out of your mind, Edmund? You could marry a lady like Lillian Kightly. Why would you want to marry a vicar's sister?" Her nose wrinkled in distaste. "She has no idea how a lady should act. She attacked a man with a lance."

"To save your life, Aunt Belinda. How can you forget that?" His jaw tightened. "If she had not delayed Tresting long enough for us to get there, both you and Vera might be dead now."

Mrs. Uppington opened her mouth, but, for once, no sound came out.

Edmund cupped Vera's chin in his broad hand. "Tell me, Vera, that you will marry me."

Gazing up into his eyes, she could read his eagerness to hear the answer he hoped for. The decision was totally hers, and she knew what the choice had to be. So softly she could hardly hear the words herself, she said, "No, I cannot marry you."

She pulled her hand out of his, turning away so she did not have to see the shock and pain in his eyes, and ran from the room. She did not stop running until she reached the rose-covered arbor. She dropped to the ground and hid her face against her arms folded on the bench. Sobs racked her.

A gentle hand stroked her back. She raised her head, even though her cheeks must have been filthy where her tears had fallen and mixed with the dust on the bench.

Edmund knelt beside her but looked out at the waves. "Everyone has told me that I need a wife who can help me learn to become the lord of Meriweather Hall. I cannot continue on with no idea what I should do next."

"I never said that you had no idea what to do next."

"But you thought it." He chuckled when she hesitated answering. "You may as well own to the truth, Vera. Just as you should accept the truth that I love you."

She stared at him, unsure if she had actually heard him say the words that had been whispered through her dreams. "You do?"

"I wouldn't have asked you to marry me if I didn't love you. I may be a baron, but I still think like a merchant. I won't settle for less than love when I marry."

His words echoed her own thoughts when she had wondered if he would give in to pressure to propose to Lillian. Happiness flared within her, then died.

"Your aunt is right about one thing," she said.

"I find that hard to believe, but go ahead. Humor me and tell me what you think she's right about." He sat on the grass so close she could feel his warmth, but he did not touch her.

"I am not the sort of woman you should marry."

"Oh, Vera, do we have to go through this again?"

"Yes." She took a deep breath, then looked deep into his eyes. "I know you see me as the vicar's helpful sister, but there are things you don't know about me."

"Things like about you and Nolan Hedgcoe?"

"You know about that?"

A sad smile tugged on his lips. "Your brother sought me out for a private conversation because he was concerned about the attention I was paying you. He did not want you to be hurt again."

She flinched as she recalled how she had seen Gregory going into the book room the day after Edmund had first kissed her.

He ran one crooked finger along her cheek. "Your brother told me how you blame yourself for the circumstances that unfolded before you came to Sanctuary Bay."

She put her hands up to cover her eyes and her

cheeks that burned with her embarrassment. She could not bear to look at him while he spoke of her greatest shame. When he put his hands on her wrists and drew down her fingers so his gaze could meet hers, she longed to lean against his strong chest and have his arms around her, shutting out the past that haunted her.

"Vera, your brother didn't give me the details of what happened. Only that you were judged harshly when you could not prevent a young man from continuing on his self-destructive path."

"Did Gregory tell you that I was sweet on Lord Hedgcoe's son? I would have done anything to protect him."

"He didn't have to. I know you, Vera. Where your heart leads you, you follow, no matter what the cost."

"The cost was my brother's living." She lowered her eyes as she told him how Nolan had been in love with a married woman and died in a duel. She could not bear to see the recriminations on his face. The same recriminations she felt in her heart. When she finished the explanation, she added, "I know you have wondered why I have been so eager to see the church rebuilt for Gregory. It's the best way I can repay him for ruining his previous living."

"You didn't ruin it."

"But Gregory lost this living there."

He tipped her face back up so she could not avoid his eyes. "No, he *resigned* that living."

She searched, but saw no accusal on his face. "Resigned?"

"He must have told you."

She was ready to say that he had not, but then she thought back to the night when he had told her they were leaving Lord Hedgcoe's parish. He had told her that they could no longer stay because of what had happened. "He never said Lord Hedgcoe made him leave."

"Your brother refused to stay there when Lord Hedgcoe tried to blame you for his son's mistakes."

"But I assumed..." She blinked back more tears. "Oh, Edmund, all these years, I have felt horrifically guilty."

"I know a lot about guilt, too, Vera. I have been guilty since I sent those men to their deaths. I don't know if I will ever get over it, but I know God knows that I honestly thought the men would be safe. He is not punishing me. I am punishing myself by pushing aside every chance for happiness." He kissed her cheek. "Until I met you. Vera, say you will marry me. I need you to help me make decisions, in spite of my stupid frustration, and I need you in my arms. Say yes."

"I have to make the decision?"

He nodded, grinning.

"But didn't you choose to ask me?"

"I didn't choose. My heart did, and I know I need to listen to my heart. I ask you to listen to yours, Vera. Marry me."

"Yes," she whispered.

He swept her up against him, sprinkling kisses on her face as he told her again and again how he loved her.

"And I love you." She caught his face between her hands and laughed. "I *choose* to love you for the rest of my life."

He pulled her to him and kissed her until she was so breathless her laughter faded into soft sighs of joy.

Epilogue

Six months later

Standing at the front of the new church, Gregory raised his hands to the sky. The walls were up, but the roof and the bell tower still needed to be finished.

"I can imagine no better place to celebrate this special day than here," he said. "And I can imagine no better people to be celebrating it with than the ones who have worked hard to build the new church. In the midst of our great sorrow, God shone a light in our hearts, helping us hold on to faith and hope. As Paul wrote in his first letter to the Corinthians, faith, hope and love are treasured gifts that abide with us, but the greatest of these is love."

He smiled at Vera. She smiled back through her veil, then glanced at Edmund, who stood beside her in front of the simple pulpit that had been finished a few days ago. The lacquer reeked, but nothing could ruin this perfect day.

She had hoped they would marry before this, but Edmund's obligations as a baron had intruded time after time. First, before the banns could be read even one time, he had been called to London to give testimony at Whitehall. Then there had been Sir Nigel's trial in North Yorkshire. The result had been as Edmund's aunt had predicted. Sir Nigel was found insane, though Edmund said he was not the only one who thought the baronet was faking being crazy to avoid being sentenced to death. Any man who had set up such a network of smugglers and even used his supposed love of painting to confer with them and give them orders must have a facile mind. His estate had been seized, and there were rumors throughout Sanctuary Bay about who might have purchased it, but nobody had come to claim it.

When Edmund had returned, he was kept busy with the group of excise officers who swarmed over the village. Seven or eight families had disappeared from the village within hours of Sir Nigel's arrest. Several others left before the excise officers arrived. A collective sigh of relief had come from the villagers when those neighbors left, because they had never fit into the close-knit village. All the cobles pulled up on the sand now were used only for fishing and bringing legal cargo to the village.

The tunnels' sole purpose was carrying the waters of beck tumbling down to the sea. No smugglers used them to avoid detection. The entrances from cellars had been sealed closed, including the one in the public house. An iron-barred gate at the entrance kept people out of the tunnels, a precaution taken after a trio of young boys became lost while exploring.

At the same time, work had continued on the church. Vera visited the site almost every day, often to escape what seemed like endless fittings with Mme. Dupont for her wedding dress. The work went more slowly than they had hoped, but the new building would be strong enough to stand up to the most powerful winds blowing in off the sea. It was a labor of love for everyone involved, which was why she and Edmund had decided to be married in the Sanctuary Bay church, even though it wasn't finished.

"The love of man for God," Gregory continued, "the love of a congregation for its church, the love of a parent for a child or a brother for a sister, and the love of a man for a woman. All of these are gifts from God, gifts we share with one another."

Vera snuck a glance over her shoulder as she savored her brother's words of all the ways love had come into her life. On the front bench, Lady Meriweather sat with Sophia and Charles, as Lord Northbridge had reminded her that she should call him now that they were going to be cousins-in-law, and their three children. The newest child, another daughter with her mother's green eyes, slept on Sophia's lap, and Gemma and Michael, the older two, were trying without much success to sit still. Near them Cat, her stomach already growing round with her first child, rested her head on Jonathan's shoulder. Lillian had arrived late, having come all the way from London where she had been feted by the *ton* as a heroine in halting the smugglers. She sat near the back because the other benches had been claimed by villagers and residents of Meriweather Hall. Those who had not found room inside looked through the glassless windows. Several youngsters sat on the sills. All the guests were smiling broadly, except Lord Ashland who shared a bench with Edmund's Aunt Belinda. He was not smiling as she kept whispering to him.

Everyone she cared about was in the church on this special day. She wondered how much happiness her heart could hold.

She discovered it could hold even more when Edmund took her hand and offered her the special smile that was solely for her. Her brother turned to the wedding service and began, "Dearly beloved, we are gathered here today…"

* * * * *

Dear Reader,

The Sanctuary Bay trilogy was inspired by both my own experiences in the military and by tales of smuggling in North Yorkshire. While visiting Robin Hood's Bay, we explored the tunnels that still are open beneath the village. The opening is tall enough for most people to walk in without ducking. The beck flowing over the stones would make for difficult walking, especially while sneaking in smuggled crates. We walked in only a short distance, because we didn't have a light other than the one on my camera. Even so, we could see what appeared to be doorways that had been sealed with concrete. It was easy to imagine my characters trying to avoid smugglers beneath the steep streets of Sanctuary Bay.

Check out the other books in this series at joannbrownbooks.com.

Wishing you blessings,
Jo Ann Brown

Questions for Discussion

1. Vera's friend's wedding is disrupted when bad news comes from Sanctuary Bay. What do you do when your plans are upset by events you can't control?

2. Edmund finds making decisions impossible. Do you find certain decisions extra difficult? What do you do when faced with making that sort of decision?

3. In the ruins of the church, Edmund is shocked to find what appear to be clues that the smugglers used the building for storage. What advice would you give him for his search for answers?

4. When Vera asks Edmund for his help in rebuilding the church, he agrees...then wishes he hadn't. Most of us have agreed to volunteer and then wondered if we are up to the task. Has this happened to you, and how did you deal with it?

5. Vera works behind the scenes to help her brother with his tasks as vicar, but she longs for recognition for her service. Do you think she is right or wrong to crave for others to know her contribution?

6. Loyalty is considered a virtue, but sometimes, as in Vera's case with the young man she once loved, it can lead someone to make a big mistake. Are

there examples in your life or the lives of your close friends/family where doing the right thing led you in what you came to realize was the wrong direction?

7. Edmund trusted a woman who betrayed him. That makes him fearful of trusting again. What advice would you have for him in overcoming that fear?

8. Both Edmund and Vera carry a heavy load of guilt. Why do you think it is so hard for them to confront that guilt?

9. The vicar hands over the rebuilding of the church to Vera. Has anyone given you a job that you feel is a huge challenge because they believe you can do it, even if you aren't so sure? How did you deal with it?

10. Vera believes that another woman would make Edmund a better wife than she would. Have you seen strengths in others that you think you would like to have? Do you think it's possible to incorporate those strengths into yourself? If so, how?

THE HUSBAND CAMPAIGN
The Master Matchmakers
by Regina Scott

They may have married to curtail a scandal, but Lady Amelia Jacoby is certain she can persuade Lord Hascot, her guarded new husband, that even a marriage of convenience can lead to true love.

THE PREACHER'S BRIDE CLAIM
Bridegroom Brothers
by Laurie Kingery

After refusing to give in to an unwanted engagement, Alice Hawthorne is determined to stake her own claim during the Oklahoma Land Rush. But when she meets Elijah Thornto can the preacher convince her to open her heart?

THE SOLDIER'S SECRETS
by Naomi Rawlings

Blackmailed into spying on Jean Paul Belanger, widow Brigitte Dubois soon comes to care for the gruff farmer. But is she falling for a man who may have killed her husband?

WYOMING PROMISES
by Kerri Mountain

When Bridger Jamison arrives in Quiver Creek, he's desperat for work and a safe place to care for his younger brother. But with the town against him, his only ally is the beautiful undertaker, Lola Martin.

REQUEST YOUR FREE BOOKS!

2 FREE INSPIRATIONAL NOVELS
PLUS 2
FREE
MYSTERY GIFTS

Love Inspired.
HISTORICAL
INSPIRATIONAL HISTORICAL ROMANCE

YES! Please send me 2 FREE Love Inspired® Historical novels and my 2 FREE mystery gifts (gifts are worth about $10). After receiving them, if I don't wish to receive any more books, I can return the shipping statement marked "cancel." If I don't cancel, I will receive 4 brand-new novels every month and be billed just $4.74 per book in the U.S. or $5.24 per book in Canada. That's a saving of at least 21% off the cover price. It's quite a bargain! Shipping and handling is just 50¢ per book in the U.S. and 75¢ per book in Canada.* I understand that accepting the 2 free books and gifts places me under no obligation to buy anything. I can always return a shipment and cancel at any time. Even if I never buy another book, the two free books and gifts are mine to keep forever.

102/302 IDN F5CN

Name	(PLEASE PRINT)	
Address		Apt. #
City	State/Prov.	Zip/Postal Code

Signature (if under 18, a parent or guardian must sign)

Mail to the Harlequin® Reader Service:
IN U.S.A.: P.O. Box 1867, Buffalo, NY 14240-1867
IN CANADA: P.O. Box 609, Fort Erie, Ontario L2A 5X3

Want to try two free books from another series?
Call 1-800-873-8635 or visit www.ReaderService.com.

* Terms and prices subject to change without notice. Prices do not include applicable taxes. Sales tax applicable in N.Y. Canadian residents will be charged applicable taxes. Offer not valid in Quebec. This offer is limited to one order per household. Not valid for current subscribers to Love Inspired Historical books. All orders subject to credit approval. Credit or debit balances in a customer's account(s) may be offset by any other outstanding balance owed by or to the customer. Please allow 4 to 6 weeks for delivery. Offer available while quantities last.

Your Privacy—The Harlequin® Reader Service is committed to protecting your privacy. Our Privacy Policy is available online at www.ReaderService.com or upon request from the Harlequin Reader Service.

We make a portion of our mailing list available to reputable third parties that offer products we believe may interest you. If you prefer that we not exchange your name with third parties, or if you wish to clarify or modify your communication preferences, please visit us at www.ReaderService.com/consumerschoice or write to us at Harlequin Reader Service Preference Service, P.O. Box 9062, Buffalo, NY 14269. Include your complete name and address.

LIH13R

SPECIAL EXCERPT FROM

Love Inspired.
SUSPENSE

*Morgan Smith is hiding in the Witness Protection
Program. Has her past come back to haunt her?*

*Read on for a preview of
TOP SECRET IDENTITY by Sharon Dunn,
the next exciting book in the
WITNESS PROTECTION series
from Love Inspired Suspense. Available April 2014.*

A wave of terror washed over Morgan Smith when she
heard the tapping at her window. Someone was outside the
caretaker's cottage. Had the man who'd tried to kill her in
Mexico found her in Iowa?

Though she'd been in witness protection for two months,
her fear of being killed had never subsided. She'd left
Des Moines for the countryside and a job at a stable because she had felt exposed in the city, vulnerable. She'd
grown up on a ranch in Wyoming, and when she'd worked
as an American missionary in Mexico, she'd always chosen
to be in rural areas. Wide-open spaces seemed safer to her.

With her heart pounding, she rose to her feet and walked
the short distance to the window, half expecting to see a face
contorted with rage, or clawlike hands reaching for her neck.
The memory of nearly being strangled made her shudder.
She stepped closer to the window, seeing only blackness. Yet
the sound of the tapping had been too distinct to dismiss as
the wind rattling the glass.

A chill snaked down her spine.

Someone was outside.

If the man from Mexico had come to kill her, it seemed odd that he would give her a warning by tapping on the window.

She thought to call her new boss, who was in the guesthouse less than a hundred yards away. Alex Reardon seemed like a nice man. She'd hated being evasive when he'd asked her where she had gotten her knowledge of horses. She'd been blessed to get the job without references. Her references, everything and everyone she knew, all of that had been stripped from her, even her name. She was no longer Magdalena Chavez. Her new name was Morgan Smith.

The knob on the locked door turned and rattled.

She'd been a fool to think the U.S. Marshals could keep her safe.

Pick up TOP SECRET IDENTITY wherever
Love Inspired® Suspense books and ebooks are sold.

OPEN TO LOVE?

After refusing to give in to an unwanted engagement,
Alice Hawthorne is determined to stake her own claim during
the Oklahoma Land Rush. But when she meets Elijah Thornton,
can the preacher convince her to open her heart?

BRIDEGROOM BROTHERS

The Preacher's Bride Claim

by

LAURIE KINGERY

Available April 2014 wherever
Love Inspired books and ebooks are sold.

Find us on Facebook at
www.Facebook.com/LoveInspiredBooks

LIH282